CW00693649

Non Fiction by the same author

Murder At The Priory: The Mysterious Poisoning of Charles Bravo. Co-author Bernard Taylor

The Pimlico Murder: The Strange Case of Adelaide Bartlett

Who Killed Simon Dale?

The Book of Hay

Journal: volume 1

THE BIRKETT BRONZE

Kate Clarke

*

Carrington Press

First published in 2005 by Carrington Press

*

*

ISBN 0 – 9530761 - 4- 8

British Library Cataloguing in Publication Data
A catalogue reference for this book is available from the British Library

All characters in this book are fictitious and any resemblance to real persons, living or dead, is entirely coincidental

Printed and bound
Antony Rowe Limited
Eastbourne

THE BIRKETT BRONZE

Kate Clarke

*

Chapter One

'I think you'll find she threw Julia Thomas's head over *Hammersmith* Bridge, not Richmond. I could be wrong but I'm pretty sure that Richmond was where she chucked the boiled torso.'

As she spoke, Leanne teased a skin-thin sliver of cucumber from the edge of her plate and dropped it delicately into her mouth.

'I beg to differ, my dear,' announced Duncan, whisking a newly starched damask napkin from the confines of his shirt collar. Dabbing at his greying moustache he looked up and smiled warmly at Mrs Doggett, the proprietor's wife, who had been hovering around the table throughout lunch. 'However,' he continued, fully aware of the pleasantly sonorous tone of his acquired actor's voice, 'as it's not one of my particular cases I'm perfectly happy to bow to your superior knowledge.'

He looked quizzically at the man slumped like a collapsed stick insect in the chair beside him. Reverend Joseph Pinny looked up, weary, preoccupied:

'Sorry, can't help,' he said. 'Not my field, I'm afraid.' He turned and raised his eyebrows at the young man to his right, now sitting astride his chair, lighting a cigarette. Oliver shrugged, thrust out his chin, pursed his lips and exhaled a mouthful of smoke into the air above his head.

Leanne, sitting directly opposite, was watching him with interest. She guessed his age to be about thirty and was surprised to find herself appraising the pleasing line of his jaw, his lean frame and his rich brown, casually cut hair. He was dressed in jeans and a worn leather waistcoat over a collarless cotton shirt, cream in colour with a feint blue stripe. He was clearly a restless young man, constantly on the move; throughout lunch, she'd noticed, he'd been tapping the table, rolling his lighter around in his hand or allowing his slightly bemused gaze to wander, continually assessing the company and his surroundings:

'Rae should know,' he said, turning towards the bar where a young woman was ordering a round of drinks. Her appearance was striking for she was tall, with a strong, almost handsome face and her hair, which was bleached nearly white, was cut very short. Like Oliver, she too was in jeans over which she wore a faded denim shirt; she had five silver earrings speared through one ear, two in the other and a small stud near her left nostril. She was talking to the landlord of *The Hare*, Leonard Doggett, an ex-Army Major. He was a diffident, self-effacing man and whilst retaining something of his military bearing he lacked the hearty bonhomie one might expect from an ex-serviceman turned licensee; in fact, his face wore an expression of weary resignation and he seemed unwilling to maintain any eye-contact with either his wife or his customers.

By contrast Thelma Doggett was small and plump and though, like her husband, in her late fifties, she was full of energy, the matronly wattles at her neck constantly reverberating with her tireless chatter; and as she moved about fussily attending to her guests her plump thighs, like well-packed sausages encased in nylon skins, rubbed together as she walked giving off a curious rhythmic Velcro-stripping rasp.

'Rae!' Oliver called across the room. 'Settle the argument for us - the maid, Kate Webster - over which bridge did she chuck Mrs Thomas's head - Hammersmith or Richmond?'

'Hang on! Just let me sort out the drinks first,' Rae protested, clenching her teeth over a bag of peanuts and two packets of crisps. Carrying the tray of drinks she negotiated a pathway through the minefield of little occasional tables, some in nests of three, dotted at random all over the floor of the lounge bar. Having successfully completed the course she handed out the drinks.

'Grapefruit juice for the Rev, whisky for Duncan, brandy for Oliver and rum and coke for Leanne - did I get it right? Great.' Finally returning to her seat Rae took a long drink of beer and rubbed her hands together:

'Right then,' she said, enthusiastically, ‘Let me see, yes, Kate Webster,1879, housemaid, murdered her employer Mrs Julia Thomas - spent the night cutting up the body - boiled the bits in the kitchen copper - went to tea with some friends carrying the head in a canvas bag and then, once it was dark, chucked it over Hammersmith Bridge. Then she jammed the rest of the body into her mistress's hat-box and threw it over Richmond Bridge....'

Pausing for breath she flicked a cigarette across the table to Oliver and lit one herself. 'Not the whole body though,' she continued. 'If I remember correctly, one of Mrs Thomas's feet was found a couple of days later on a compost heap on an allotment in Twickenham.'

'God, how absolutely *frightful!* It makes my theatrical villains seem quite civilised,' exclaimed Duncan, leaning back and wrinkling up his nose for the benefit of Mrs Doggett who had positioned herself close to the bar so that she could more easily eavesdrop on their ghoulish conversation. 'But it would make a marvellous play. I must mention it to one of my producer friends...'

'Oh, yes, but this is the best bit - it was rumoured at the time that, after spending the night boiling the body, Kate made a tour of the local pubs the next morning trying to flog jars of 'best dripping'. Some tough lady. Great case.'

Thelma Doggett, looking startled, gave a little gasp. She was a well-meaning but somewhat shallow woman programmed to respond in a wholly predictable way, rarely troubled by an original thought or the need to question the conventional values she shared with her familiars. Or so it seemed. But there was one aspect of her orderly, mundane existence that she kept hidden even from her closest friends - in her mind too awful, too distressing and shameful to divulge and impossible to share. She stood with her dumpy feet turned in - the excess flesh easing over the edges of her patent leather pumps (the ones with the gold filigree buckles) like unleavened dough over a baking tin - and the fingers of her small, tap-touchy hands, encrusted with eternity rings, were pressed against her open mouth. For further effect she raised her shoulders and gave a little shudder, closing her eyes in an exaggerated show of disgust.

Oliver looked across at her and whispered, 'Oh, Christ Almighty! Fetch the smelling salts, girls - the old duck's having the vapours again...'

'She's loving every minute of it,' said Leanne, draining her glass. 'She's been listening all through lunch - didn't miss a word. Can't you just imagine her holding court after we've gone, telling all her corseted and crinkled cronies every lurid detail over a pint or two of sherry?'

'One thing's for sure - it'll do wonders for her street cred,' said Rae, raising her glass. 'Well, here's to the winner, whomsoever it might be. I won't say may the best man or woman win because we all know that won't be the case.'

'You can say that again,' said Oliver, bitterly, tapping the top of the table with his fingertips and catching the edge of his ring on every third beat.

A flicker of irritation passed over Rev Pinny's face as he leaned forward to take a sip of his fruit juice.

'God, not only is that wretched woman coming over again, she's got those disgusting pugs with her. Oh, *honestly*, it's too much...' Duncan groaned, covering his eyes with his hand. But as Mrs Doggett approached he rose to his feet, positioned himself by the ingle-nook and managed to muster an appreciative smile.

'Ah, Mrs Doggett', he said, 'how nice... you're an absolute angel looking after us like this. Yes, I think you're right, let's have our coffee by the fire - nice and cosy. Thank you so much. *Too* kind.'

'No need to thank me, Mr Wainwright, it's all part of the service. I like to have people like you - my '*extra special'* guests' - here in the Lounge Bar so I can look after you properly. Not over there...' she waved her hand dismissively towards the Public Bar, 'with the local riffraff.'

She giggled girlishly as she handed round the cups of coffee after which she hovered around the periphery of the group, smacking the odd cushion, re-arranging the line of pottery dogs along the mantelpiece, clearly working up to an interrogation. The two pugs, as overweight as stuffed piglets and quite hideous to look at, had settled themselves on the rug by the fire and were already dozing, their contorted faces resembling disgruntled gremlins. Duncan shuddered as one of them, emitting a disgusting nasal snore, rolled over onto his foot, its fat body quivering with every intake of breath, its trotters held out stiffly, slightly raised, as though it had been shot. Looking up, Duncan saw that Mrs Doggett was gazing at them with nothing less than maternal devotion, and quickly transformed his expression of revulsion into one of amused tolerance.

Her response was to smooth the antimacassar behind his head and insist for the third time since his arrival that she was sure she'd seen him somewhere before. He suggested she might have seen his photograph on the fly-leaf of his latest book but she adamantly dismissed that idea declaring that she never had time to read books and only occasionally flicked through a magazine.

'I can't remember when I last read a book,' she said. 'But now I've met you I'm going to make the effort and get one of yours from the library - I might even pop down there tomorrow.'

'Well, Mrs Doggett, what can I say? I'm honoured,' muttered Duncan, easing his foot, which was now quite numb, from under the body of the pug. By way of response it made an awful guttural noise deep in its throat and from then on each time it breathed out a bubble of mucous formed round its right nostril, only to be sucked in again with each new intake of air. Fighting to overcome a wave of nausea Duncan returned his attention to the landlady who was now twittering on about the hotel arrangements for the Literary Festival, held annually in Chiselfordam for the past nine years.

'Of course, the publicity people - well, the lady in charge at this end - I expect you know her - Fiona Bridewell - she's *ever* such a nice person - she told me just a little bit about you all when she made the booking. When she said I was getting the crime writers this year...well, to be honest, I was just a *teeny*-weeny bit worried, not knowing what to expect. Not to worry, she said, you'll like them, they're ever such nice people - they're not all psychopaths or anything that like that, you know. I had to laugh, didn't I?' She put her hand to her neck and made a rapid snuffling noise not unlike that made by one of her pugs. 'And I hear you've all been short-listed for some prize or other?'

'Yes, that's right - the *Birkett Bronze Award'*, said Rev Pinny, making an effort to be pleasant. 'It's awarded annually for the best - well...' He hesitated and looked apologetically at the others, '*supposedly* for the best crime book of the year - factual, of course, not fiction. It's a specialist field, you see, and we each have our own particular subject.'

'Oh, I see,' said Mrs Doggett, moving her weight from one foot to the other.

'Mine's company law and corporate fraud - embezzlement, that sort of thing. I know most people think it's boring but in fact it's terribly interesting when you really look into it. Duncan writes mainly on murder in the theatre...'

'May I just say at this point, Mrs Doggett, writing is only *one* of my preoccupations,' Duncan said. 'I think I might say without any false pride that I am a reasonably successful actor. Currently between jobs but, nevertheless, a life-long devotee of the performing arts.'

As the only response was an appreciative nod from Thelma Doggett, Pinny went on: 'Oliver concentrates on Fifties' mobsters - well, amongst other things...' At this point he seemed to either lose track of his flow or run out of wind for his voice faded away and he stared fixedly at the gaudy pattern of swirling orange and gold leaves on the carpet by his feet.

'My speciality is nineteenth century poison,' Leanne continued, 'and Rae here, she only deals with female killers.

She's doing a doctorate on the role of hormone imbalance in female criminality.'

'Not quite - genetics and aggression and the significance of testosterone and serotonin,' explained Rae.

'Well, I never,' said Mrs Doggett, resting her thumb under her chins, splaying her fingers across her cheek and adopting a thoughtful expression.

'And as for Aubrey Atherton, the sixth finalist, he's a specialist on fuck all,' finished Oliver, avoiding Rev Pinny's startled look.

'In spite of which, Mrs Doggett, it may surprise you to know, he's won the prize for the last two year's running,' said Duncan, peevishly, *'and* he's the most successful – ie. popular - crime writer of our day. If he wins this time he gets to keep the original bronze bust Birkett had made when he retired as Lord Chief Justice - it's a truly hideous thing but worth a few bob, I can tell you. He'll also get the £25,000 prize money and go down in the Record Books for winning three times in a row. And what's more, I bet he walks away with the lot.'

'And he's the nastiest sod you could imagine,' Oliver said. 'Loathsome. Well, you know what they say - the Devil looks after his own. Isn't that right, Pinny?'

Joseph Pinny, reluctant to be drawn into an argument with Oliver, merely lowered his eyes and contorted his lips.

'Oh, it all sounds very exciting. When will they announce the lucky winner?' prattled Mrs Doggett, her right hand pulling at the bits of raised fluff on the front of her mauve mohair jumper, fully stretched to accommodate the amorphous spread of her matronly breasts.

'On Saturday. But in the meantime we've got a week of lectures, seminars and workshops to get through, I'm afraid,' Duncan moaned, affecting an exaggerated yawn. 'The whole thing's a crashing bore!'

'It's all right for you,' cried Leanne. 'Yours isn't till Wednesday - mine's first thing tomorrow morning and I'm absolutely dreading it...'

'Oh, don't you worry - it'll be *ever* so nice. We get a lot of what I call 'booky' people down here for the Festival; would you believe it, there's even more this year than last.' She turned to look at her husband, who was mechanically, unobtrusively stacking glasses behind the bar. 'We get a lot of 'booky' people staying here, don't we, Leonard?'

'Oh, we do that - yes, a lot. All sorts.'

'All the hotels and Bed & Breakfast places are fully booked - from what I've heard there's not a room to be had anywhere. My friend Geraldine's got eight children's' writers staying with her down at *The Three Oaks* and there's a whole load of poets at *The Dog & Whistle*. The romantics - well, we call them the Bodice Rippers - you know, the Mills & Boon lot, they were at *The White Hart Hotel* last year. To be honest I'm not sure where they're staying this time - I must find out. Just a mo - I'll ask Leonard...'

'Len! Who's got the Bodice Rippers this year?' she called. 'Is it *The Wheatsheaf* or *The White Hart*, same as last?'

'No idea.'

Mrs Doggett made a tutting noise. 'Hopeless man. Useless.' She frowned with ill-concealed irritation before turning once more to Duncan, who was looking uncomfortably hot. He had moved away from the fire, acutely aware that the air was ripe with the foetid smell emanating from one of the pugs as it grunted, snuffled and farted at his feet.

'Just a *teeny* bit too warm, Mr Wainwright?' asked Mrs Doggett. 'What about another coffee while you're waiting? Tell me, has Fiona told you yet where you'll be giving your little talks?'

'No, we're waiting for her now - she's supposed to be giving us a guided tour,' said Rev Pinny. He looked peevishly at his watch. 'She said she'd be here by one-thirty and it's three minutes to two already.'

'Oh, didn't you know? She's already here; she arrived while you were having lunch. She's upstairs with Mr Atherton, trying to sort things out.'

'Don't tell me that the old bastard's staying here as well!' exclaimed Oliver.

'Sorting out what?' asked Rae, suspiciously.

'Well, unfortunately, there's been a bit of a mix-up,' Mrs Doggett replied, glancing towards the stairs and lowering her voice to a stage whisper. 'Fiona was supposed to book him into *The Crown Imperial* - that rather grand place in the centre of town, where all the Bigwigs stay - no offence, but you know what I mean - all the best-seller authors, Adrian Henley, Samantha Egerton and that lot - but she booked him in here instead, thinking all the crime writers would be staying in the same place. It was a perfectly understandable mistake but now he's sulking and refusing to come out. Len took him up a little bit of lunch on a tray but he won't touch it. And now he's threatening to go back to London.'

'Good riddance!' said Rae, laughing.

'God, that's just so typical of him,' sneered Oliver. 'Why the hell can't he stay in the same place as the rest of us without making such a song and dance out of it? He's such a drama queen.'

Duncan proceeded to describe a particularly colourful tantrum thrown by a well-known theatrical personality but although she laughed shrilly on cue it was clear that Mrs Doggett was upset by Aubrey Atherton's behaviour for a slight flush of pique had transcended the layer of chalky powder on her face. Atherton's attitude left no doubt whatsoever that he considered *The Hare* infinitely inferior to *The Crown* - which it was. Although Thelma Doggett was willing to admit that her establishment was nowhere near as grand (and it was more than two miles out of town) she did her best and it was perfectly respectable. At least the sheets were brushed nylon, fitted, not those old scratchy linen ones they had at *The Crown.* She knew for a fact they still used them because Geraldine had told her and, what is more, they only provided a choice of three breakfast cereals whereas her clientele could choose from no less than four. And she was quite prepared to make proper coffee for her special guests - they only had to ask.

'Ah, well, they do say there's 'nowt so strange as folk', she said, as though that explained everything. 'Now I shall leave you to natter in peace. But I must say you do talk about some horrible things. Makes me go all funny.' She gave a little fastidious shudder. 'Just give me a little tinkle on the bell, won't you, if you need anything. Anything at all.' Standing on tip-toes she reached across the bar and lifted up a small brass bell in the shape of a lady in a crinoline. Lifting it delicately between forefinger and thumb and with her little finger crooked, she gave it a demonstration shake. 'There,' she sighed. 'Just a little tinkle, that's all it takes.'

Retrieving her tray and Rev Pinny's empty cup and glass she eased herself behind the bar where her husband was hunched over a copy of the local newspaper. She pushed his arms from under him and said, in a voice loud enough for everyone to hear:

'Oh, for heavens' sake, go on upstairs, Len. I thought you said you had some paper work to do? These people have important things to discuss and they don't want the likes of you hanging around looking like a wet Sunday and listening to every word they say. And change out of that horrible cardigan. Makes me sick at the sight of it.'

With that she gave him a sharp nudge with her elbow before sweeping aside the multi-coloured bead curtain on her way through to the kitchen.

*

Chapter Two

It was ten past three by the time Fiona Bridewell came downstairs. She was looking flustered and her nest of permed red hair was looking positively wild; her large eyes were further magnified by the thick lenses in her assertive, turquoise-framed glasses, which blended perfectly with the transparent plastic hearts dangling from her ears. She wore a loose-fitting purple tunic over a green silk blouse and under her long black skirt she was wearing high-heeled, buttoned ankle boots. In one hand she held a clipboard and in the other a copy of Aubrey Atherton's latest book, *The Ultimate Chronicle of Crime*. Her neck was festooned with several ropes of multi-coloured glass beads and on the end of a purple leather thong there hung a green plastic jumbo pen in the shape of a dolphin.

Gathering up her skirt she perched on one of the bar stools and slammed Aubrey's tome onto the bar. Turning to face the other finalists she began by apologising for the delay; her voice was breathless and as she waved aside Oliver's offer of a drink she adjusted her glasses and studied the list on her clipboard.

'The whole thing's an absolute dis*aster* - everywhere's booked up. I really don't see what Atherton expects me to do. The room's perfectly adequate.' She ran her fingers through her tousled hair and closed her eyes. 'He can be the absolute limited sometimes - really.' For a moment she looked as if she might burst into tears. 'If he does go back to London they'll sack me...oh, *God!'*

'Oh, come on,' said Oliver, walking over and putting his arm around her shoulders. 'He won't go back. You don't honestly think Aubrey would forgo all the adulation? As far as he's concerned all these people will have come all this way, from all corners of the country, for one purpose only - to see *him*! The man's a megalomaniac, we all know that...'

'He's right, my dear,' said Duncan, fiddling with his Paisley bow-tie. 'He can't resist a captive audience. Smell of the greasepaint, roar of the crowd and all that. He'll not be going anywhere you can be quite sure of that! He did the same thing last year - found some reason to make a fuss, anything to be the centre of attention.'

Rev Pinny chose not to comment. Having noticed a particle of the Quiche Lorraine he'd eaten at lunch stuck near the top button of his flies, was engrossed in rubbing it with the end of his finger which he had surreptitiously wetted with spittle.

'Hey, steady on, Pinny - what *are* you doing, man?' Oliver quipped. 'The lounge bar of the *Hare'*s hardly the place. Shame on you, a man of the cloth and in mixed company too...'

Rev Pinny raised his eyes but ignored the remark and refused the paper tissue offered by Leanne. 'May I ask, my dear,' he said, directing his attention to Fiona Bridewell, 'if you have been given the names of the judges yet? Or anything about them? I should like to know in whose hands our destinies lie, as it were.'

'I can, at least, give you their names,' said Fiona, leafing through her notes. 'Yes, here we are - Mr Theodore Rigby...'

'Surprise, surprise!' exclaimed Rae.

'As you know,' went on Fiona, 'it was he who instigated the *Birkett Bronze Award* some years ago and is the current President of the *Crime Club Committee.* It's his last year, I think. He's due to retire in the summer.'

'Where, no doubt, he'll rummage around fumigating his potting shed while he waits to hear about his knighthood,' scoffed Oliver, lighting a cigarette and handing one to Leanne.

'The second judge is...let me see...the critic, Max Wilbur.'

'Critic! Is that what you call it?' exclaimed Duncan, huffily crossing his legs and folding his arms like a truculent schoolboy. *'Machete Max'* more like it - the man's a butcher! And he wouldn't know a decent play if he saw one.'

'And totally without talent himself, of course,' added Leanne. 'He really tore my first book to shreds - not only that, the comments he made were so bloody inaccurate. It was obvious he hadn't even bothered to read it!'

'Think yourself lucky,' said Rae, 'he said one of my books was completely unreadable. It wasn't brilliant, I grant you, but it wasn't *that* bad.'

'Who's the third assassin?' asked Oliver.

'Beverley Holden can't make it so there'll be a replacement coming on Wednesday - no, I don't know who it is.' As she said this Fiona slipped off the stool and gathered up her things. Looking at her watch she tutted and reached over to give the brass bell an imperious shake.

Always pleased to be summoned, Mrs Doggett swept through the bead curtain, wiping her hands on a piece of kitchen towel, her head tilted expectantly.

'Now Mrs Doggett,' began Fiona, decidedly bossy now that her confidence had been restored. 'Will you please ensure that Mr Atherton has everything he requires to make his stay as comfortable as possible. I have to go now as I'm running terribly late. If there are any problems you can always get me on my mobile...' She inserted one of her cards between Thelma's plump little fingers. 'Please don't hesitate to get in touch with me if there's the slightest problem - I'd really much rather know straight away. As you may have already gathered, Mr Atherton is a man of particular tastes and heightened sensibilities and in consequence can sometimes be a little difficult - and yet, as you will no doubt soon realise, he can be an absolute sweetie when he so chooses.'

Turning to the group by the fire, she said: 'Right, I'm off. Bye for now. I'm sure I'll run into you during the week. You do know your venues, I presume?'

'Of course we don't,' Rae protested, standing with her hands on her hips. 'We've only just got here! We thought you were going to give us a guided tour and go over the final arrangements.'

'Well, I'm sorry. You can see how things are. I just haven't got time.,' Fiona said, shaking her head. 'You'll just have to find them on your own - I'm sure you're perfectly capable - Chiselfordam is, after all, a very *small* town, hardly a swarming metropolis.' Turning to Duncan, she said, 'You were here last year - surely you can find your way around? Anyway. if there's a problem I'm sure Mrs Doggett will gladly help you out.' By this time Fiona was already by the main entrance, her hand on the door.

'What's that, dear?' asked Thelma Doggett on hearing her name mentioned.

'Be an angel and tell them where to find *The Schoolroom*, *The Church Hall* and the *Marquee*. They've got a special map and a list of times for the lectures and workshops in their information packs. But the truth is, I suppose, they haven't even bothered to look at them. Writers never do. They're all the same. Tunnel vision.'

'Fancy. Better things to think about, I suppose,' Mrs Doggett said, folding her arms as she winked at Duncan.

'Mr Atherton's just as bad. He's scheduled to appear at the conference hall in *The Crown Imperial* along with our other best-selling authors. But there's no need to panic. His principle lecture isn't till Wednesday but no doubt he'll make a few guest appearances and I know he's got several book signings lined up.'

'What a busy man!' exclaimed Thelma Doggett, admiringly.

'He's always in great demand at the literary festivals. He's got a press conference at ten tomorrow morning. But don't worry, I'll be here with his car at nine-thirty. Don't forget to wake him by seven-thirty. He likes to have at least a couple of hours to prepare himself, mentally and physically, for an appearance. His lectures are sold out, of course. He's *terribly* popular. Well I'm off. 'Bye, now. Good luck for tomorrow.'

With that Fiona was gone leaving the group in the lounge feeling aggrieved and abandoned as they listened to the wheels of her car slicing up the gravel as she turned in the drive and headed back towards the town centre.

'Well, that's nice - left to our own devices,' muttered Oliver, 'though I can't say I'm surprised.'

'I suppose we'd better make our own way down to the town and find out where these God-forsaken places are ready for tomorrow,' said Duncan. 'What a crashing bore. What about another drink before we go?'

'Now don't all hit me at once,' Leanne said as she passed a glass of bitter lemon to Rev Pinny, who was still fretting about the stain on his trousers. 'but I must say I think Aubrey Atherton sounds intriguing, in a horrid sort of way.'

'Intriguing!' sneered Rae. 'I can think of better adjectives.'

'But to be fair to the man, despicable though he may be,' conceded Duncan, downing his second whiskey. 'He actually started out as a very good writer, very good indeed. Not many people know this but he wrote a play many years ago and I actually had a small part in it when they put it on in Sheffield. It was quite good, as a matter of fact, and his first three books were excellent - first rate.'

'I grant you that,' agreed Oliver. 'But the success went to his head big-time and, in my opinion, he hasn't written anything worth reading since.'

'Oh, I agree,' said Leanne. 'I'm not arguing with that. But I'm still looking forward to meeting him.'

'I think I'm right in saying,' Rev Pinny suddenly interjected, 'that he couldn't find a publisher for his first book and a friend subsequently paid for it to be privately printed...'

'Really? I didn't know that,' replied Oliver.

'No, well, he wouldn't broadcast the fact, would he?' scoffed Rae. 'I suppose he might consider it a bit of a smack in the eye for his over-inflated ego.'

'You see - we're doing it again! Whenever we get together we always end up talking about bloody Aubrey Atherton!' Duncan groaned.

'Anyway, Leanne, you'll meet him soon enough - *if* he decides to make an appearance...'

'Which of course he will. I told you, he can't resist an audience,' muttered Duncan.

'That's right - he simply laps it up,' said Oliver, passing a glass of beer to Rae and another coke to Leanne. 'I had to interview him once at the Frankfurt Book Fair when I was with the *Manchester Recorder*. What a fiasco that was - dozens of reporters scrambling all over the place, flash bulbs popping. He loved every minute of it. I bet he spends hours practising those spontaneous, witty one-liners.'

'Well, why not?' said Leanne, wistfully. 'Let's quit the sour grapes, everyone. The fact is we're only jealous because he's so successful. We should be so lucky...'

'Yes, but we all know *why* he's been so successful,' sneered Rae. 'Unknown to the average reader he just pinches everybody else's work and re-hashes it - *verbatim,* in some instances, I might add.'

'He doesn't even do that,' explained Oliver. 'With all the money he made from the book royalties and the film rights he can afford to employ a bevy of researchers to dredge up all the info - as you say, usually from other people's books. I know for a fact he just bleats into a tape recorder for a couple of hours a day and then gets a fleet of secretaries to type it out for him. I'm telling you, it's money for old rope. Besides which, he's well and truly clinched the market, the lucky bugger.'

Rev Pinny shook his head sorrowfully: 'But, for all his wealth, you know, by all accounts he's not a happy man - one must have compassion.'

'Must one? Why?' asked Oliver.

Before Rev Pinny could answer, the conversation was cut short by someone calling:

'My good woman!'

Turning, the group saw that someone was standing at the top of the curving staircase that led directly into the centre of the lounge.

'Talk of the devil - it's Aubrey.' Oliver whispered into Rae's ear. 'That's odd - I thought vampires only came out after dark.' At this Rae snorted into her beer glass, sending showers of froth onto Rev Pinny's knees. The only one of the group yet to meet the celebrated writer was Leanne and she was intrigued.

Joseph Pinny had met Atherton on several occasions and each time his dislike had been reinforced. Still busily dabbing his trousers with his handkerchief he only briefly glanced at the figure on the stairs.

Aubrey Atherton stood very upright, his head slightly tilted towards the ceiling, the better to look down on his inferiors. He was a large man, tall and upright with dark chestnut hair, carefully waved. He was dressed in a pale yellow polo necked jumper, made of the finest cashmere, light grey slacks, silver moccasins and white socks. An expensive camel coat hung from his shoulders and his eyes were shielded by pink tinted glasses. He stood perfectly still, making no attempt to descend.

Realising that he required her assistance, Mrs Doggett scuttled over and stood at the foot of stairs. The man at the top held out a limp, manicured hand and waited as she skipped up the stairs to meet him. Only then did he descend, very slowly. On reaching the bottom step he stopped and, with exaggerated disdain, drew the neck of his jumper up over his nose. Flapping his free hand in the direction of the pugs, still somnolent by the fire, he complained, in a nasal whine:

'Mrs Doggett, my dear, I must ask you to remove those creatures. It's really too bad. Fiona should have told you that I am allergic to dogs - in fact I am allergic to animals of any kind and they have the most *devastating* effect on me. Please order them out immediately.'

Len Doggett darted from behind the bar and, scooping one wriggling pug under his arm he dragged the other across the floor of the lounge by its collar. It protested pig-like as its backside processed the pattern of swirling orange leaves on the thick pile carpet and the rolls of excess skin on its neck were pulled into pleats over its bulging forehead and moist, gobstopper eyes. It was only when the Doggett had pushed both dogs out of sight that Aubrey Atherton allowed Mrs Doggett to lead him towards the most comfortable chair by the fire. Once she had plumped up an extra cushion, placed it in the small of his back and brought him a Bacardi and rum, he dismissed her with a wave of his hand. A fleeting smile of satisfaction passed over his flaccid face as he crossed his legs and lit a gold-tipped cheroot.

Looking round the assembled group he gave a little squeal of amusement:

'Well, my dears,' he said, in his distinctively high-pitched, querulous voice. 'What a hoot! Don't tell me *you're* the competition. It's quite, *quite* ludicrous. They might just as well hand over the sodding bronze and the loot right now and let me get back to London and away from this bloody awful hole.'

*

Chapter Three

The moment Aubrey Atherton sat down both Oliver and Rae stood up, feeling somehow at a disadvantage sitting, as it were, like acolytes at the great man's feet. Rev Pinny, after a nod of acknowledgement to Atherton, sank further between the wings of his chair and, lowering his head, was soon lost in thought. Duncan rose to order another drink from Len Doggett, who, obviously primed and poked into action by his wife, was looking more lively than before, having changed into a smart navy blazer with brass buttons and a gold thread logo on the breast pocket. His hair now slicked back, he was standing to attention behind the bar.

'I'll have another as well, Duncan, while you're there,' said Aubrey. 'Stick it on my bill, Doggett, there's a good chap.' Ignoring the others he turned his attention to Leanne:

'Well, you must be Miss - or does one say *Ms* Philips these days - you must be gratified, not to say surprised, to find yourself short-listed this year. I suppose some might consider even so small an accolade marks a certain degree of success. Personally, I find this whole business of promotional tours - prizes, signings, readings - frankly rather a chore.'

As he took off his glasses and launched into a monologue on those aspects of fame he found most tedious Leanne was able to watch him closely. She saw at once that the others had not been exaggerating - there *was* something disturbingly repellent about him. He was clean-shaven and his pale skin, smooth and soft and stretched over his subcutaneous fat, gave the impression of a *full* maggot. His face, in fact his whole body, though of more than average height and weight, seemed strangely boneless whereby his features were indistinct, unfinished, almost embryonic. His head was topped with a toupee made of wavy, chestnut brown hair that was too thick and too glossy for a man turned fifty and failed to blend with his own which was pale in colour, neither blond nor grey and plainly visible above his fleshy ears. His eyes, too, were virtually colourless, slightly protruding, the pupils contracted to pin-pricks, as devoid of expression as those of a reptile - indeed, the analogy was apt for as he talked they gave the appearance of revolving, like the eyes of a chameleon. His teeth were small, uneven and nicotine-stained and his hands looked limp and sweaty. One or two beads of perspiration had formed on his upper lip. As he crossed and re-crossed his legs Leanne noticed that, whilst his feet were unusually small for a man of his size, his ankles, encased in white silk socks, were unusually thick and as he moved he exuded what she could only describe as a sweet, decomposing smell that even his potent after-shave and expensive array of body lotions failed to mask.

'Oliver, dear boy,' Aubrey was saying. 'Do sit down, you're making me quite dizzy pacing about like that - why don't you sit here and tell me all about your latest tome, I'm simply dying to hear all about it.' He raised his hand for Doggett to replenish his glass, lit another cheroot, balanced his heavy gold lighter on the arm of the chair and continued: 'What is the title, by the way, I've completely forgotten?' He paused for a moment, looking intently at Oliver, as though, despite the contempt in his voice, his interest was, in fact, engaged.

'Villains or Heroes - The Fifties Mob', said Oliver, his face set, waiting for the inevitable put-down that would follow.

'Ah, yes. Well. Almost as eminently forgettable as your last. Tell me - do you honestly think people are the slightest bit interested in reading about muscle-bound morons?' He lowered his eyes; 'More to the point,' he continued, 'why on earth is a *wildly* attractive creature like you bothering to work at all? I could name countless men - and women for that matter - who could quite easily fall madly in love with you and provide you, for a while at least, with everything you could possibly want. We must talk about it at some length before the week is up.'

'Wow, now that's an offer you can't refuse, dear boy,' whispered Rae, squeezing Oliver's arm. But before he could answer Atherton had turned his attention to Rev Pinny.

'Oh, heaven's above,' he said in mock surprise. 'I see the Praying Mantis is here! Well, Pinny, fancy you getting short-listed. What's the title this time? *Last Minute Confessions* or *The Devil At Work in The Criminal Mind*'? Having said this he raised his hand to his mouth, closed his eyes and gave an exaggerated yawn.

'It's called *Easy Money - The Counterfeit Trail,'* replied Pinny. 'I think you already know my speciality. You also know full well that my religious convictions are a quite separate matter.'

'Oh, yes?' sneered Atherton. 'Do tell me, I'm dying to know, why this loving God you've conjured up from the depths of darkest mythology allows the pernicious spread of evil without lifting so much as an omnipotent finger to end the most inexcusable suffering that has been the lot of billions and billions of people throughout history, poor souls unlucky enough, and through no fault of their own, to have been born at all? The word *'sadistic'* springs to mind.'

'As well you know, Atherton,' said Rev Pinny, at last looking directly at his would-be tormentor. 'To even begin to address the whole premise of good versus evil would take a very long time - certainly more than we have at present - nor do closed minds make for constructive dialogue,' he added, rising from his chair. As he walked towards the stairs, Atherton called after him:

'Now, now, Pinny, stop trying to sneak off! Stand firm and fight, man - Onward Christian Soldiers and all that.'

'I am merely going to my room to fetch my Macintosh.' Pinny said. 'I think we might be in for a shower.'

'God, that man's the wettest creature I've ever met and he's worried about a bit of rain - *pathetic,*' remarked Atherton as he watched the stooped figure of Rev Pinny mount the stairs.

'At least he doesn't go around upsetting everyone,' said Leanne, defensively.

'Why should he?' Atherton said, with a shrug. 'He's in the business of placating, not confronting. Creeping around hoping to pounce on any unsuspecting soul that doesn't foolishly fall for all that mumbo-jumbo - hell-fire and all that. He's full of it, it's jamming up what may once have been a half-decent brain. Though I doubt it somehow. The man's a ninny. A spineless jelly.'

Drawing on his cheroot, he sighed loudly. 'God, I'm *unbelievably* bored.' He watched with irritation as Duncan, who was sitting opposite, rummaged through the contents of his shabby brief-case looking for Fiona's list of venues.

'And what about you, Duncan?' he went on. 'Ah, is that a copy of your book? Do let me see.' He reached over and lifted the book from the table, glanced at the cover and then replaced it. 'Ummm - *The Theatrical Portrayal of Murder*. I must say I was surprised to see you'd been short-listed. To be honest I thought you'd given up on the writing lark for good after your last attempt. How's the acting, by the way?'

Duncan hesitated: 'Oh, I've been extremely busy for the last couple of years so I can't complain.'

'Oh, really? You surprise me. What have you been in?'

'Well, one or two fairly small but challenging parts in rep. Wonderful scripts, marvellous company of actors, great fun...'

'Which companies were those?' Aubrey's reptilian eyes, fixed on Duncan's flushed face, were coldly enquiring.

'Oh, you know - various provincial theatres - wonderful repertoire. Excellent productions. First rate,' babbled Duncan, as Atherton watched him flounder.

'Come now, Duncan, don't be so modest - we're all dying to know the details - dates, companies, runs, reviews, etc. I know for a fact you keep a damned great scrapbook - Christ, you've bored enough people with it in the past.'

'I did bring it, as a matter fact. I like to browse through it in the evenings - there's nothing wrong with that, is there?'

'Nothing at all - as long as you don't expect other people to look at it and die of terminal boredom. But, more importantly, what next - have you got anything else lined up or are you err-rum, *resting*, as you people say in the theatre?'

Duncan reddened and did not reply.

'Well?' demanded Atherton.

'Ah, no, nothing at the moment. Nothing at all, I'm afraid.'

'Oh, dear, what a shame - and nothing in the pipeline either, I suppose.'

'Well, there is a *slight* possibility of ...' Duncan began, acutely ill at ease at Atherton's cruel interrogation. He did, in fact, have something coming up at the end of the year - in pantomime - but he had no intention of telling his tormentor.

'Yes, I thought so. Nothing at all. May I suggest you might be wiser to concentrate on one or the other, either acting or writing, and not, as it were, spread what little talent you possess too thinly. That's only my opinion, of course, and I only say this for your own good for, correct me if I'm wrong, thus far success seems to have sadly escaped you in both fields.'

Duncan was clearly upset by Atherton's remarks and Rae was quick to defend him: 'Well, I'm sure Duncan can do without your advice, Atherton,' she said. 'My book's called *The Genetic Factor in Female Criminality* by the way - perhaps you'd like to say a few words about that as well?'

Aubrey's awful eyes swivelled in her direction:

'That's the trouble with you, my dear, and, may I add, with your sort in general. You're so confrontational and, moreover, singularly averse to criticism. And I fear you will find this an insurmountable failing, not only in your ill-chosen career but in life in general.'

'What d'you mean - my sort? Why don't you come out with it and say what you mean?'

As Rae got up and moved to the bar Atherton gave a little laugh.

‘'My dear soul,’ he said, ‘your sexuality is entirely your own business and of no interest to me one way or the other. Of that, my dear, you may rest assured - no interest *what*soever.'

He took a sip of his drink and cast a conspiratorial smile at Thelma Doggett who had come over to replace his ashtray with a clean one. 'So kind; thank you so much. My goodness, is that rain again? It really is too depressing - the first of May tomorrow and no sign of spring. Thank goodness you keep a good fire, Mrs Doggett, I can assure you it's greatly appreciated.'

'Insufferable pig,' Rae muttered, putting down her glass on the bar and heading for the stairs just as Rev Pinny was descending, his beige raincoat folded neatly across his arm. 'I'm just going up to my room to get my things. Leanne, Duncan, d'you want lift in my car?'

'Oh, yes, please. I'm ready when you are,' said Duncan, gratefully, shoving everything back in his case. Placing it on his knees he leaned forward, rested his chin on the handle and sighed.

'Me, too,' said Leanne, rising to her feet and following Rae. 'I'll just drag a comb through my hair and I'll be with you.'

'Well, Rev,' Oliver said, giving Joseph Pinny a tap on the shoulder. 'Looks like you're coming in my car.' Turning towards Atherton he said, ‘I won't offer you a lift, Aubrey, just in case it gave you some degree of pleasure to refuse.'

'My goodness, Oliver, such cynicism from someone with such a *heavenly* face! Dear heart, what ever gave you the idea that I should take pleasure in rebuffing your advances? On the contrary I should simply love to accompany you in your wonderful little motor car - if, that is, it was my intention to visit the mini-metropolis of Chiselfordam. To be frank, wild horses wouldn't drag me there - except for money, of course. I find the place quite loathsome. Naturally my publishers provide me with a chauffeur-driven car which will transport me wherever I wish to go. It goes without saying that I always have it written into my contracts and I shouldn't dream of setting foot outside London without it. But,' he added, his strange face twisted into a smile, 'I look forward to your return. Perhaps we might spend the evening together, discussing the latest line in knuckle-dusters, your love life or something equally riveting?'

Oliver caught Duncan's eye, frowned and whispered: 'Jesus, you don't think he fancies me, do you? Hell.' He pulled at Rev Pinny's lapel before he had the chance to sink back into his chair. 'Come on, Rev, chop-chop, let's get going - and you, Dunc. Ever played a chaperone before?'

Atherton gave them a perfunctory farewell flick of his hand and then beckoned to Mrs Doggett. She hurried over, her thighs rasping and her hands already clasped in a gesture of subservience.

'Now, Mrs Doggett,' he cooed. 'Thelma - what a pretty name - might I trouble you to assist me to my room where I should like you to bring me a glass of warm milk, a red apple, a copy of *The Times* and a little champagne. And perhaps you could ask your husband to transfer the television set and video machine to my room for the length of my stay? I intend to have my usual afternoon nap at four-thirty. I would appreciate not being disturbed, on *any* pretext, until seven twenty-five. Please ensure that you do not use a Hoover or any other domestic appliance between the hours of four and seven-thirty. Is that too much to ask? Am I being a *frightful* nuisance, my dear? Do say if I am. I have no wish to put you out in any way.'

*

Chapter Four

Rev Pinny's heart sank when he saw Oliver's nifty Aston Martin two-seater parked in the drive next to Rae's battered Volvo Estate. He hung back with palpable trepidation as Oliver undid the canvas top, rolled it back and told Duncan to climb into the space between the seat and the boot. To Pinny's profound relief, Duncan proved to be too large and too inflexible to fit into such a small space and was allocated the passenger seat instead. It was decided, therefore, that he, Pinny, should travel into town with Rae and Leanne, who, incidentally, would have loved a ride in the Aston Martin and had hoped Oliver might change his mind at the last moment and offer to take her instead of Duncan.

Though mercifully spared a nerve-racking spin in the Aston Martin, Rev Pinny's journey was, nevertheless, far from comfortable for the back seat of the Volvo had been folded down to accommodate what looked like a load of mucky builder's gear - tools, lengths of timber, piles of piping and several bags of plaster. He found himself wedged between a nest of dirty buckets and the bottom half of a dilapidated sink unit, encrusted with rivulets of grease studded with bits of vegetable matter. Fortunately the journey into town was short - Oliver and Duncan were already there - and within ten minutes

Leanne was helping Rae pull Pinny free from a piece of rope that had wound itself around his foot.

Unfortunately, Joseph Pinny's inelegant release was witnessed, not only by both Oliver and Duncan, but also by a small group of open-mouthed, adenoidal children, who, watching with mild interest as he disentangled himself, passed wads of bright pink gum around their loosely-hanging mouths. Their attention was soon diverted, however, by the sight of Duncan, red-faced and flamboyantly dressed in his floppy bow tie and checked jacket, with his grizzled hair blown askew by the wind. One of the children pointed at him, muttered something unintelligible and they all sniggered. Rae took one look at him and could see why.

'They probably think you're Ken Dodd,' she said, slamming down the hatch and locking it.

'Right - where first?' said Leanne, relieving Duncan of his briefcase so that he could sort out his hair as they made their way along a pedestrian walkway to the main street. 'Does anyone know where the church is - *The Church of St Ignatious*? Somewhere near the centre, apparently, not far from the Library. Is that right, Duncan?'

'Yes, it's somewhere along here - let me get my bearings - I think you'll find it's at the end of this street, in Bishop's Close. The Hall's right next to the Church. Look, there's the spire - if we keep going we should reach it - no problem.'

'Well, Duncan, I'm impressed,' Rae was saying as she led the way through the busy narrow streets. 'It's really nice here - your actual eighteenth century market town - some wonderful shop fronts. So much for Aubrey's opinion. And all these little tea-shops with those scrumptious cakes and that gorgeous smell of freshly ground coffee...'

*

It didn't take them long to find all three venues listed by Fiona. Leanne's seminar, it appeared, was scheduled for the following day in a Marquee which had been erected not far from the church on the banks of the river that meandered through the old part of the town. They could hardly have missed it; it was a massive pale green canvas structure, for some reason in the shape of a medieval castle, designed to seat some four hundred. Oliver had also been selected to lecture there on the following Thursday. As they walked around it, peering into the eerie green interior, workmen were still adjusting the ropes and marking the entrance with a wooden placard and chairs were being unloaded from a large lorry parked close by.

*

By mid-afternoon the town was crowded with visitors and there was a definite feeling of excitement in the air. There were bill-boards and fly posters everywhere heralding not only the forthcoming *Literary Festival* but also the *Grand May Day Parade* to be held the following day, Monday 1 May. The procession was due to start from outside *The Crown Imperial* and would be accompanied by side-shows, speciality rides for children, street theatre performances, buskers and Morris Dancers. Every building, it seemed, had been decorated with bunting and coloured lights and many of the shops sported special window displays - some with mock medieval scenes with gaily be-ribboned Maypoles whilst others marked the forthcoming *Festival* with windows celebrating the theme of books.

Passing down a narrow cobbled alley they came out into a secluded, tree-lined square in the middle of which stood the *Church of St Ignatious*, once a fine fourteenth century building, now an amalgam of various restorations carried out over the years in a number of conflicting styles. In its shadow stood a small, two storey church hall with a corrugated roof topped, incongruously, by a pretty cupola, round which strutted a group of sleek and quarrelsome pigeons. It was here that Reverend Pinny was due to give his talk on the following Tuesday. Having tried the door and finding it locked he scuttled off in the direction of the church and with a cheery wave, heaved open the massive oak door and went inside.

About five minutes walk away was *St Saviour's Junior School* where Duncan's workshop was scheduled to be held on Wednesday 3 May - on the same day Aubrey Atherton was due to deliver his much-hyped lecture at *The Crown Imperial* which was in the next street. Mrs Doggett had earlier described the place as 'big and posh and slap in the centre of town'. It was that all right. It was a fairly grand thirty-room building, with an ornate, early Victorian facade, heavy with cast-iron buttresses and balconies and an entrance heralded by an impressive iron and glass walkway.

By this time the group had lost Oliver as well as Joseph Pinny. Seeing Fiona Bridewell escorting a small group of women writers - one of whom Oliver recognised - up the steps of the hotel, he had sprinted across the road and joined them. Leanne watched him effortlessly infiltrate the group and burst out laughing at something Fiona had said. She was surprised to feel a twinge of envy as she watched him take the agent's elbow and guide her along the walkway and through the swing doors.

Feeling flat and out of sorts, Leanne followed Rae and Duncan, who were happily peering into the windows of antique shops and, at the same time, hoping to catch sight of various well-known authors who had also braved the showers to take a leisurely stroll before the hectic schedule ahead. On one corner they came across Rev Pinny listening intently to the Town Crier, who was proclaiming the events of the following day. For this purpose he had been wheeled out and trussed up in a bright red uniform, his usual place of employment being behind the '*Cooked Meats*' counter at Tesco's.

His audience consisted of a bemused group of tourists, cameras poised and an unsavoury bunch of local teenagers gathered, arms akimbo, merely to mock. Unperturbed and unabashed by their inane remarks he leaned back, unfurled his plastic parchment roll, and roared his message with astonishing vigour, not one word of which - except the perfunctory '*Oh, yeh, oh, yeh*!' at the beginning, was even remotely intelligible.

At the corner of every street, it seemed, there were entertainers of every description practising for the *Grand Parade* - young men with painted faces on monocycles, smiling jugglers, female buskers playing violins and even a man in a silly hat, bow-tie and striped trousers walking awkwardly on stilts.

Suddenly, from the church hall there came the strains of a practising jazz band, causing the arrogant pigeons to scatter and squawk.

Gathering up Rev Pinny, who had struck up a conversation with the Town Crier, Rae led the way through the maze of streets and after another hour's browsing they felt justified in making a bee-line for the coffee shop in the main street, well pleased with their afternoon's progress.

*

By a quarter to six there was still no sign of Oliver so they all piled into Rae's car for the journey back to *The Hare*. In fact, they only just made it for the Volvo shuddered and groaned ominously for the last hundred yards. When they reached the hotel they found the Lounge Bar empty and the fire out. Leonard Doggett had already opened up for the evening and was serving his regulars in the Public Bar. There was the low murmur of formatted conversation and the first rendition of *'My Way'* was already spinning on the deck. But there was no sign of Mrs Doggett nor, they were relieved to see, of Aubrey Atherton.

'I doubt if Oliver will be back tonight,' commented Rae. 'This happens every time we attend festivals - literary ladies love him and he'll have charmed his way into whatever's going on tonight. He always manages to get himself invited to the best parties. He's an incorrigible womaniser, you know. He's known in journalists' circles as "radical, restless and randy". That's right, isn't it, Duncan?'

'And the rest,' Duncan said. 'But he's got a lovely girlfriend - well, more than one if the truth were known. I don't understand it, myself. There was a chap in the theatre at Newquay, you know, he had a beautiful wife, lovely woman, but he just couldn't resist the ladies...'

'Like a child with sweets,' suggested Rev Pinny, as they went upstairs to their rooms, weary after their afternoon's excursion. Rae and Leanne were sharing a room, so, too, were Duncan and Pinny, but Oliver had insisted on a single.

Leanne settled down to go through her lecture notes before supper and Rae did the same. Duncan promptly fell asleep while Rev Pinny sat by the window reading and making notes. A little later, feeling hungry, they went back downstairs to the Lounge Bar expecting to find Mrs Doggett preparing their evening meal. Finding the room still empty, with only a small side-light left on, Rae rang the bell twice. It wasn't until the third ring that Mrs Doggett appeared, her cheeks flushed and her eyes decidedly glazed. It was evident that she had been drinking. Resting her palms on the bar she cocked her head on one side.

'Yes?' she asked, forgetting to smile.

'Might we have the menu, Mrs Doggett?' ventured Leanne. 'It's gone eight so we thought we'd better come down for supper.'

'Supper?' replied Mrs Doggett, looking surprised. 'Oh, I hadn't planned on providing supper tonight. Mr Atherton said he'd be going out to eat so he told me he didn't think it was worth while bothering to cook.' She slapped her hand against her cheek by way of retribution. Then she said, 'Shall I get Len to heat up a couple of pork pies? Would that suit you? Honestly. It's no trouble, no trouble at all.'

*

Chapter Five

Thelma Doggett seemed to have recovered by the time the group descended the stairs to the Lounge Bar shortly before eight next morning. Leanne had been up since seven, having slept badly, worrying about her contribution to the seminar, having intermittent dreams in which she found herself completely tongue-tied before an audience of thousands, some of which were jeering and cat-calling whilst others were laughing outright at her frantic efforts to speak. She had also been worrying, probably unnecessarily, about her son, Joe, whom she'd left with neighbours for the week. Coming up to thirteen he was well able to take care of himself but this was the first time they'd been separated for more than a day or two and he was constantly on her mind. She'd already phoned twice the day before, the moment she arrived and again as soon as they got back from town in the afternoon. She had been asked to attend the *Festival* two years before, when her first book came out - which was an excellent study of the Madeleine Smith arsenic case of 1857 - but had declined on account of Joe. Should she have turned down the invitation again this year? It was only because her latest book, *The A to Z of Nineteenth Century Poison*, had been short-listed for *The Birkett Bronze* that she'd decided to accept - was that selfish of her? Wasn't her responsibility as Joe's mother more important than pandering to her own vanity?

By the time she had washed and dressed, quietly so as not to wake Rae in the other bed, her nervousness had increased rather than diminished. Waiting until seven-thirty, when she knew her neighbour in London would be up, she crept downstairs to the public telephone which was mounted on the wall in the passage by the kitchen - next to a garish picture of a dog with soppy, myopic eyes sitting inside a fluffy slipper. The smell of frying food wafted through the half open door accompanied by the sounds of Len and Thelma Doggett arguing and the angry clatter of cutlery being flung into a drawer. Their voices rose even higher. The actual words were indistinct but the tone was clearly acrimonious. Feeling a little uncomfortable, as though she were eaves-dropping, Leanne dialled her friend's number and was soon assured that all was well. Joe was reluctant to come to the phone but when he did pick up the receiver he seemed irritated.

'Oh, hi. Want d'you want?' he said.

'Are you sure you're OK?' asked Leanne.

"Course I am.'

'Make sure you get to school on time and...'

'Don't fuss. Is that all?'

'I'll ring you this afternoon,' she said, 'when you get back from school.'

'What for? There's no point. I might be late. I've got to go now. I'm eating my breakfast. It's getting cold.'

That was it. He put the phone down. Well, at least he's still in one piece, Leanne thought, as she tiptoed back upstairs to find Rae already dressed, sitting on the edge of the bed, reading. She looked up as Leanne came in.

Everything OK?' she asked, slipping a torn strip of paper between the pages of the book.

'Yes, I suppose so,' Leanne said, gathering up her notes and files and jamming them into her jumbo-sized shoulder bag.

'Oliver's back,' Rae said, 'I just heard him talking to Duncan outside the bathroom. Nursing a hangover by the sound of things. He had to leave the car and get a taxi back in the early hours.'

'Well, let's hope he doesn't throw up over Mrs Doggett's fried eggs. Come on, let's go down and get it over with.'

When they reached the Lounge they were surprised to see Aubrey Atherton sitting at the table in the dining alcove, flanked by Duncan and Rev Pinny. Whilst they broke up their bread rolls and spread them with butter, Atherton was delivering one of his scathing monologues between sips of black coffee.

'Ah, the ladies!' he called as they approached. 'Well, I use the term euphemistically, of course. Come and sit near me, Leanne, my dear. Move along, Pinny, there's a good man.' But before she could sit down he raised his hand in protest. 'Forgive me for asking, Leanne, but surely you're not intending to give your little talk in that outfit? Just tell me it's not true. Disastrous, quite *disastrous*. Or is it the latest fashion to spend the morning rummaging through a box of Oxfam rejects and come out looking like an emaciated crow? And all those dingly-dangly things hanging from your ears lobes - just *too* awful! I get the whiff of a joss-stick just by looking at you.'

He patted the seat next to his and then, stirring his coffee, continued. 'You have a child, do you not?'

'Yes, a son of thirteen - why?'

'How fortunate that your husband has been able to stay behind in London to look after him.'

'I have no husband. I'm a single parent.'

'Oh, really, I didn't know.'

Silence while her interrogator paused to dismantle his croissant: 'Thank you so much,' he said, as Thelma arrived on cue with another dish of curled butter balls. 'They do tell me,' he went on, looking directly at Leanne, 'that it's quite the thing these days to be an unmarried mother. Is that so?'

Feeling too demeaned by his unprovoked assault on her appearance to offer an adequate reply to this facetious remark, Leanne remained silent. Rae, however, was quick to defend her.

'Don't bother to answer, Leanne,' she said, then turning to Atherton she snapped: 'Why don't you shut up, Atherton? You're a despicable bully. I might have known you'd make the effort to get up especially early just to annoy somebody. You know, you should arrange to have your food pushed under your door on a stick...'

'Ooooh, we *are* waspish this morning,' Atherton observed, clearly delighted at Rae's response. 'I wonder why?' He was just about to elaborate but stopped when he saw Oliver coming downstairs and gave a delighted shriek. 'Oliver, dear boy! Only *you* could be nursing a king-sized hangover and still look divine. Duncan, give the poor boy some black coffee and Pinny, pass him a croissant quickly, before he passes out before our adoring eyes.'

'Atherton,' Rae announced, 'has just been demolishing Leanne's fragile self-esteem by telling her she looks awful. Very helpful, I must say, just before she has to make a public appearance.'

Oliver took a long drink of coffee, rolled up the sleeves of his shirt and half-turned to face Leanne. He looked at her appreciatively for a moment then reached over and lightly touched her knee.

'Well, I think you look wonderful,' he said. 'Don't take any notice of Atherton - he wouldn't know a good-looking woman if he saw one. Anyway, he's stuck in a time-warp and has been for years. I should think a nice pleated Goray skirt, twin set and pearls is more his line. Mind you, I must say, he does look rather nice in a wrap-over pinny and a hair-net.'

Duncan chuckled behind his napkin but Rev Pinny frowned disapprovingly. Everyone was looking at Aubrey Atherton, expecting him to throw a tantrum or flounce out and lock himself in his room for the rest of the day. But, he did nothing of the sort; instead, he gave Oliver a roguish smile.

'Well, *fancy* - I had no idea you were into cross-dressing,' he said. '*How* exciting. We must have a long chat about it later on when we have our little tête à tête. I can't wait, and I have the prettiest little blouse you can try - shell pink satin, cap sleeves, with just a *teeny* bit of crochet round the collar.'

Rev Pinny's eyes widened. He looked lost. Duncan began to splutter, having swallowed an un-chewed portion of bread and both Leanne and Rae, despite their antagonism, found themselves smiling. So engrossed were they in the effects of

Atherton's remarks that no one noticed the look of disgust on Thelma Doggett's face as she circled the table handing out plates piled high with sausages, eggs and bacon. The moment she left the room Oliver shovelled his food onto Duncan's plate and poured himself more coffee.

'Getting too much for you these days?' asked Rae, resting her arm on Oliver's shoulder. 'You look terrible. Needless to say we saw you smarming round Fiona and her precious 'best-sellers' yesterday. Worth it, was it?'

Oliver shrugged. 'So-so,' he said. 'Got invited to dinner last night and another tomorrow. Funny, I'd always imagined Samantha Egerton to be an ancient crone, at least sixty. I had no idea she was relatively young - you know, early forties - attractive, too.'

Atherton made an exasperated noise and banged his knife onto his plate. 'I've told you before,' he whined. 'Why must you waste your talents fawning over these redoubtable literary ladies when I can get you in anywhere - *anywhere* at all. You only have to ask and I'd be delighted to oblige.'

Rae, who was tucking into her breakfast with some relish while the others, finding the greasy fare unpalatable, simply picked at theirs, let out a snort of disgust. 'Blimy!' she said. 'Which would be worse? *Him* or a crinkly old duck with a moustache!'

'More up *your* street one would have thought, my dear. Or did you say 'duck'?' murmured Aubrey, dabbing his mouth with his napkin and reaching for his lighter.

By this time Leanne was feeling very nervous about the seminar, which she had been secretly dreading for weeks. She looked at her watch again - nine o'clock. Realising that she'd be on the platform and facing an audience within the hour, she felt sick and thoughts of escape flashed through her mind. Basically fairly shy, her fragile self-confidence had been further deflated by Aubrey Atherton's disparaging remarks. Her stomach began to churn. Just as they were about to leave she had to make a last minute dash to the lavatory.

While she was upstairs she stopped to exchange her loose, black-fringed top for a simple silk shirt and replaced her heavy silver and garnet earrings with some plain silver hoops. Taking a last look at her tense reflection in the mirror she was reminded of a frightened rabbit, with the only discernible features being two staring 'boiled gooseberry' eyes. Desperate to add some emphasis to her face she applied more blusher before reaching for the mascara.

Then, on impulse, she decided to put her hair up for a change. Gathering the long, dark tresses in her hands she piled it on top of her head, letting several strands fall prettily over her ears. Securing it with an antique tortoise-shell comb she took one last look before joining the others downstairs.

In the short time Leanne had been upstairs the weather had changed completely - from cloudy with a slight drizzle to a brisk wind and sudden heavy showers. She groaned, knowing what a good drenching would do to her hair. There was also something wrong with the Volvo.

Duncan, Rev Pinny and Oliver were hanging around looking useless while Rae, with Len Doggett's help, had lifted the bonnet and was fiddling with the engine. The next moment Aubrey's Bentley arrived, chauffeur-driven and with Fiona Bridewell in the back.

'Morning!' she called as she swept past the forlorn group in the driveway, coats over their heads, backs to the wind, like a posse of wet cockerels. She gave a cheery wave as she caught sight of Aubrey watching from the window of the lounge bar. He was standing beside a bright red pelargonium in a pot on the window sill, sipping a glass of fresh orange and smirking at their misfortune.

'I think it's the fan belt,' Doggett was saying. Turning to Rae he asked her if she had a stocking he could borrow.

'Certainly not,' she replied, sharply.

'Hang on - I'll get some tights,' Leanne said.

Returning a moment later she gave them to Doggett. 'Here, use these - and please hurry. It's nine twenty already and it starts at ten.'

Ten minutes later the Volvo was lurching reluctantly through the wrought iron gates of *The Hare* with Rae, Leanne and Rev Pinny in the front and Duncan and Oliver wedged in the back with the builders' gear.

A sprinkling of bystanders were already lining up along both sides of the street eager to watch the first of the *May Day* floats easing their way from the outlying districts towards the assembly point in the centre of the town. Already people were sounding their car horns and from half a mile away came the muffled sound of a brass band starting out from the Territorial Drill Hall on the other side of town.

'Let's hope we don't get caught up in all the extra traffic,' said Rae.

'Oh, God, that's all we need,' Leanne groaned. 'What time does it start?'

'I think you'll find the procession proper starts from *The Crown* at ten,' said Rev Pinny, leaning against the sink unit, bent double like a ventriloquist's doll.

'We'll just miss it if you put your foot down,' said Oliver.

Leanne, clutching her bag of notes, looked through the rain streaked windscreen and crossed her fingers.

Two minutes later, three hundred yards down the road, the

car coughed and groaned and finally came to a halt outside a café.

'Shit!' shouted Rae, furiously turning the key in the ignition. 'The bugger's died on me.'

'Oh, God, why's this happening to me?' cried Leanne. 'Why? I just don't believe it.'

Rae tried the ignition again but the engine was dead. 'Sorry,' she said, shaking her head. 'It's no good. It's had it, I'm afraid. I'll have to get it to a garage.'

They all looked at their watches. Nearly a quarter to ten. Leanne let out a moan of misery.

'Don't worry, we'll get you there somehow or other,' said Oliver. 'If all else fails that creep Atherton will have to take us in the Bentley.'

'Shall I go back and ask him?' offered Duncan, not very enthusiastically.

'Why don't you go, Oliver?' suggested Rae. 'You're good at sucking up to people. Surely you could try to be nice to him just this once - for Leanne's sake?'

'Sure,' he said, without conviction. He ran all the way back to the hotel and was relieved to see that Aubrey Atherton hadn't left. Fiona was talking to the chauffeur in the driveway and Atherton was huddled in the doorway with Thelma Doggett. Oliver quickly explained their predicament but Fiona merely tutted irritably and shook her head.

'Please, Oliver - not now,' she said. 'I really haven't time to sort it out. I've got enough on my plate with Mr Atherton. My instructions are to concentrate on *his* engagements, not the rest of you. He has a very heavy schedule and my first priority is to get him to a press conference by ten. Needless to say we're running late.'

'Okay, fair enough,' Oliver said, 'but why can't we all pile into Aubrey's car and go down together?'

'Out of the question, I'm afraid.' Fiona replied. 'The publishers have provided the car for the sole use of Mr Atherton which means exclusively for his use and his use only - it's written into his contract. The insurance doesn't cover any other passengers...I'm sorry. Excuse *me!*' she snapped, deftly positioning her body between Oliver and the door of the Bentley as he reached for the handle.

'Oh, come *on*!' Oliver protested. 'Be reasonable for Christ's sake. Surely you can bend the rules for once? It's pissing down with rain, there's a ten force gale and Leanne's due at the *Marquee* in ten minutes.'

'Take your hand off that door,' Fiona hissed, looking like a fractious hen under her plastic rain-hood. Turning, she smiled and beckoned to Aubrey who was still hovering in the doorway of the hotel, refusing to come out until Len Doggett found an umbrella to hold over his head as he walked the five yards to the car.

Infuriated, Oliver raced back to the Volvo, still stationary outside the café, all its windows completely steamed up and its miserable occupants huddled in glum silence.

Moments later they had been offered, and were in no position to refuse, a lift from a man driving a vintage steam roller gaily bedecked with streams of bunting. Attached to the roof were clusters of bobbing balloons on which were painted moronically smiling faces. To the rear of the massive engine was a trailer cleverly camouflaged to look like a giant hot-dog, complete with a sausage the colour of diarrhoea down the middle of which was painted a garish strip of yellow mustard. The whole contraption was destined for the *May Day Parade* during which the driver, the local fishmonger, would offer to give children rides at twenty-pence a go.

Red-faced and numb with embarrassment the bedraggled group of crime-writers climbed into the 'hot-dog trailer', amid cheers and whistles from the crowds in the street, not to mention the jeering group of teenagers with their noses pressed to the window of the café.

To further excite the onlookers and draw their attention to the embarrassing spectacle, as the driver re-started the hissing and cranking contraption he repeatedly sounded the whistle. It was a truly piercing noise, guaranteed to make people turn and stare whilst oily smoke belched from every nut and bolt and wafted back into their faces.

'I must be dreaming - it's one of those bizarre nightmares, it must be,' groaned Leanne, being jolted from left to right as the steam roller, churning up the asphalt as it went, lurched its way down the main street towards the centre of the town.

Recovering from her initial embarrassment, Rae stood up near the rear of the roller and was soon chatting to the driver and roaring with laughter.

Rev Pinny sat white-faced and withdrawn, oblivious to the cheering crowds lining the route, cat-calling and waving. Children, obediently waggling their flags, smiled and shouted out to them as they rattled past.

Oliver, though acutely embarrassed to be seen in such a ridiculous mode, put on a show of jolliness but his smile was fixed and he was cursing Fiona under his breath.

But Duncan, it seemed, was genuinely enjoying it, waving back at the children and bowing ceremoniously to groups of old ladies who'd paused in their shopping to watch the parade as it passed.

And so it was that, amid the noise and mayhem, only

Oliver and Leanne noticed the Bentley sweep past them a few minutes later and caught a fleeting glimpse of Aubrey Atherton, seated beside Fiona Bridewell, waving benevolently from the rear window.

*

Chapter Six

Several minutes later, as the clock on the Church Tower was striking ten, Leanne was pushing her way through the crowds converging on the town centre. It was chaotic, with hordes of street entertainers gathered outside *The Crown Imperial* and officious men with loudspeakers trying to coerce the drivers of the floats into some sort of order before the start of the Grand Parade. Unleashed and unruly children were causing havoc by charging through the assembled bandsmen, knocking into empty instrument cases and scattering sheets of music in their wake.

When Leanne reached the *Marquee*, closely followed by Oliver, Rae and Duncan, there were still a few people trickling through the entrance, first shaking the surplus water from their umbrellas and then rummaging in their bags and pockets for mislaid tickets. Not daring to look at the audience she climbed onto the platform and sidled into the vacant seat at the end just as the compere, Claire Fenton, was introducing the other three speakers, dry and smugly in situ a full ten minutes before.

'Firstly,' she said, 'I should like to congratulate you all for finding your way through all the May Day shenanigans to attend our little meeting this morning, the first in a long list of lectures, talks and seminars on offer as part of this year's

Literary Festival. Secondly, let me present our guests in the order they will speak - on my far left Professor Ian Wyndham, Pathologist, next to him Dr Deirdre Swann, Toxicologist; to my right, Mr Ralph Smithson, Forensics, and next to him, having made it just in time I'm glad to say, Ms Leanne Philips, whose latest book deals with some fascinating cases of poison, the topic of our seminar this morning.'

There was a slight round of restrained clapping during which last minute arrivals scuttled to their seats. It was only at this juncture that Leanne dared to look up and confront the audience - all forty-eight of them. Fiona had warned them not to expect the vast audiences attracted to the main events - staged by well-known authors like Aubrey Atherton and Samantha Dunbar - but even taking into account the unsettled weather and the simultaneous start of the May Day Parade it was a pretty pathetic turn-out. In truth the number was so small that the first three rows were barely filled. Although Leanne had tried to dissuade Oliver, Rae and Duncan from coming to witness her tremulous debut, in the circumstances she was quite relieved to see them sitting in the front row, smiling and nodding in encouragement.

'Although it is our intention,' continued Ms Fenton, 'to keep this seminar fairly informal, I wonder if I might ask each of you to introduce yourself at the commencement of your talk, giving us a few salient details of your life, the titles, maybe, of your previously published works and any current projects - that sort of thing?'

She turned to smile at the four on the platform and they all nodded obediently. Seeing Oliver smiling up at her not four feet away Leanne was acutely aware that her sodden hair must have looked like a lump of soggy seaweed dumped on the top of her head. Water was trickling in rivulets down her forehead to collect copiously in her eyelashes, like rain water in a gutter. She kept her eyes wide, trying not to blink, thereby causing her mascara, which she had applied more thickly than usual that morning, to run in black streaks down her face.

She looked desperately at Rae, indicating her cheeks with her finger. Rae nodded. Oh, hell! She was aware that Oliver, sitting with his arms folded, was looking directly at her with a disarming smile. Fishing out a mangled piece of blue tissue from the bottom of her shoulder bag she dabbed at her face as each blackened river of soot descended, unhappily aware that her cheeks must now resemble the mottled red skin of a pomegranate.

Acutely discomforted at looking so foul for her first public performance, not to mention being the object of Oliver's amused surveillance, she tried hard to concentrate as Claire Fenton, having come to the end of her introduction, turned to the gentleman at the far end of the table.

'Now, may we start with you, Professor Wyndham?' Having said this, Claire Fenton sat down, her hands together and an encouraging smile on her face. This was the cue for the arrival of another group of latecomers, pealing off their dripping raincoats and sodden headscarves as they took their seats, mumbling their apologies.

The professor was a seasoned speaker. He rose, assembled his notes and then looked up, taking his time, appraising his audience, perfectly at ease.

'Good morning, ladies and gentlemen,' he said. 'Welcome. My name is Professor Ian Wyndham and I am quite sure none of you has ever heard of me.'

There was a ripple of polite laughter and the chance for the latest arrivals to re-align their bottoms more comfortably on the rigid plastic seats and drop their folded raincoats to the floor.

'Let me first give a brief explanation of my function. I am the County Pathologist - that is to say, I am attached to Staunton General Hospital and part, but by no means all, of my clinical work involves...'

Having been assured by a discreet thumbs-up from Rae that she had managed to mop up the last of the wet mascara, Leanne tried to concentrate on Professor Wyndham's words - but she was already familiar with his most recent text-books and found that within minutes her mind was wandering.

Looking once more at Rae with affection she remembered that winter, nearly eight years ago, when she first saw her at a meeting of the South London Women Writers' Circle in Fulham. She'd never been one for joining clubs - hated them, in fact. As a child she had never belonged to the Brownies or anything of that sort, much preferring her own company, alone in her room, drawing and reading.

Not surprisingly perhaps, as the only child of a teacher and a librarian, from an early age she had developed an insatiable appetite for books. She read anything she could lay her hands on and took to writing long complicated stories about children who lived in the country and had ponies and dogs - something she knew nothing about seeing as she'd been born in Hammersmith and had lived all her life in London.

It had been sheer desperation that had led her all those years later to join the Writers' Circle, not only to discuss the creative process with other writers but simply to get out of the flat once a month. At the time she had been incarcerated in a flat on the eleventh floor of a Battersea tower block with her son, Joe, for four and a half years. Though she had a number of colleagues who had become friends she had very little practical help. Her mother had died soon after Joe was born and her father was already sinking into premature senility and therefore of little use. Now, eight years later, she and Joe were still there and with no immediate prospect of moving to a more congenial setting. Leanne was still teaching history at one of the local schools and Joe had just started his second year at a comprehensive in Southfields.

Teaching in an inner-city school was hard and incredibly frustrating and after fifteen years in the job Leanne had become permanently exhausted, worn-out and disillusioned. She'd only taken three months leave when she had Joe - she couldn't afford to take more and often felt cheated of the first five years of his childhood. And now, after each day's struggle to attempt to socialise her charges, as well as teach them, she was burnt-out and irritable by the time she got home. She knew it wasn't fair to Joe but there was no way she could afford to work part-time or significantly reduce her work-load.

Their shared interest in writing had created an instant rapport between Leanne and Rae; they'd become friends and before long Rae introduced her to her partner, Sarah. Sarah felt in no way threatened; in fact it was she who volunteered to sit with Joe so that Leanne could attend the monthly meetings over a period of several years.

In many ways Leanne envied the lives of Rae, Sarah and the four other women who shared a three-storey house in Ealing. Though maintaining the privacy of their various partnerships they were, in effect, an extended family, offering each other tremendous companionship and support. Two of the women were mothers and much of the responsibility for the three children, all under ten, was shared.

Leanne had often envied them at times of crisis, when for instance either she or Joe was ill, or worse, when they were both ill together; and yet, though they'd tried to persuade her to join them, something, her dislike of groups perhaps, or the fact that she was alone whilst the others were in relationships, had held her back. Even so, she greatly admired the way they organised their lives so that the burden of child rearing was shared and even the mothers with youngsters were free to go out either to study or simply to enjoy themselves occasionally. Not like some of the wretched women on Leanne's estate, trapped, isolated not by choice but by circumstance.

Breaking her reverie Leanne made an effort to concentrate.

'Sadly,' she heard Professor Wyndham saying, 'we are seeing an increase in this type of injury in the youth of today.' At this point he held up a gruesome photograph of a young man on a mortuary slab with a stab wound to the heart.

Leanne looked away, thinking once more of Joe. Did ten minutes ever pass when she didn't think of him? Didn't think of his touchingly pubescent body, changing but still so vulnerable; the mind of a child too despite the street-wise attitude he'd recently acquired.

Especially vulnerable without a father, prey to the callous, careless or downright evil influences all around him, especially on the estate. Faced with the constant pressure to join one of the rampaging lawless gangs of petty thieves, or the ranks of the pathetic glue-sniffing kids, some as young as seven, slumped against the walls of the hollow alleyways between the blocks or squatting amongst the stinking rubbish bins, just another piece of human refuse. Or drugged out of their minds, crashed out cold on the fluted steel floor of a lift, face down in a pool of stale urine, more sprayed up the walls as far as the ceiling, the air thick with an appalling, stomach churning stench, courtesy of someone's need to defecate just inside the door.

Not Joe. Please, not Joe. She thought again of his youthful body, slight and soft, the still lively look in his eyes and their treacherously long lashes. Many a time she'd wept as she watched harrowing documentaries about drug addicted runaways and rent-boys and saw, not the anonymous blurred blob on the television screen but the face of her own son - Joe's face.

She shivered and became aware that Professor Wyndham had sat down and that Dr Swann, a slight, mild-looking woman of middle age with bobbed grey hair and half-glasses, was addressing the audience in a surprisingly forceful voice.

'...perhaps emphasises,' she was saying, 'our need to educate the young in the use of toxic substances, not only in the home but also...'

Tell me about it, thought Leanne, and tell me how to prevent kids like Joe being sucked into it all. It had been easier when he was young. She'd taken him around London, all the places children love to go - the Tower of London, The Science Museum, The Natural History, Madame Tussaud's, everywhere. But he was nearly thirteen now and there was no way he'd been seen going places with his mum. She could understand that. It was different with a girl. It shouldn't be - it just was.

Fortunately, he still saw the point of working hard at school but once his homework was finished what did she expect him to do? Stay in with her? What could he possibly do jacked up a hundred and seventy feet in the air? No place to kick a football, no shed to tinker about in. She could tell that sometimes he felt caged, trapped. He had to go out. God knows who he was mixing with and what he was getting up to. When it came down to it, how was she to know? He was probably lying half the time anyway - like she'd lied to her own mother since the age of twelve.

'And that, I firmly believe, is where the emphasis must lie if we are to continue to make advances in this particular field...' announced Dr Swann, for some reason waggling her finger at the people in the front row. It was then that Leanne noticed that Oliver had disappeared. Rae was still there, in body at least, though she was looking a little abstracted. Duncan, sporting an owlish pair of glasses, was reading from a sheet of paper laid across his knees, and appeared not to be listening at all.

Nor was Leanne - she was still thinking about Joe. Perhaps life on the estate didn't affect him as badly as she imagined - as it did her. After all, he'd never known any different. The tenancy of her bedsit in Notting Hill had run out soon after Joe was born and she'd been allocated the high-rise flat in Battersea, which at the time was classified as emergency housing. Leanne, thankful to find somewhere to live, could see nothing wrong with it - at least for the first hour or two. Until, that is, the music from the flat to her right penetrated the party wall at full blast, and continued non-stop for what seemed like eighteen hours a day.

Not only that, she soon realised that her new neighbour, Kelly, was not only anti-social but she was also an unpredictable, foul-mouthed and unusually bad-tempered tart. This thick-set and tacky harpie, whose age was difficult to assess, though coarse and volatile was, nevertheless, extremely popular, entertaining a never-ending stream of desperate punters. Whenever Leanne caught a brief glimpse of her as she shunted out one client and yanked in another, she was always dressed in a grubby baby-doll nightie, exposing her bruised and shapeless legs, under a soiled pink candlewick dressing gown.

She invariably had a cigarette hanging from her mouth, a succession of partly healed and fresh cuts mainly on her face, and what appeared to be a permanent gash on her head which showed through her unwashed, matted hair. Whenever she opened her door there was the unmistakable smell of stale semen, sweat and warm booze, which she made no attempt to dilute, not even with a dab of the cheapest perfume.

Over the years Leanne had often wondered when Kelly found time to go to Tesco's or the launderette, for her door was open to her clients from nine each morning until the early hours of the next. Any sympathy Leanne had initially felt for the wretched woman had soon gone, for living next to her was sheer hell.

By way of recreation, when she wasn't busy on her back, she was engaging in vicious fights that usually erupted around two in the morning. During these bouts she would alternately throw her opponent across the room, cursing him with loud and colourful expletives as she slammed him against the party wall with death-defying ferocity or, if the tables were inexplicably turned, she'd scream 'MURDER!' like one demented, a cry for help, needless to say, that the other tenants chose to ignore. In fact, most of them were fervently hoping that her unknown assailant would eventually finish her off. But no such luck. Kelly always managed to survive and live to fight another day.

Leanne soon learned that it was a common practice to remove all potential weapons and missiles at the first sign of a fight. At the first thud of body-hitting-wall she would cautiously open the door of her flat which faced a wide corridor, empty, echoing like the vault of some ghastly cathedral - and bring in all the milk bottles. Looking along she'd invariably see the hands of the other tenants, equally furtive, reaching out for their bottles, whisking them inside, before quietly closing their doors.

Kelly would never know how many gashes in the head she was spared by this weird, altruistic ritual. Those silent, faceless people who lived along the same corridor, never coming face to face with their neighbours, only surveying all the comings and goings through the spy-holes cut into the dull, feature-less doors that wouldn't look out of place in a nineteenth century Lunatic Asylum.

Avoiding any direct contact they would make a dash for the lift when the coast was clear and be carried away into the anonymity of the city streets without ever bumping into anybody, without ever having to speak to anyone, to pass the time of day or offer any account of themselves. And everyone dreaded meeting Kelly. Everyone on the estate was scared of her when she was shooting her mouth off and her temper was up, even the men.

In the nine years she'd lived there Leanne only made friends with one other tenant, Jean, who lived on the floor above with her fourteen year old daughter, Linda, and her son, Donny, aged eight. It was through Donny that she'd met Jean.

A couple of years back, on her way home from school one day she'd found him cowering behind the rubbish chute, hiding from a gang of lads and too frightened to come out in case they were waiting to duff him up in the lift. Leanne found out he lived on the next floor and took him up to his mother and the woman was so desperate to talk to someone that she sat Leanne down with a cup of tea and didn't stop for the next two hours.

She and her husband, Dougie, were divorced, she'd said. She'd chucked him out for playing around. But everyone on the estate knew he'd walked out and was living with another woman in East Dulwich. For months Jean had believed him when he said he was working nights as a mini-cab driver but all the while he was seeing the other woman. The other woman had money, too, and was really keen on him - God knows why.

Leanne saw him once in the lift and she was surprised to see what an insignificant little runt he was. His fancy woman had even given him money to take back to Jean, so he could pretend he'd earned it from the mini-cabs.

Before the incident with Donny, Leanne had never seen Jean before but she and the whole estate as far as Battersea Bridge had heard her all right. At intervals, especially at weekends, like some strident call to prayer from the top of a minaret, she'd lean over the concrete balcony above Leanne's flat and holler at the top of her voice.

'Lin-DAAAAAA!' or 'Don-EEEEEE!' whichever offspring she needed to wash, chastise or run an errand. She had perfected the knack of throwing her voice so well that her call echoed around the soaring forest of towers with amazing clarity, much to the embarrassment of Linda and Donny, burdened with this highly efficient tracking system. Leanne had been surprised, therefore, when she met the rest of Jean.

She was not, in fact, an Amazon with a high-velocity voice box but a softly-spoken mouse of a woman struggling heroically to keep her family together, terrified that she wouldn't be able to cope and that the children would be taken into care. Every day was a lonely battle to survive her own private hell of humiliation.

Leanne had befriended her and later helped her get a job as a dinner lady in her school but, except for the shared deprivation of life on the estate, they had little else in common and the friendship was never close. She was glad to accept, however, when Jean offered to look after Joe for the week of the festival, knowing that, for all her shortcomings, Jean was a woman she could trust.

No wonder Leanne longed to leave the estate, leave the likes of Kelly, the depressing life-style, and move somewhere like Rae's place, to a ground floor flat in Ealing, Chiswick or somewhere like that. And a garden would be nice, no matter how small, as long as there was room enough for a shed where Joe could take his mates and tinker about, doing up bikes or whatever boys of that age do. She didn't expect nor even remotely hope that she might win *The Birkett Bronze*. She thought longingly of the £25,000 prize, the deposit on a new flat, a new way of life.

Looking up she saw that Oliver still hadn't returned. In a way she was glad he wouldn't be there to witness her speech. She knew that she'd be hopeless. It wasn't that she didn't know her subject - she did, but she liked *writing* about poison cases, not talking about them.

Her first book had taken a year to research and a further two years to write, typing it out on the kitchen table night after night from the moment she got back from school until twelve-thirty, stopping only to give Joe his supper and check he'd done his homework.

All those hours of work, the recurrent attacks of migraine brought on by eye-strain studying the minuscule print on old documents and then, when the book was finally published, the bitter disappointment. The jacket design was so banal and uninteresting it could never inspire anyone to pick up the book, let alone buy it. She looked enviously at the copy of Dr Swann's book placed next to hers on the table - although it had not been short-listed for the prize it looked good - the jacket design was simple, restrained, impressive.

Leanne felt suddenly depressed; she guessed she was looking pretty hideous. Just when she wanted to look good for Oliver. Strange that she should care what he thought. She had to admit that she found him attractive. Pity he had this reputation as a womaniser. Mind you, most good-looking men were the same. Why not? In some ways Joe's father, John, was similar - not so much playing the field with women necessarily but desperate for adventures, new horizons. They'd started going out together at college and sort of drifted into a long term relationship - congenial, easy-going, with some passionate moments.

But then she'd become complacent, careless and, at twenty-three, when she found she was pregnant with Joe she assumed John would accept it as a natural, if unplanned, outcome of the relationship.

That night, in the restaurant, he said he had something to tell her. And I've got something to tell you, she'd said, lovingly squeezing his hand.

She was still holding it when he told her he'd met someone else, another botanist. It was sickening. He was full of hope and enthusiasm. They had so much in common, he'd said. He really thought he was in love this time. They were setting off on an expedition to South America and they'd be gone for a year at least. After that, he'd said, who could tell? Maybe it'd be a good thing for them, he and Leanne, to have some space, some time apart. See a bit of the world, meet new people, new experiences... Right, that's my news. Sorry it's a bit of a bombshell. I'll be leaving at the end of the week. What's your news, by the way?

So she'd found herself with a baby son living in a box in the sky with an empty corridor and *'All Night'* Kelly for company. No joke. As for affairs with men, after John there had been no one else for more than five years. She'd always been too tired, too tied, too uptight. Then she'd met Bill - in some ways Oliver reminded her of him. He had the same restlessness, always playing the field, terrified he'd miss out on something.

But it hadn't worked out. In fact, despite appearances, he turned out to be incredibly boring. Leanne hadn't had any lovers since Bill left.

Joe, at seven, had quite liked him and had enjoyed a dose of male bonding - going to football matches and such like - and was difficult and withdrawn for a while. He soon resigned himself to his mother's company, however, and had accepted the status quo. But it wasn't ideal and she wished it had been otherwise. They were both trapped, depleted, incomplete.

Leanne sighed and forced herself to concentrate on Dr Smithson who was talking enthusiastically about the latest developments in DNA coding. Realising that she was due to speak next she felt a surge of adrenaline. Oh God, he'll stop talking in a few minutes and then I'll have to stand up and start speaking. Perhaps the microphone would pack up and they'd have to cancel.

Instinctively, her eyes searched for the entrance and she noticed that Oliver had come back and was leaning against one of the poles. He smiled and gave a little wave. A feeling of panic overwhelmed her and her skin felt cold. She began to tremble - she just knew she was going to make a complete fool of herself. What if she fainted and collapsed in a sprawling heap on the platform like a pile of old rags? Her mouth felt dry. What if, when she tried to speak, nothing came out, only gobbledy-goop, like Stanley Unwin?

'And lastly, Ms Leanne Philips, a writer of great promise...' Claire Fenton was saying. Leanne looked up but had difficulty in focusing. 'You will remember, perhaps, her first book on the Madeleine Smith case of 1857, which was received with considerable acclaim... Ms Philips?'

Leanne was aware of the blurred shape of Claire Fenton's face turned towards her and her heart lurched painfully against her ribs, causing her body to break out in a fresh wave of sweat. The next minute she found that she had stood up and could hear her own voice, as though belonging to a stranger.

'My name is Leanne Philips,' she found herself saying. 'I am thirty-six years old and at present I live in Battersea with my son, Joe, who's nearly thirteen. Although I have always enjoyed reading and writing stories I was encouraged to start work on my first book some years ago by a group of women writers whom I met...'

Thinking about it later, Leanne couldn't really remember what she had said during the twenty minutes she was on her feet. Some of the people in the audience seemed to be listening and at one point, when she made a feeble joke about putting drops of arsenic on a sugar lump, several of them actually laughed. Even so, she was greatly relieved when her talk came to a natural and fairly satisfactory end and she saw Claire Fenton rise to her feet.

'Well, ladies and gentlemen,' she said, 'that brings our individual talks to a fitting close. And how informative they have been! I am sure you will agree with me that all four speakers have given us a great deal to think about. Before I ask you to show your appreciation in the usual way may I thank you for being such an excellent audience. After a short break we will commence with our question and answer session ...'

Ms Fenton looked up sharply as an official wearing a yellow badge was hurrying towards the platform making frantic shooing gestures with his hands. A sizeable queue of persons waiting for the next event had already formed at the entrance of the Marquee; some individuals were already breaking ranks and craning their necks to look inside. Ms Fenton was not pleased and raised her hands in protest.

'Oh, dear, well I'm sorry to say we seem to have run over our time and shall have to forgo our questions. What a shame! Never mind. Now, how about a quick round of applause for our speakers?'

The audience, the number of which, Leanne noticed, had

dwindled to no more than twenty, clapped enthusiastically but briefly, for the appearance of the official leading a crocodile of replacements urged them to start wriggling into their raincoats, gathering up their umbrellas and heading for the exit, another official hot on their heels.

It was with tremendous relief that Leanne jammed her notes into her bag and hurried to join the others outside. After arranging to meet them later near *The Crown Imperial* she scuttled away in search of a public telephone. When she did manage to find one that was working she had to wait for nearly twenty minutes as there were five other people waiting their turn. There was a lot of rummaging in handbags and studying of shoes in an attempt to appear *not* to be listening to the somewhat inane conversation from inside the kiosk. Leanne cursed herself yet again for forgetting her mobile and judging by the irritable expressions of the others in the queue they were doing much the same. When she finally heaved open the kiosk door – the stale air inside was very unpleasant – and dialled Jean's number she was surprised when Joe answered.

'Why aren't you at school?' she demanded, suspiciously.

'What d'you mean?'

'I said – why aren't you at school?'

'I wish you'd stop checking up on me!' he said.

'I said, why aren't you at school?'

'I've got a bit of a sore throat, that's all.'

'A sore throat?'

'That's what I said.'

'You don't sound as if you've got a sore throat,' Leanne said.

'Well, I have. Don't fuss.'

'When did it start?'

'This morning. Whenever.'

'You didn't stay up all night!'

'Don't fuss.'

'Has Jean given you anything for it?'

'Course not.'

'Why not?'

'Haven't told her.'

'Why not?'

'No need. Can I go now?'

'Where is she, by the way? Let me have a word with her.'

'She's not here.'

'Not there?'

'Nope.'

'Where is she, then?'

'Dunno.'

'Don't tell me she's gone out and left you children on your own?'

'She's out shopping or something. How should I know? It's no big deal. Stop fussing.' A pause. 'Anyway, there's no school today.'

'What d'you mean - no school?'

'I dunno. Bank Holiday? May Day or something. Look, mum, I've got to go now.'

'Why? What's the hurry? What are you doing?'

'I'm making some toast.'

'So you didn't have any breakfast?'

'Nope.'

'Why? Because you got up too late?'

'I dunno.'

'Joe - can you hear me?'

'Gotta go. 'Bye.'

'I'll ring tomorrow.'

There was an audible sigh. 'Whatever.'

‘What d’you mean - whatever?’

'Whatever. Do what you like. You can ring if you want to but there's not really much point, is there? I'm perfectly all right.'

The click of the receiver. And an unaccustomed sense of redundancy.

*

Chapter Seven

The first thing Leanne did after leaving the telephone kiosk was to find a public lavatory and there repair the damage done to her face by the effects of wind, rain and near-terminal stage fright. Her initial relief at having come through the ordeal of her first public performance was followed by the shock of seeing, from her reflection, that she did indeed look as awful as she'd imagined. A complete reconstruction job was necessary, starting from scratch.

When she had finished she pulled out the combs holding up her rain-flattened hair, drew it over her head and gave it a thorough brushing until it shone. It looked so good she decided to leave it loose. Fifteen minutes later she inspected her reflection and was reasonably satisfied. Not bad for a thirty-six year old - small, slim, long glossy hair, gentle face, good bones, large grey eyes, a pretty mouth.

As she stood appraising herself she realised that this new and unusual preoccupation with the way she looked was purely for Oliver's benefit. She hadn't felt so attracted to anyone for years and, partly due to the relief at having finished with the seminar without any great disaster, she began to feel quite light-headed.

Gathering up her things she took one last look in the mirror before hurrying off in search of the others; she found them gathered round a group of street entertainers in medieval dress performing a loud, knock-about sort of play near the Church Hall.

As she joined them Oliver turned to look at her. The obvious appraisal, and, she had to admit, surprise, in his eyes left her in no doubt that the effort she'd put into her appearance had been worth while. Leanne was delighted, moreover, that Oliver chose to stay with the group all afternoon even though on several occasions they came across other writers whom he seemed to know. These impromptu meetings invariably resulted in a lot of gushing exclamations, enthusiastic air-kissing and fervent elbow clutching and Leanne felt sure he would once more attach himself to some celebrity or other and disappear.

But he didn't. It was Rae, and not Oliver, who eventually defected. She met up with a group of friends, one of whom offered to help her fix the Volvo, and went off to spend the rest of the day with them.

Leanne, Duncan and Oliver attended a couple of lectures, had a light, mainly liquid lunch and then spent the afternoon wandering through the town which was still humming with activity. Thankfully the actual *May Day Parade* was over but they did see the *'Hot Dog'* trailer pass by packed with squealing tots and one or two embarrassed-looking fathers.

By four o'clock the weather had brightened considerably - in fact the showers had stopped and there had been a short spell of weak sunshine - so they walked down to the river where they came across Rev Pinny sitting on a concrete bench wedged between a group of school kids who had somehow mastered the art of jamming fistfuls of crisps into their mouths whilst continuing to screech dementedly at the same time. Pinny, however, seemed unfazed by the phenomenon but, on catching sight of the others, allowed himself to be gathered up and propelled towards a teashop close by.

They lost him again, however, as they passed the church on their way to the side-street where Oliver had left his car the night before. Duncan was all for trying to get a taxi back to *The Hare* but when this proved impossible he was obliged to take the passenger seat while Leanne, still slightly whoozy after the wine at lunch, crawled into the space at the back.

On their return to the hotel they passed the café, the scene of their earlier humiliation, and saw Rae and her friend bending over the bonnet of the Volvo. As Oliver jammed his finger on the horn Rae gave them a thumbs-up sign and a cheery wave.

When they reached *The Hare* they saw that Aubrey Atherton's Bentley was parked in the driveway but there was no sign of the driver. As soon as they entered the hotel they could sense an atmosphere. The smell of lavender polish and *Arctic Pine* Air Freshener failed to mask the underlying smell of stale beer and cigarette smoke.

Other then the low murmur of two regulars deep in conversation over a pint in the Public Bar, the place had an incriminating quietness and the air of resentment was further reflected in the set of Thelma Doggett's face. She was fiddling with the castor oil plant in the hallway, her little fingers dipping and plucking compulsively while her lips were compressed and her eyes cold.

Receiving a simple nod in reply to his cheery 'Good evening', Duncan sidled past her and made straight for the Lounge Bar where he ordered a double whiskey from Len Doggett, whose thin face seemed even more apologetic than usual. Leanne had an orange juice to keep Duncan company for a few minutes and then, unsure how to spend the two hours before dinner, she decided to ring Joe before going to her room to read.

As she replaced the receiver after a monosyllabic exchange with her son she saw Oliver going back through the front door and a moment later she heard the sound of his car as it roared off. Feeling suddenly tired and flat she went upstairs and lay on the bed, remembering nothing more until she heard Duncan knocking on her door shortly before eight, to tell her that dinner was ready.

A little later, after a quick repair job on her face, Leanne felt ridiculously pleased to see Oliver sitting with Duncan and Rev Pinny in the small dining alcove at one end of the Lounge Bar. Mrs Doggett was serving the soup, the expression on her face no less frosty than it had been earlier. She did make the effort to smile, however, as Leanne entered the room and greeted the others.

Taking a seat opposite Oliver, Leanne noticed that he'd combed his hair and changed his clothes. He was now wearing a waistcoat made of mattress ticking over a cream shirt, raw silk by the look of it, and tobacco-coloured linen trousers. He was also looking very pleased with himself.

'Thank you so much. I have to say - this is excellent soup,' Duncan said, as Thelma approached the table with fresh rolls. 'Tell me, how was your day, Mrs Doggett?' he asked.

'Oh, so-so, but I've known better what with the crowds and the terrible weather,' she said, mustering a perfunctory smile before compressing her lips into a millimetre slit once more. 'And a bit of help around the place wouldn't go amiss neither.'

Her husband came from behind the bar, took the tray from her hands without a word and followed her back into the kitchen.

'God, poor old Len's in the dog-house,' whispered Oliver. 'I wonder what he's done to upset her? Mind you, I shouldn't think it takes much.'

'As far as I can gather it's something to do with Aubrey Atherton...' Duncan confided, leaning forward and keeping his voice low.

'That figures. What's he done now?' asked Oliver.

'I dread to think,' Duncan whispered. 'All I know is that Len disappeared up to Atherton's room for a couple of hours this afternoon. Thelma was absolutely *furious* - she'd been looking for him everywhere. What made it worse, whatever it was he'd been up to certainly agreed with him because he came back down with a big smile on his face and smelling – or so she says - of booze.'

Duncan stopped speaking as Len came through to the bar to serve someone in the other room. When he had returned to the kitchen, Duncan added. 'You should have heard her - she really tore into him. Reduced him to a jelly. That's why he's going around as if he's had a lobotomy, poor sod.'

The group fell silent as Thelma Doggett came back with the roast lamb. When she'd gone Leanne said.

'Strange - I can't think what Aubrey Atherton and Len Doggett would have in common, can you? Where is he, by the way?'

'Right behind you,' muttered Oliver.

Duncan gulped and Rev Pinny looked up sharply.

Leanne turned to see Atherton smiling down at her. He then turned his attention to Oliver.

'Pour me a drink, dear boy - I'm gasping. I'd ask Mrs Doggett but I fear it might be laced with arsenic. What a strange woman she is. Such an odd creature. Tell me,' he said, settling himself close to Oliver whilst addressing Leanne, 'why is it that women can't abide seeing their men folk enjoying themselves? Poor Doggett, can't even have a drink and a shriek without she's flaying him alive. It's just too depressing for words.'

Looking across at Rev Pinny, who was struggling to cut through a piece of gristle, he dipped a finger into his glass and flicked a little of the wine in his direction in a gesture of benediction.

'That's not funny, Atherton,' Rev Pinny said, wearily, without looking up.

'I couldn't agree more, Pinny, old thing. All that mumbo-jumbo's downright pathetic. Nothing funny about it at all.'

Then, unable to get any reaction from Pinny, he turned once more to Leanne.

'Tell me, Ms Philips, how was your little talk this morning? Such a shame. I heard that only a handful of people turned up. How terribly disappointing for you. Of course, *The Crown Imperial* was simply *heaving* for my press conference. Packed out with chaps from all the nationals, all the TV companies, the BBC, the lot. Oh, you can't imagine the noise, all that pushing and shoving, questions, questions, questions, till my head was spinning. And those infernal flashlights! No doubt about it, all this razzmatazz, it's the B side of fame. Five minutes only, I said to Fiona, you know I'm a martyr to migraine and have been since the age of six.'

'Oh, come on, Atherton, you love every minute of it!' cried Duncan, belching as delicately as he could into his napkin as he lay down his fork and reached for his glass.

At that point Mrs Doggett came into the room and, seeing Aubrey, she whisked his glass from under his nose.

'Excuse me!' she hissed. 'I'll have you know this wine is part of the set dinner and not for the consumption of guests who are dining elsewhere.'

Atherton stared at her, open-mouthed in mock surprise.

'Come, come, my dear, there's no need to be so waspish,'

he cooed.

‘And if you wish to partake of alcohol,’ Mrs Doggett continued, glaring back in return. ‘I'm sure my husband will be only too happy to serve you from the bar.'

With that she gathered up Duncan's plate and went back into the kitchen where she could be heard slamming it into the sink. Duncan, by now fairly well-oiled, started giggling into his napkin and Oliver, too, had a broad grin on his face.

‘What an extraordinarily touchy woman,' Atherton remarked, huffily drawing his coat around his shoulders. 'Positively menopausal, if you ask me.’ He gave a little shiver and raised his eyes to the ceiling. ‘Oh, my God, what a ghastly thought.'

Depositing his cheroot in the ashtray, he turned to Leanne.

'You know, I was thinking about you a little earlier on,’ he said. ‘Correct me if I’m wrong, but did you say you lived in one of those horrendous tower blocks that look like dingy pigeon coops in the sky?’

'Yes - why?' asked Leanne, warily.

'Well, it's beyond my comprehension, it really is. Why on earth do women have children in such ghastly places where they can't possibly look after them properly?'

'How can you say that?’ Leanne protested, feeling her face flush. ‘It may not be ideal but we do our best and Joe's the most important thing in the world to me.'

'I don't doubt it,’ Atherton sniffed. ‘Far be it from me to pass judgement. All I'm saying is it's hardly commendable to inflict such a ghastly environment on your poor offspring.'

'It's not from choice I can assure you!' Leanne cried, anger now draining the colour from her face.

'Come now, there’s no reason to get upset,’ Atherton went on. ‘Though I realise, of course, that as a single parent you are at a distinct disadvantage - concerning money, amongst other things.'

He looked her up and down, his head slightly to one side.

'I'm surprised you haven't married. Surely a reasonably attractive - well, I imagine you might be to some people's taste - woman like you could have found some poor sop to marry her by now?'

Looking up he saw that his driver was standing in the doorway. He started to pull on his soft leather gloves.

'Well, I'm off,' he said. 'I trust you will enjoy the rest of your meal. I shall be dining with Samantha Egerton, Fiona Bridewell and a rather attractive lady journalist this evening - aren't I the lucky one?'

Turning to Leanne he said. 'I don't mean to be rude, my dear. I'm sure you try very hard but frankly, whatever you may say, living as you do is hardly the *best* start in life, now is it?'

Perhaps it was the tension of the morning's performance, or the drink at lunchtime and again at dinner, whatever it was, Leanne suddenly burst into tears and, pushing back her chair, stood up to face Atherton.

'Oh, for God's sake, why can't you leave me alone!' she cried.

Pushing past him she ran upstairs, followed by Oliver. Duncan had risen from his chair to assist her but, now slightly pissed, he slumped back again making sympathetic noises.

Rev Pinny simply shook his head sadly as he watched the smirk spread on Atherton's face.

Seeing his expression of disapproval, Atherton gave his wrist a light slap with his glove which he followed with a little shriek.

'Oh, dear, have I been a terribly naughty boy, Reverend?' he lisped. 'It's not my fault if the truth hits home. Surely one's entitled to have an opinion once in a while?'

'You don't have to go out of your way to hurt people's feelings, Atherton,' Pinny said, sternly. 'You go too far. You always do, and it's quite unnecessary. I think you owe that young woman an apology.'

'I have no intention of apologising to anyone, and certainly not for speaking my mind,' announced Atherton. 'The very idea.'

With that he flounced out of the room, calling for his driver.

Oliver caught up with Leanne just as she was opening the door to her room. He put his arm around her shoulders and briefly held her. She noticed that he had a clean smell about him and his body felt lean and warm.

'Don't let him get to you,' he was saying. 'The man's a pig. Just remember he loves nothing better than to reduce a woman to tears. Don't give him the satisfaction.' He put his hand under her chin and lifted her face. For a moment Leanne thought he was going to kiss her. He looked at her for a few seconds, then tapped her gently on the nose.

'Got to go - will you be all right?' he asked. 'Come on, cheer up. I expect Rae will be back soon. I tell you what, let's go out for dinner tomorrow night. What d'you think?'

Leanne nodded. 'Thanks, Oliver. I'm sorry, it's just that I'm already worried sick about Joe and everything and I certainly don't need someone like Atherton rubbing it in. He has no idea how real people live - or he pretends he doesn't.'

'He's perfected the art of sussing out people's vulnerability,' said Oliver. 'And goes for the jugular every time.'

'How come he goes out of his way to be cruel? Why?'

'God knows. It's just him.' Oliver said. 'Don't worry about

it. He does it to everyone. Forget it. It's not important. I'll see you in the morning.'

On reaching the landing, Oliver turned and blew her a kiss before running back downstairs. Five minutes later Leanne heard the slam of the front door and, looking out, she saw him driving off towards the town. Still upset, she rang Jean, who said Joe was already in bed and everything was fine.

That night she had a strangely disturbing dream in which she was making love on an ancient tombstone - in full view of the guests at the wedding between Rae and Rev Pinny - to a person halfway between Oliver and her tormentor, Aubrey Atherton, and, most embarrassing of all, with Joe and his friends laughing helplessly in the background..

*

Chapter Eight

As soon as Rev Pinny pushed open the warped door of the Church Hall the next morning his sharp nostrils recognised the familiar smell of dusty hymn books and wet floor mops. He was early, a good twenty minutes before he was due to begin his lecture, so he could put up his flow-chart indicating some of the more obscure money-laundering networks in Eastern Europe.

He was neither surprised nor dismayed to find himself alone. Someone had been kind enough to put out the chairs though he thought seven rows of ten was being a little optimistic. He didn't expect a large turn-out for although he seemed to inhabit some other dimension he was, nevertheless, quite aware that his subject, fraud, counterfeit and embezzlement, couldn't compete with the public's current fascination with sexual and social psychopaths and serial killers.

Duncan, bless him, had promised to come along but he felt sure that Leanne would prefer to go to Rae's performance rather than his. That was perfectly understandable. Nor did he expect to see Oliver. He was quite sure that the younger man found him a bit of a bore, too serious, too slow, too cautious in his assessments of people and situations, not altogether *'au fait'* with the modern world. Though he might deny it, choosing to remember only the feeling of security given to him by the constraining reins of his early years and the certainty afforded by his conventional and in some ways old-fashioned upbringing, he had suffered a restrictive childhood.

Surprisingly, for the reverse is often the case, he became a repressed adolescent, not a rebel in any sense of the word, not one to kick against the system, to take chances or lose control. And he was fully aware that now, as a man in his late forties, he was not an attractive personality, one that drew people to him. He knew that he appeared awkward and dull and in some ways he envied Oliver for his open, effortless charm and Duncan for his ability to draw on seemingly endless theatrical anecdotes whenever the conversation palled.

By contrast Pinny was a man of few words and often ill at ease in company. In that respect his wife, Joan, was a great help. She was more outgoing than he, an invaluable asset in a social setting and, moreover, whenever he needed help in composing his weekly sermons she'd always come up trumps with some amusing, innovative and, occasionally, inspirational idea. He couldn't imagine life without her and thanked God on a daily basis for sending him such a stalwart shipmate as he steered his ill-equipped craft through the stormy sea of life.

Undoubtedly his religious fervour distanced him from other people, it put them off and left him open to ridicule. And so he had learned to hide his feelings and innermost thoughts, cut himself off and rise above the scepticism. It was his way of coping. It was the only way.

The clock above the platform had a loud, almost menacing mechanism. As each minute passed the large hand jerked forward - *whurrr-snnnap* - quivering slightly as it stopped before resuming its hypnotic *tick, tick, tick*. Through the dusty glass of the lattice windows he could see local women walking by, chatting to each other, having a moan or a joke, their offspring trailing behind, whining, bored with shopping.

He thought again of Joan. They had no children. Not from choice, it must be said, but, they told themselves, it was not part of God's plan, it just wasn't meant to be. Pinny's brother, Andrew, had become a Benedictine monk in his mid-twenties and, he assumed, had kept to his vow of chastity, so that was the end of the Pinny line. He smiled inwardly as his mind switched to the underground and the end of the Piccadilly Line.

He must tell Joan when she phoned that evening. That would make her chuckle - '*the end of the Pinny line*' - she'd like that. Joan was a good woman, God bless her soul. She'd always been good, born to make sacrifices, and had never been drawn to the flippant, cruel or carnal side of life. Even as a teenager she knew what she must do - serve the Lord in whatever part of the world the Spirit sent her.

When Pinny met her she was engaged in active missionary work but gave it up when she felt called to his side and now she made an excellent vicar's wife - he couldn't ask for more. They were both still very much involved in the work of the Church abroad, Somalia mainly, where they had established a small medical centre with a mission attached.

There was never enough money, of course, for all they wanted to do - like update the sewerage and fresh water system and build a school. He and Joan prayed together every night for more funds to continue their work but it remained a struggle; endless jumble sales, *Bring & Buy* bazaars, coffee mornings, sponsored walks and swims - it took up all their time but they didn't care. After all it was the Lord's will, not theirs, and they'd try anything to make money to further the work of the mission.

He thought of *The Birkett Bronze Award* and the £25,000 in prize money. Just think what he and Joan, with God's help, could do with it! Would, he wondered, the Lord intervene and allow him to win the money they so desperately needed? Or would that heathen Atherton, the devil's own disciple, win the lot and squander it on all manner of debauchery and sinful pursuits? Pinny saw it simply as a question of good versus evil and reminded himself that he firmly believed that God worked in mysterious ways and stranger things had happened...

Rev Pinny was shaken from his meditations by the arrival of two elderly ladies. They stood awkwardly in the doorway and, seeing Pinny's dog-collar, they nudged each other to be quiet like school girls in assembly.

Rev Pinny's eyes, half-hidden under his bushy grey eyebrows, were so small and deep set the women thought he was either asleep or praying. They'd seen him through the window as they were passing on their way to the butcher's and for some reason they thought he was the new locum at the doctors' come to give a talk on *Hypothermia - The Hidden Killer*, free admission for pensioners and a cup of tea at the end.

That's what usually happened - they always came in of a Tuesday to see what was going on. There was always something on offer - a talk, a sale, an exhibition of kiddies' paintings, WI Flower Arranging Competitions - it made a little break, a chance to rest their misshapen feet and have a nice cup of tea. It never occurred to them to look at the notice on the door to see what was on the agenda. They didn't really care to be honest. It all went over their heads anyway. A lot of gassing about nothing half the time. Still, fills up an hour. Gets you out. Something to do.

As they hobbled towards the front row of seats they saw that Rev Pinny was not asleep or praying but looking directly at them and as they sat down he held out his hands to them.

'Good morning, ladies, so glad you could come.' They

nodded and smiled, their rheumy old eyes, crafty as a collie dog's, looking around the room for the tea urn. They noted with disappointment that the trestle table that was usually covered with a crisp white cloth and rows of pale green cups and saucers had been folded away and stacked alongside the spare chairs near the side door. A bad sign.

The old ladies looked at each other and were just wondering whether to get up and go out again while they had the chance when several other people came in. They watched them suspiciously, arms folded, mouths set. Two men in suits carrying notebooks, both strangers, two couples, never seen them before, a young Italian woman on her own, she's not from round here, that's for sure, one of the local coppers, hasn't he got anything better to do?

Next was one of their familiars, an old man called Will Morgan, from down the almshouses in Pig Lane. He came along to the hall every Tuesday as well. He sat down heavily, moaning, more out of habit than anything, placing a canvas bag full of vegetables by his feet. He, too, was looking around for signs of a brew. One of the old ladies caught his eye, pursed her lips and shook her head. The old man looked confused and, folding his arms, stared inquiringly at Rev Pinny.

A moment later Claire Fenton arrived carrying an armful of books and a bulging Filofax. She frowned as she noted the poor attendance. Joining Rev Pinny on the platform she dropped her things onto the table and, bending down, whispered in his ear.

'Not a very good turn-out, I see. Quite honestly I don't know what I can do about it. Fiona's off organising the television coverage of Aubrey Atherton's lecture tomorrow and I've got to go over to the schoolroom to sort out the projector for Rae Roberts's thing at eleven.'

She looked at her watch. 'I can hang on for a couple of minutes and say a few words by way of introduction, if you like. I tell you what, I'll just nip round to the *Dog & Whistle* and see if I can rustle up a few of the Romantics. What d'you think?'

Rev Pinny was still smiling gratefully as he watched Claire hurry from the hall. He counted the faces in the audience. There were now nine and each one was staring at the wall behind him. Looking round he saw that one corner of his flow-chart had already come away from the wall. As he watched, another followed suit. Everyone was waiting for the third corner to come away, which it did, very slowly, as predictably as a tired strip-tease, leaving the chart hanging by one small lump of blue-tack, which everyone knew, including Rev Pinny, would eventually give way and the whole thing would crash to the floor. It did - the thick edge of the card hitting the floor with a resounding *'thwack'*

After a moment's contemplation of the rolled-up chart the local bobby, one of the men in grey suits and the Italian woman came forward and helped Pinny re-position it on the wall. He thanked them as warmly as he could and then sat with his fingers tips touching, his eyes withdrawn yet glimmering deep within his skull, waiting for Claire to reappear.

A full five minutes later the silence was broken as she pushed open the door and hurried in with five grim-faced 'Bodice Ripping' authors in tow. By the looks on their faces it was clear, even to Rev Pinny, that Claire had resorted to some unjust threat or blackmail, for they took their seats in grudging silence.

As they did so Pinny saw Fiona's head pop round the door for no more than a second before disappearing again. Claire called out to her and then ran out into the street but returned a moment later having lost her. It was therefore with ill-concealed impatience that she banged an ashtray on the table to call order before rising to introduce Rev Pinny.

'May I welcome you on behalf of the organisers of this year's *Festival.* With so many events vying for your attention I must thank you all for coming along to the Church Hall this morning to hear Rev Joseph Pinny speak. I'm sure you won't be disappointed. As some of you will already know, in addition to being the curate of a busy parish in Derbyshire, he is, of course, one of our leading writers on company law, fraud, embezzlement, etc, and his latest book, *Easy Money - The Counterfeit Trail* has been short listed for this year's *Birkett Bronze Award*, sponsored by the Crime Club Committee. May I just remind you that there will be a short question and answer session at the end of his talk and I'm sure you will have plenty of queries to raise with Rev Pinny who will, I know, do his very best to answer them.'

As Claire Fenton gathered up her things and hurried out of the hall, Rev Pinny rose, his mouth twisted into an embarrassed smirk. It was at this point that those in the audience saw his eyes for the first time. He cleared his throat, clasped his hands together and looked toward the ceiling - which, he noticed, was badly in need of re-plastering. This reminded him that he'd promised to help Joan slap some distemper on the ceiling in the porch as soon as he got back. The hallway would need doing as well before long and...

Rev Pinny forced himself to focus on the matter in hand. Putting on his glasses he looked down at his notes.

'What do we mean when we use the word '*counterfeit*'?' he began.

The two old ladies put their heads together and murmured into each other's hats. Just then, the door was flung open and Duncan came in as though propelled from behind. Apologising in his best actor's voice he unwound his long silk scarf as he slunk into a seat at the back and then tried to flatten his wiry hair with his hands. He gave Pinny a little wave and smiled encouragingly.

The two old dears were still talking and as the room warmed a little there was a strong smell of leeks rising from Will Morgan's vegetable bag. As Rev Pinny continued he was surprised to see that one of the grey-suited men was taking notes and the Italian lady actually looked interested.

As for Duncan, he was soon happily engrossed in *The Times* crossword and Will had fallen asleep, his drooping head resting on the local copper's shoulder. From the room above came the sound of someone sweeping, the rhythmic swish of the broom accompanied by shrill singing. The tune was random and indecipherable, interrupted every so often by the sound of chair being dragged across the floor.

After talking for a further fifteen minutes Rev Pinny turned his attention to his flow-chart. As he gingerly indicated certain points with his ruler he saw that an audience had begun to form *outside* the hall. Several middle-aged women were peering through the window, shielding their eyes with their hands for a better view.

After a few nudges and giggles they moved on only to be replaced by a group of raucous lads of eight or nine. As they peered through the glass they pushed and shoved each other and shouted, laughing loudly at some idiotic remark.

'...one of the biggest problems faced by cross border security...' Rev Pinny stopped mid-sentence and frowned at the miscreants.

They responded by sticking out their tongues and jumping up and down like deranged monkeys. Whilst one boy squashed his face against the glass until it resembled a grotesque gargoyle, another started scraping the window with his dirty finger-nails. One of the group, unaware that his mother was passing, suddenly let out a piercingly indignant yell as he felt her hand land across his ear, causing his familiars to screech with laughter at his expense.

Losing patience, Rev Pinny waved them away with his hand and shook his head sorrowfully. One of the boys immediately imitated him and then called out with remarkable originality, '*Piss off, four eyes!*'

Feeling the sweat breaking out on his brow, Pinny turned his back on the boys and addressed himself once more to the flow-chart.

'WANKER!' called one of the brats, very loudly.

Rev Pinny froze, his ruler poised.

Duncan looked up from his paper in surprise as the local bobby jumped up and made for the door by which time, of course, the gang of boys had already disappeared and were halfway through the alley to the main street.

The two old ladies chewed their tongues and sorrowfully shook their heads just as the wall-chart fell for the second time landing with a loud report like a pistol-shot. Old Will Morgan awoke with a start and looked around, feeling for his vegetables, unsure of his surroundings.

'...and in conclusion, ladies and gentlemen, the full complexity of the problem is confronted at some length in my book, *Easy Money - The Counterfeit Trail*. I have a few copies here should any of you care to purchase one - signed, of course. But first may I ask if you have any questions?'

There was an awful silence. Rev Pinny resumed his seat and waited, his finger tips together and his eyes downcast. Able now to tune into the muttering of the old ladies he realised that they were discussing the prices at the new supermarket. He looked up expectantly at the sound of a chair being pushed back. A question perhaps? The Italian woman was leaving.

'Could you tell me how much your book is, please?' asked one of the other women.

'Ah, £12.99. I'm afraid,' apologised Pinny, fingering a copy.

'Is it out in paperback?'

'No, I'm afraid not.'

Silence. A prolonged silence during which everyone listened to the sound of someone walking across the floor above and then, after a succession of muffled tinkling noises, the sound of a chain being yanked and a cistern refilling. A moment later the sound of singing resumed and the scraping of chairs being moved from one side of the room to the other.

Rev Pinny looked at the clock. Ten forty-five. He was scheduled to run until eleven. He looked at the blank faces in the audience and they stared back.

'Well, as there aren't any more questions perhaps we'd better vacate the premises,' Pinny suggested. 'I believe there's another meeting here at eleven-fifteen and something else upstairs at eleven-thirty. Thank you for coming. Thank you.'

Duncan helped Pinny gather up his notes and the ubiquitous flow-chart. He patted his arm as they made for the door.

'Splendid lecture, Pinny,' he said. 'Good man. First rate.' Then, holding open the door for him to pass, he added, 'What about a nice drink at *The Dog & Whistle*?'

'Well, why not?' said Pinny, unexpectedly. 'And while we're there, remind me to phone my wife, Joan. I promised to ring when it was all over. She'll be relieved to know it went down so well.'

Chapter Nine

Meanwhile Leanne and Rae were in *Glad Rags*, a chic, very expensive boutique in an alleyway just off the main street. Leanne had already confided in Rae that she found Oliver extremely attractive, so much so that she'd accepted his invitation to dinner that evening. Rae was amused by this development and was helping her choose a new outfit before dashing off to give her lecture in the Schoolroom. She selected a long, blue raw silk tunic and held it against Leanne, shook her head and changed it for a cream jersey sweater. Leanne had several pairs of trousers and two long cardigans over her arm, ready to try on. Rae looked at her watch.

'Christ, it's ten-fifteen already.' she cried. 'I'll have to go in a minute. Claire's meant to be helping me sort out the overhead projector. Here - try these...' she added, pushing two more tops through the curtain of the changing room. 'I can't believe you're really thinking of starting something with Oliver - you *are* joking, aren't you?'

'Not at all. And I told you I haven't really fancied anyone for years - well, for the last three at least - but now everything's changed, the animal, as they say, has been unleashed!' called Leanne, stifling a giggle as she lost her balance getting out of a pair of size 10 jeans. 'Mind you, that's if he's interested...'

'Interested?' Rae exclaimed. 'Anything that moves from what I've heard. Here, try the size 12 - the colour's great.'

'Oh, come on. He can't be that bad. Stop exaggerating!'

'I'm not kidding. He even tried it on with *me* once when we were both on a weekend writing course in Brighton a couple of years ago.'

Leanne laughed. 'Well, if that's the case I'm surprised he survived - what happened?'

'I told him to go and squirt his genes over someone else. I mean, the arrogance - can't they tell when someone's just not interested?'

'He probably saw you as a special challenge. You know, like all those women who think they can change gay guys into raging heteros...'

'Something like that,' Rae said, laughing. 'But we're still great friends so presumably his precious ego didn't take a terminal bashing. Anyway, I must get going...'

Leanne came out from behind the curtain. 'Quick, before you go - rust trousers, cream top?' She did a quick twirl. 'Or black trousers and purple top?'

Rae stood back, raking through her hair with her fingers: 'I reckon rust and cream... hang on, turn round again... or cream and black ...oh, God, I don't know. D'you honestly think he'll care? Just throw on an old bin-bag and be done with it. See you later. Try to get there before the end?'

Leanne went back into the changing room feeling excited, ludicrously so, laughing at herself for attaching so much importance to a dinner date with a notoriously fickle young man several years younger than herself and infinitely more sophisticated. She wondered if she'd remember how to flirt, how to enjoy an evening out in the company of an interested male. Since her break up with Bill she'd only been out for the occasional meal or a drink with old friends, most of whom were gay. As for the heterosexual men she'd known at college, most were now married with young families and inevitably some of these friendships had gradually been weakened by the demands of work, home and jealous wives.

As it was she preferred the company of her gay friends and welcomed the chance for a 'bit of grub and a screech' without any sexual expectations. It suited her fine - not least because her life was quite complicated enough, working full time and coping with the pressure of school, writing for several hours each evening, the awful living conditions on the estate and bringing up Joe on her own. Always exhausted and worried about something or other, she was hardly the most scintillating companion - and, even if she'd found someone who was remotely interesting or interested, there were the impracticalities.

It was no easy matter starting an affair in a flat so small that her bed, though separated by a wafer thin wall, was literally only four feet away from Joe's sleeping head. Added to which, she knew from experience with so many of her pupils at school, that a succession of 'uncles' was not only confusing for children, it could also cause untold friction and misery within the family.

All in all she was glad that she hadn't met anyone since Joe was nine so the problem had never arisen. But now, knowing she would be away for a few days, amongst new acquaintances, she felt free and determined to enjoy herself for once, abandon herself to a bit of fun, away from work, away from that bloody awful tower block and above all, away from the perpetual scrutiny of a thirteen year old boy. The sense of freedom she felt was exhilarating!

Ten minutes later she was hurrying from the shop carrying her new clothes, having spent far more than she could afford but not caring. She went straight across the road to the chemist's shop and, selecting a small bottle of her favourite Yves St Laurent perfume, she handed it to the young girl behind the counter and gave her a conspiratorial smile.

'And a packet of condoms, please,' she said. '*Gossamer de Luxe*.'

She wasn't late for Rae's lecture - in fact, when she reached *St Saviour's* at ten to eleven she had to join a queue that had extended across the tiny playground and into the street outside. Bits of burst balloons were hanging like limp tongues from the spikes of the railings and strips of coloured tissue, crumpled raffle tickets and cardboard beakers were strewn along the gutters, a dreary aftermath of the *May Day Parade*.

She took her place behind a group of local women, equipped with rolled up carrier bags under their arms, from whose conversation it became clear that they thought they were queuing for a jumble sale.

As the line crept towards the main entrance Leanne looked up and noticed that the words - St Saviour's Infant School - Built 1876 - had been carved into the stone lintel and underneath in bold letters, the word BOYS. She was sure that Rae had also noticed and would no doubt bring it up in her lecture - the injustice of denigrating the GIRLS entrance to a small, single side door, which she would interpret as yet another example of the ingrained ethos of secondary citizenship for the female of the species.

And Leanne had to agree with her. Through knowing Rae, her eyes had been opened to so much insidious prejudice against women and made her realise how upbringing, hers included, not only brain-washed most men into assuming that they were the superior sex, but also conditioned women to accept the notion as an irrefutable fact. She had done her best, therefore, to remedy this with Joe, deliberately setting out to instil in him from his earliest years the preposterously simple and fundamental fact that men and women were born equal.

Thinking of Joe she suddenly realised she'd forgotten to phone him - she had rung after breakfast but the line was engaged. She'd intended to ring back, of course, but then, busily buying new clothes, she'd forgotten.

Feeling guilty, she toyed with the idea of rushing off to find a telephone box but as she was being propelled from behind by a couple of redoubtable dons and the lecture was due to start she decided to wait until later. Joe probably wouldn't notice anyway. She was just about to slip into a seat at the back when Oliver came up behind her and, taking her elbow, eased her down the central aisle, around the bent figure of Claire Fenton as she fiddled with the projector, towards the front row where Duncan was saving their seats.

Rae was already on the platform, sitting at a long table with the other speakers. She was looking stunning, her long lean body shown to good effect by the black T-shirt and jeans she was wearing and her blond hair, olive skin and pale eyes were set off to perfection by an exotic array of antique silver jewellery. She gave them a broad smile and winked.

Fiona Bridewell was seated in the middle, and in between anxiously watching the latecomers filing in and mentally assessing the number of empty seats that were left, she fiddled obsessively, first with the bottles of Perrier water and then straightening the piles of notes in front of her. She gave Oliver a quick smile and nodded in Leanne's direction and then, looking round at the school clock on the wall behind her she rose and gave a little cough:

'Ladies and Gentlemen - er, may we begin? Thank you.'

She stared at the audience with a fixed, bright smile. They responded with a last low murmuring and a final shuffle of bottoms on seats.

'Firstly,' she said, 'may I welcome you all to our discussion this morning. As you see we have managed to enlist the services of three most eminent speakers and I think it might be helpful if I introduce each one before we begin. On my far left we have Dr Mary Reynolds, Chief Medical Supervisor of Her Majesty's Prisons. She has contributed to several White Papers on the medical provision for women serving long sentences and works closely with the back-up services for prisoners on release.

'Next to her, the Governor of Holloway Prison, Ms Ruth Carruthers, a very experienced administrator who has written extensively on the subject of the incarceration of women, especially on all aspects of their rehabilitation.'

'And on my right, Ms Rae Roberts,' she continued, 'who, as you will know, has a book entered for this year's *Birkett Bronze Award*, entitled *The Genetic Factor in Female Criminality.* She is, at present, and I hope she will elaborate further in her address, engaged upon research for her PhD on *The Role of Serotonin and Testosterone in Aggressive and Anti-social Behaviour in Women.* She has recently returned from a tour of women's prisons in the United States, interviewing women serving life sentences for murder. Copies of Ms Roberts's book will, of course, be available for purchase after the customary question and answer session.'

'And now,' Claire Fenton concluded, 'I shall sit down and allow our guests to begin what I can guarantee will be a most invigorating discussion, one that will, I am sure, give us plenty to think about - Dr Reynolds?'

Looking down from the platform Rae noticed how pretty

Leanne appeared, more relaxed, lively, younger. She glanced at Oliver, who had his right foot resting casually on his left knee and as he inclined his head to inspect his fingernails, his long hair had flopped down, obscuring his face. Aware that she was watching him he looked up and winked. Then, looking sideways at Leanne, he raised his eyebrows and nodded, before breaking into one of his most disarming smiles.

On his other side, Duncan was sitting bolt upright, with his hands folded in front of him, his customary bow-tie replaced with an extravagant cravat and instead of his usual, flamboyantly-checked jacket, he was wearing one made of wine red velvet. His baggy cord trousers were olive green and his socks, an expanse of which was visible above his black moccasins, were both bright yellow only one was plain and the other was covered with a series of blue half moons.

Both Rae and Oliver saw them at the same time and giggled. Oliver nudged Leanne and indicated the phenomenon with his eyes. Duncan, realising the cause of their amusement, stretched out his left leg and admired the half-moon sock, waggling his ankle around a few times before changing over and doing the same with the other. He seemed more than pleased with the effect.

As Dr Reynolds talked in a low, soothing, ad ministerial voice, Rae looked around the hall, at the long, drab curtains, heavy with chalk-dust, the well-worn horse and box stacked in one corner, the red and green hoops held together with a blue PE band, hanging from the wall-bars. Was it her imagination or could she detect a reminiscent waft of that awful smell of schools - warm, wet wool, the biscuity smell of old books, the sickly stench of stale milk bottles, the close cabbagy farts of children...it all came back to her with sickening clarity. She even imagined she could taste the rancid tang of the midmorning milk that had been left standing too long in the playground. The sharp, irony taste of nibbled wax crayons and the gritty texture of little bits of chewed-up rubber on the tongue.

Looking down at Duncan's socks Rae fell to thinking of her own childhood and of her father's rages the morning after a night's boozing when he couldn't find two socks that matched. She remembered him with loathing and, even at thirty, she still experienced a sickening sense of fear. He had been a selfish, violent man and it hadn't taken much to set him off, make him lose his rag completely, become incoherent with rage over the slightest thing.

'...the inescapable fact that many of the most violent women currently serving long sentences in our prisons are themselves the products of violent, abusive family units where the pattern of aggressive behaviour is not only condoned but accepted as normal. I'm sure Ms Roberts, with all her experience of abused women who have been convicted of violent crimes, will agree with me here?'

Rae, suddenly aware that Dr Reynolds was addressing her, looked up and nodded.

Tell me about it, she thought. She'd been so used to seeing her father brutalise her mother she thought all fathers did it - that men hit women and that was the way it was. And she and her two brothers grew up *expecting* their father to come home blind drunk on Friday and Saturday nights. It would have seemed odd if he hadn't. Sometimes he'd get drunk during the week as well if he could get his hands on some money. He'd even rifle their mother's purse before she had a chance to get the food in for the week.

One year their aunty Pat went to Margate for the day and when she came back she gave Rae and her brothers a small tin money-box in the shape of a No 22 double-decker bus and a fifty pence piece in each one. But two days later their father had rifled all three to buy some booze and they never bothered to try to save up again. There wasn't any point. He'd only take it off them soon enough.

Their mum had a terrible row with their dad when she found out about the money boxes. It started as soon as he got in from the pub late on the Friday and went on half the night.

Rae didn't know which was worse, the actual fighting - the hollering, the thumps, the swearing and the cursing - or the next morning, with him full of remorse, sobbing like a great blubbering baby with his head on her mother's lap, begging her to forgive him - her mother's trembling, mottled hand, still clutching soggy bits of pink lavatory paper, stroking the back of his head, her eyes either downcast or scanning the tops of the walls as if searching for answers - never quite able to look Rae in the eye and confront the confusion and rage she knew would be there. And she'd put his shirt to soak in the sink and the water would be all bloodied and horrible and when they'd finished cleaning their teeth they'd have to spit into the lavatory instead.

She could still feel the awful silence broken only by the sound of her father throwing up and see her mother's white face, freshly-bruised, her hand still shaking as she waved them off to school. A school very much like this. God, the memories, that awful, tragic, suffocating helplessness of small children at the mercy of uncaring adults, who, she now realised, were damaged children themselves.

Rae was aware of a short, appreciative round of applause as Dr Reynolds sat down and Ruth Carruthers stood up. Even her strident, authoritative voice was unable to staunch the flow of memory that flooded Rae's mind as she looked around the hall. She felt small again, insignificant, frightened. Miss will shout at me, always late, never any breakfast when there'd been a bloody great row - so tired, eyes drooping heavy, want to curl up on the PE mat by the radiator and go to sleep. Find a corner in the cloakroom and cuddle up under a pile of coats, stay there for ever and ever, nice and safe.

Miss Hunt was nice, she'd give her extra milk if there was any left over. Rae, dear, she'd say, why don't you take the spare milks and put them away in the crate by the cloakroom? You know where it is - go along, now, there's a good girl and don't be long. She liked Miss Hunt. She wondered where she was now. Married, probably, with kids of her own, or still working in some God-forsaken school like this, being nice to little girls like Rae, trying to undo all the harm done the night before, and the night before that... no chance, too much hurt, too much fear, too much hate.

She remembered those Friday afternoons, watching the classroom clock relentlessly jerking towards three-thirty, not longing for the bell like the other kids, but wishing Miss Hunt would let her stay, warm and safe amongst the cushions in the library corner, listening to the squeaks and rustling of the class gerbils in the hamster cage.

As the memories came flooding back she found herself on the verge of tears; still remembering the supply teacher who didn't know what her home life was all about, didn't know that Miss Hunt used to let her put her head down on her desk for ten minutes after lunch and have a little sleep. She thought Rae was pretending and told her off - but she really *was* asleep and didn't hear and the teacher came and lifted her head from the desk by her hair. And when Rae ran all the way home her dad was watching the racing on the telly and gave her a thrashing for bunking off. She was only frightened of him then. It was only later that she grew to hate him.

By the time she was sixteen she hated him enough to kill him. She'd actually picked up a knife to jam into his great hulking back once when he was hitting her mum only she'd screamed at her, *'Don't, Rae, don't!*' so she put the knife away and ran out of the house. She left home soon after and never went back. She knew that if she'd stayed she'd have killed him.

He was dead now, thank God. Run over by a transit van in Fulham Broadway when he came staggering out of the subway in the middle of the afternoon, drunk as a lord, walked straight out into the road. Serves him bloody right.

Her mother had been more relieved than bereaved but so diminished by his brutality over the years she couldn't really cope with the freedom - a bit like a tortured bear released into the wild - and she started to drink as well. It was because of her, seeing what he'd done to her, that Rae, Sarah and a group of like-minded women had set up a refuge for battered women in Ealing. Her mother, though often shaky and tearful, helped them keep the place clean, sort out the cooking rotas, that sort of thing.

But they were desperate for more space, they could fill a dozen houses and were already turning away women who were desperate for a place of safety for themselves and their children. And now the house next door was coming up for sale. Being at the end of the terrace it was slightly larger and had a garden. If only they could raise the money for a mortgage. There was so much they wanted to do. It sickened her to think of Aubrey Atherton and his millions and the £25,000 he'd be clasping in his sticky little hands at the end of the week.

'Thank you so much, Mary, that was really most informative,' Claire Fenton was saying. Then, turning to Rae, she said, 'and now Ms Roberts, over to you.'

Chapter Ten

At seven o'clock that evening Oliver was waiting for Leanne in the Lounge Bar of *The Hare*. He'd actually bothered to shave for the occasion and had changed into a pale grey linen suit and cream shirt. He joined Rae and Duncan at the bar just as Rae was telling Thelma Doggett about another Mr and Mrs Doggett who had featured in one of her favourite murder cases. As she spoke, Thelma clutched at her throat with her little picky fingers and widened her eyes expectantly.

'Are you sure it was Doggett spelt the same - with two T's?' she asked, her eyes wide.

'Quite sure,' Rae said. 'Fred Doggett was the landlord of the house in Claverton Street, Pimlico, where Adelaide Bartlett supposedly poisoned her husband with liquid chloroform in 1886. I say, supposedly, because she was, in fact, acquitted at the Old Bailey but everyone thought she did it.'

'Despite Sir Edward Clarke's phenomenal speech for the defence...' added Duncan, fingering his glass and blowing the smoke from his cigarette into the air above Rae's head.

'Well, I never, just fancy - *famous* Doggetts! cried Thelma Doggett, who was, of course, delighted. 'I must tell Len.' Her plump hand flitted around her throat once more and she patted her breast as though suffering from shortness of breath. 'Oooh, it makes me go all funny!' she whispered.

'Wasn't Adelaide Bartlett the really pretty one that ended up as a nurse in the First World War?' asked Oliver.

'That's right - half-French,' agreed Rae. 'Born, as they say, the wrong side of the blanket. The illegitimate daughter of an undisclosed member of the English aristocracy - all good stuff. She had an affair with a Methodist preacher and killed her wimp of a husband by pouring chloroform down his throat - can't say I blame her. The defence maintained it was impossible. She was quite an extraordinary woman.'

'Certainly it's one of the great late nineteenth century cases - poison being the method favoured by a number of women, of course,' added Duncan, already on his second whisky. 'More appropriate to their sensibilities, I suppose - and, maybe not surprisingly, with their access to a range of pharmaceuticals, quite a few doctors.'

'That's right,' Rae said. 'I reckon there were five really classic cases. Besides the fiery Adelaide, there was Constance Kent - now there was a strange girl - the tragic Florence Bravo, Florence Maybrick and, of course, that canny Scot, Madeleine Smith. All quite fascinating. It's a great shame. Now it's all guns, knives and garrotting,' moaned Rae, wistfully. 'There's no finesse anymore - no real style.'

'Oooh, you people talk about such nasty, *horrible* things...' chided a delighted Thelma Doggett, whose smile was quickly replaced with a frown as she saw Aubrey Atherton come swanning through the swing door of the foyer with Fiona Bridewell and Samantha Dunbar in his wake.

Although Samantha made a point of smiling sweetly at Oliver, Atherton ignored the three at the bar and, taking his guests to sit by the fire, squealed with laughter at something one of them had said. Whilst replenishing Duncan's glass, Mrs Doggett looked across and gave Aubrey's back a dagger of a glare.

'My, my, Mrs Doggett, if looks could kill. Have we, perchance, a Cassius lurking in our midst?' whispered Duncan. 'I see you've changed your mind about the monstrous Aubrey.'

The landlady's body stiffened. 'Have I?' she snapped. 'I really don't know what you mean...'

'Oh, come on, Mrs D,' Duncan teased. 'When he first arrived you thought he was too wonderful for words. He could do no wrong - so what happened? Whatever has he done to annoy you so? Come on, do tell, we're dying to know.'

Thelma Doggett pressed her lips together but was unable to keep silent.

'The man's a pervert,' she whispered scornfully, 'and I've a good mind to let the pugs in, allergy or not.'

'My goodness, Thelma, that's fighting talk!' cried Duncan, chortling into his glass. 'I reckon he'd best gird his loins forthwith.'

As Mrs Doggett had made no effort to take his order, Aubrey Atherton came over to the bar and asked for three glasses of chilled white wine; then, turning to Oliver, he drew back in a gesture of exaggerated admiration.

'Well, young Oliver,' he lisped. 'I must say you're looking particularly ravishing tonight.'

Looking round at each of the women present in turn, he went on,

'So who's the lucky lady, I wonder? It's not you, is it, Fiona, my dear? Samantha? No, of course not, silly me - it was your turn last night, wasn't it? Oh, my goodness, he's *such* a busy boy!'

He paused to feign a puzzled expression. 'It can't be Rae,

of course, not her scene, as they say. Surely, Oliver, you're not intent on having your wicked way with Ms Philips, feminist sympathiser, stalwart pedagogue and single mum? How extraordinarily perverse of you!'

'Just drop it, Atherton, will you?' said Oliver, turning his back on him. He passed a glass of whisky to Duncan and ordered another lager for himself and Rae.

Finding himself ignored, Atherton picked up the tray of drinks and went back to Samantha and Fiona by the fire but despite maintaining a continuous flow of chatter it was obvious he was also trying to listen to the conversation at the bar. On hearing Oliver congratulate Rae on her lecture he was unable to restrain his vicious tongue and called across the room.

'Rae! Rae, darling, don't pretend you can't hear me,' Atherton chided. 'Fiona's just been telling me about your performance this morning. Would you say it was a success or a dismal failure? So hard to tell, I suppose. Rather an odd subject if you don't mind my saying so. *Hormones*! Oh, Lord, spare us! I mean, who the hell wants to know, duckie?'

He dipped his nose into his glass and sniggered. Samantha Dunbar had the grace to look embarrassed whilst Fiona took the opportunity to get up and go in search of the lavatory.

Rae looked across at Atherton with loathing. She muttered 'revolting great lump' under her breath, before giving him a bright smile.

'You know, Aubrey,' she said, 'you really are a prime example of Neanderthal man - minus the muscles, of course. He, too, would have mocked the principal of penicillin because, with his under-developed brain, understanding how it worked would have been quite beyond him. Know what I mean?'

Atherton, delighted by the waspish exchange, let out a little derisive squeak.

'Oh, *do* retract your claws, dear heart,' he squealed, 'all this penis envy is really *quite* bizarre!'

'He should know, freak that he is,' Rae muttered. 'D'you think that's why he's like he is - because he hasn't got one?'

'You could be right - he is oddly *a*-sexual, isn't he?' Oliver agreed, speaking very softly, so Atherton couldn't hear. 'You know what I mean? He's sort of not quite human in a way that defies definition, like some awful mythical creature, a strange composite, neither man nor woman nor beast. One almost expects him to have cloven hooves or a forked tongue. On the other hand any journalist who has followed his exploits for years could tell you a dozen stories that dispute any notion of neutrality. He's a very active bisexual by all accounts. Whichever takes his fancy, the ultimate opportunist, I suppose.'

He paused and then drained his glass. 'God, let's not dwell on Atherton's sexuality - it's quite putting me off my drink.'

Duncan giggled happily as he ordered another round. 'What'll you have?' he asked Rev Pinny, who had crept up to join them at the bar.

'Oh, just a fruit juice will be fine - no, really, I've got a sermon to write tonight. I daren't leave it till I get back on Saturday. What's so funny?' he asked, seeing their smiling faces.

'Oh, nothing,' said Oliver. 'We're not laughing at you. We've just been speculating about Atherton's sexual preference. Rae's just had a go at him as well. Not that it makes any difference; the man's so reptilian he's got a skin like an alligator. But he must have an Achilles heel somewhere I suppose.'

Turning round, Atherton caught sight of Rev Pinny and made a point of crossing himself.

'Ah, Pinny, old thing!' he called. 'I've got a bone to pick with you. I was reading a terribly boring article in the *Readers*

Digest in my hairdresser's establishment the other day. It was all about a group of missionaries in Papua, New Guinea. I think they were from Stoke Newington. I do hope you're nothing to do with that shower! I was horrified. All those bloody busy-bodies rampaging through every damned corner of the world upsetting people, making luscious native girls wear *Marks & Spencer* braziers, spreading a load of mumbo-jumbo and generally causing absolute chaos.'

'And doing a lot of good, as you very well know, Atherton. You're just being silly...'

'What?' Atherton protested. 'Sorry, Pinny, but that really doesn't wash. Sticking needles in little black babies? Who took bloody measles there in the first place? They're only patching up their own mistakes after all - too late, my friend, too late, the damage is already done,' crowed Atherton, triumphantly, rubbing his hands together.

Joseph Pinny, determined not to be drawn into a futile argument, turned his back on Atherton, who, equally determined to be heard, merely raised his voice.

'Which reminds me,' he said. 'I also read a screamingly funny article about a very naughty man of the cloth. I think he was the vicar of some wretchedly impoverished parish in the back of beyond - somewhere in Derbyshire, I think it was. Now there's an amazing coincidence for you! Isn't that where you come from, Pinny?'

He paused to take a sip from his glass before continuing.

'Anyway,' he said, 'he died in 1848, and you'll never guess what he left all his money to - go on, Pinny, have a guess.'

'I have no idea, Atherton,' replied Pinny, wearily closing his eyes. 'But I'm sure you're going to tell me.'

'Can you believe it? He left nigh on twenty-eight thousand pounds, which was a hell of a lot of money in those days, to provide - wait for it - *knickers* for little boys! Honestly, no word of a lie. Isn't that an absolute *hoot?* What a splendid chap.'

Duncan giggled at this but Rev Pinny merely nodded and said, 'Fancy. Ah, well, I expect he had his reasons.'

'You bet he did!' squealed Atherton, slapping his thigh. 'Perhaps there should be an eleventh commandment? What d'you reckon, Pinny? What about *'Little Boys Shalt Not Enter The Kingdom of Heaven Without Knickers'*? Not before time, if you ask me.'

Then, bored with trying to rile Rev Pinny, he turned to his attention to his guests.

'Now, then, Fiona, Samantha, another glass of wine before we go? Yes, why not?'

He raised his hand to attract Len Doggett's attention but Thelma immediately appeared through the bead curtain, her face like a mask.

'The same again, Mr Atherton?' she asked, speaking through closed lips, with the expertise of a professional ventriloquist. Roughly shunting her husband along the bar, she smiled at Duncan as she poured the drinks.

'Your turn tomorrow, Mr Wainwright?' she asked.

''Fraid so,' replied Duncan. 'My turn to face the lynch mob, as it were.'

'Oh, you'll be all right!' exclaimed Thelma, brightly. 'What with all your theatrical experience behind you. Bet *you* never get stage fright.'

'Well, no, not really, Mrs D,' agreed Duncan. 'I can't honestly say that I do. Just one or two flutters before I get up to speak, that's all. It's so much easier when you've been used to a really large audience. When I was in *Romeo & Juliet,* for example, I was...'

He stopped, aware that Atherton had come over to the bar to buy more drinks and was standing directly behind him. He felt the other man's limp hand on his shoulder and his heart missed a beat.

'Allow me to finish that sentence for you, Duncan, dear boy.' Atherton trilled. "When I was in *Romeo and Juliet* at Brighton Amateur Theatricals, I was a cloak carrier in one of the crowd scenes."

He wagged his finger in front of Duncan's face. 'I know,' he said, 'I was there, I saw you, though if I'd closed my eyes for a split second I should have missed you. Oh, for Christ's sake, all this pretence; you always were a bit part player - and not a very good one at that - and always will be.'

He moved towards Mrs Doggett and smiled broadly. 'Thank you so much, Thelma, my dear.'

Looking across at Len Doggett, who was wearing a new pale blue sweater, he winked.

'Good evening, Leonard,' he said, '*Love* that shade of blue. You know, you were right, it really does bring out the colour of your eyes...'

Len, his sallow features unusually flushed, said nothing in reply but hurried into the other bar. Slamming Atherton's change on the counter, Thelma stood with her arms folded, successfully spurning any further remarks with the look of hostility cold enough to freeze water.

But Atherton merely laughed and as he turned to walk back to his table he saw Leanne coming down the stairs. She was wearing the outfit she'd bought that morning - russet silk trousers and a cream tunic top - and although she had put her hair up it had already begun to fall in delicate tendrils around her ears. She was also wearing more make-up than usual and an elaborate silver choker at her throat. Atherton did a double take and smirked as he handed round the drinks:

'Fiona, dear, your wine,' he said. Nodding his head towards the stairs he murmured: 'Just look at her - now there's a case of mutton dressed as lamb if ever I saw one.'

'You look great!' Rae whispered in Leanne's ear as she joined the others at the bar. 'A knock-out. I'll just finish my drink and then I'm off. There's something on at the *Dog & Whistle* - a live band of some sort. Probably crap but never mind. I promised to meet some friends there.'

'Might I join you, my dear?' asked Duncan. 'I don't much fancy a night in here staring into the fire.'

'Course you can, Dunc. No problem. Come on then, drink up and let's go. We'd better walk down and get a taxi back. Daren't risk taking the Volvo.'

Turning to Leanne she squeezed her arm. 'You look great, honestly. Drop dead gorgeous. Now go and have a good time for a change.'

Still smiling to himself, Atherton draped Fiona's fake ocelot jacket around her shoulders.

'Leonard,my man,' he called, 'tell the driver we're ready.'

As he strutted towards the door, one arm linked in Fiona's and the other in Samantha's, he thrust his nose into the air and trilled. 'Bye, luvvies, have a simply *wonderful* time.' He paused next to Oliver and touched his arm. 'Oooh, what a terrible waste,' he whispered.

Then, turning to Fiona, he whined.

'Fiona, dear, you must put my mind at rest, I trust you booked the very *best* table at Giovanni's? And don't forget what I said - I meant every word - if I see so much as the shadow of a press photographer lurking in a corner, I promise you I shall lie on the floor and scream. Now, don't say you haven't been warned.'

*

It had been Oliver's intention to take Leanne to Giovanni's for dinner that evening but as neither of them fancied the idea of eating in close proximity to Aubrey Atherton, they decided to go to a Pizza Bar instead. The food was okay, nothing special, but there was one advantage, they were able to talk freely amid the general hubbub coming from the kitchen and were not inhibited by the diners at the next table seemingly tuned in to every word.

Not that there was any awkwardness between them for they shared the same fascination with writing, crime writing in particular, and had plenty to talk about. They found they also shared a similar humour and, far from coming out with the usual cliched repartee of a well-practised Lothario, Oliver turned out to be an interesting conversationalist, naturally charming and not nearly as full of himself as Leanne had, at first, imagined.

After they had discussed all six books short-listed for the award they naturally fell to fantasising about spending the £25,000 prize money. Oliver was refreshingly frank about his desire for the money. He wanted it, he said, purely to spend on having fun. He'd buy a nifty new car, midnight blue, he thought, chuck out everything in his flat and replace it with some really choice custom made, minimalist furniture; after which, if there was any money left, he'd take a marvellous holiday in Barbados.

They also talked at length about their work. She about the hell of working in a run down inner-city school and he about the hectic, cut-throat business of writing for a national newspaper. Telling him about the horrendous tower-block in which she and Joe lived and the proximity of the pugnacious Kelly, she found it such a relief to talk about it that they ended up roaring with laughter. Write a book about it, he said, it might turn out to be a bestseller.

Though she tried to make light of it he seemed to understand her despair at having to live like that and listened sympathetically as she told him of her concern for Joe as he approached adolescence in such depressing surroundings. He even said that, in a way, he hoped she would win the award if it meant she'd be able to get off the estate and start afresh.

When she asked him if he was married or had any children he paused for a moment before saying no.

'None of my girlfriends have children, either,' he said. 'Just as well, really, as I don't quite see myself as an 'Uncle Oliver', somehow.'

She asked him if he could see himself married at some time in the future, to which he replied, 'Well, it's all a question of timing, isn't it? What I mean is, if I were looking for a long-term commitment, which I'm not, I'd probably look for someone like you - independent, tenacious, intelligent and compassionate.' He paused and reached for her hand. 'But at the moment, I'm really not into family units, kids, all that sort of stuff.'

'I can understand that. It certainly isn't for everyone.'

'In some ways,' Oliver went on, 'I wish I were. I see friends of mine in that kind of set-up and it looks great. It's just not for me, I'm afraid. Not at the moment, anyway. So you see, my sweet Leanne,' he said, lifting he hand to his lips. 'I can offer you no more than an evening's amorous adventure, no strings, no ties, no recriminations, no regrets. What d'you think?'

He looked at her closely. 'It's just a thought. I can't pretend

I'll be heartbroken if you refuse. I just think it'd be nice - it'd be okay - a pleasantly stimulating diversion.'

He looked at her directly, with those devastatingly expressive eyes. 'I can't believe no one's made love to you for three years - you're kidding me - what a diabolical waste, as Atherton would say. God knows, life's dreary enough - we deserve a little fun now and again. Don't you agree?'

Oh, yes, she agreed all right. She felt light-headed, young again, happy.

A couple of hours later they decided to join Rae and her friends at *The Dog & Whistle* which was packed out. The band was playing with the amplifiers at full blast and they had to push their way through the crowds to reach the bar. Duncan was perched on a stool, quite pissed, with his back leaning against a pillar, and Rae was dancing - or rather, shuffling on the spot - with one of her friends.

Oliver and Leanne stayed for a couple of drinks but, finding it impossible to hear each other speak, they went for a walk by the river instead.

The light was just fading as they made their way down the narrow sloping street to the riverside but the tree-lined walkway was strewn with coloured lights initially put up for Monday's *May Day Parade* and then left for the duration of the Festival. The peaceful setting was in sharp contrast to their normal city habitat although there were still small groups of tourists strolling about, interspersed with solitary, local people out walking their dogs before nightfall.

After a while, Oliver and Leanne sat in silence on a bench, his arm laid casually across her shoulders. As they watched people passing and listened to the movement of the river,

Leanne could feel waves of cold air coming off the water as it softly licked the base of the parapet at their feet. She felt so relaxed and realised that she'd quite forgotten how nice it could be just being with an attractive man like Oliver. It felt so good. Her mind was made up. Why not, for heaven's sake? They were both old enough to know about safe sex and as he said, there would be no conditions, no strings, just good grown-up fun.

When they got back to the hotel the place was in total darkness. Laughing and clutching each other like children, they groped their way through the foyer and then crept through the Lounge Bar to reach the stairs.

At first they thought the room was empty but Oliver grabbed Leanne's arm and pointed to a figure slumped in the wing-chair near the ingle-nook.

It was Duncan, lit by the soft glow of the dying embers, sleeping like a baby with his mouth open, his cravat hanging over the arm of the chair and, for some reason, his shoes standing side by side in the grate. He shifted slightly in his chair as they passed, made a soft, grunting noise deep in his throat and closed his mouth, but did not wake.

Despite taking care to feel their way round the unlit bar, Oliver, nevertheless, managed to walk into one of Thelma's wretched occasional tables, causing him to curse loudly.

To their surprise, they realised that Thelma Doggett was, in fact, not in bed upstairs as they'd imagined, but was still in the kitchen, presumably sitting by the light of the television set but with the sound turned down.

Hearing Oliver shout, she called out.

'Len? Len, is that you?'

Oliver and Leanne stood stock still like naughty children and Leanne actually had her hand over her mouth.

'Stop sneaky about, you silly old fool,' the landlady cried.

Silence. Oliver and Leanne holding their breath.

‘Where the hell have you been?' Thelma called.

The scrape of a chair in the kitchen and the sound of Thelma Doggett’s footsteps spurred Oliver into action. Grabbing Leanne’s hand they sprinted up the stairs and along the creaky corridor leading to his room.

As they passed Rae's room they could hear the low murmur of her radio and from Atherton's the babble of voices and a sudden burst of laughter.

Then, as ill-luck would have it, they bumped into Rev Pinny coming out of the bathroom. He was a pathetic sight, hair awry and wearing green Paisley patterned pyjamas; on his long, rat-like feet were threadbare slippers, one of which was minus its pom-pom, and he was holding a lemon yellow sponge bag to his stomach in the manner of a bashful debutante with a clutch bag.

They stood and stared at him, feeling like guilty teenagers, as though he knew their intent.

But he hadn't even recognised them. His eyesight was so poor he could see very little without his glasses and simply peered at whatever stood in his path like a startled micro-ophthalmic shrew.

'Goodnight,' he said, into the space between the two, before shuffling off in search of his room.

Leanne and Oliver, grinning stupidly, dived into Oliver's and collapsed on the bed, stifling giggles. Then, suddenly looking at her watch, Leanne got up.

'I must phone Joe,' she said. 'Dammit, I meant to phone when we left the Pizza Bar...'

But Oliver had reached over and, taking hold of her shoulders, pulled her down on the bed beside him.

'Later,' he said, placing his hand gently behind her head

and easing it down to meet his face. His lips felt cool, he smelled of soap and linen, his other hand was caressing the small of her back and he felt taut, exciting and incredibly sexy.

*

Chapter Eleven

Rae woke next morning shortly after seven and smiled when she saw that Leanne's bed was empty. She lay with her arms behind her head, thinking about Sarah, wondering whether she was awake yet. How much time they spent together depended on her shift rota and when she was on nights they saw little of each other. Closing her eyes she could see so clearly the tall, shabby house in Ealing and their poky flat under the eaves. If Sarah was on a day shift she'd be up by now, standing around in the tiny galley of a kitchen, still in the *'Grumpy'* T-shirt she wore in bed, her tawny hair a mess, waiting for the coffee to percolate.

She'd probably be standing by the window, listening to the radio, nibbling Ryvita and staring down onto the rows of back gardens with their collection of ramshackle, make-shift sheds, thrown together with bits of old doors daubed with white paint and bits of corrugated iron, havens for mice and spiders and jam-packed with bikes, rusty tins of hardened paint, old lawnmowers, defunct electric fires, broom handles and burnt out saucepans.

And, it seemed, every broken-down wall, every tree stump, dustbin and lean-to had a cat sitting on it - pretty, delicate ones, bent-eared old bruisers, nondescript, ill-marked moggies - they were everywhere. Their own two cats would be winding themselves around Sarah's bare legs, begging for food by pressing their whiskers against her shins and needling what was left of the *'rabbit'* slippers Rae had given her last Christmas, begging for food. Thinking of Sarah made her feel warm. Rae loved her deeply for she possessed not only physical beauty but also incredible loyalty and integrity. She couldn't imagine not loving her, not being part of her life, and never stopped marvelling that, after her rotten childhood and turbulent adolescence, she, Rae, had finally found someone completely in tune with her inner self, someone who saw and continued to see, something worthwhile and beautiful in her and with whom she would entrust her life.

Feeling a sudden longing to be back home Rae jumped out of bed and tried to channel her thoughts on the events of the day ahead. She'd go to Duncan's lecture at two and then look in at Aubrey Atherton's, which, she imagined, would be his usual sickeningly polished performance for his besotted fans.

On her way to the bathroom she saw Mrs Doggett hovering outside Duncan's room, stroking one of her little occasional tables with the end of her duster. They exchanged a brief greeting and as Rae reached the end of the corridor she heard her confronting Duncan as he came out of his room.

'Ah, Mr Wainwright,' Thelma was saying. 'I'm so glad I've caught you. Do you know, as soon as I went to bed last night I remembered where it was I'd seen you before. Didn't I say your face was familiar? Well, it was the voice that did it! I just *knew* I'd heard it before.'

She rolled her eyes at him in a grotesquely familiar way and thrust her dumpy digits into his arm. 'It *was* you, wasn't it?'

'Mrs D, *please,*' protested Duncan. 'I haven't the faintest idea what you're talking about.'

Mrs Doggett brought her face a little closer.

'The Yummy Breakfast Bunny!' she breathed, in a triumphant whisper. 'It was you, wasn't it? On the telly. It was the voice that did it. There's no mistaking that voice. Very distinctive, I must say. I *knew* I'd heard it before.'

'I assure you, madam, it was *not* me,' Duncan lied. He looked defiantly at his interrogator. 'The voice is not dissimilar, I grant you,' he added, grudgingly, 'but please, I beg you, do not mention my acting in front of the others - especially Aubrey Atherton - you know what I mean, he loves to mock and talks such nonsense about the theatre, a subject he knows little about. It's a case of *'pearls before swine'* and all that. Let's keep it our little secret, shall we?'

He reached down and squeezed Thelma's hand raised now in the manner of a surprised mouse. She let out a little squeal of pain as her jewel-encrusted fingers were crushed together in the grip of Duncan's hand.

'I'm so sorry, my dear,' he said. 'Do forgive me. Now, don't forget...' He knowingly tapped the side of his nose. 'I feel sure I can rely on you. Mum's the word, Mrs D, mum's the word.'

*

A little later, when she had joined the others downstairs for breakfast, the look on Leanne's face prompted Rae to whisper: '*That* good, eh?'

Leanne presented her best enigmatic smile and looked across at Oliver, who was hungrily demolishing a plate of scrambled eggs. Returning her gaze he held it for a moment and then smiled back. He was just about to say something when Mrs Doggett called Leanne to the telephone.

'Someone called Joe. I've left the receiver hanging,' she said, coming over with a pot of coffee and fresh rolls.

Leanne, looking anxious, got up from the table and hurried along the passage and hoisted up the receiver.

'Joe? Is anything wrong?' she cried. 'What's the matter?'

'Where were you yesterday?' The pitch of Joe's voice sounded much higher than usual and it was petulant in tone, like that of a much younger child. 'You said you'd phone.'

Leanne felt her face flushing. 'Well, darling, it was a bit difficult. Try to understand. For a start I was terribly busy and I have a lot of lectures to attend. It's really quite a hectic schedule fitting everything in.'

'You said you'd phone...' Joe repeated, sulkily.

'Well, I did phone in the morning. I forget when exactly, but I did phone and the line was engaged...'

'So why didn't you bother to phone back.'

'Oh, Joe, don't be silly...' The guilt she was feeling lent a defensive edge to her voice. 'It wasn't a case of not bothering.'

'Well, what about last night?'

'What d'you mean? What about last night?'

'Why didn't you phone like you always do? You said you would. So why didn't you?'

'I'm sorry, Joe.' Leanne paused for a moment. 'Look, I'll be honest with you. I went out and I forgot.'

'*Forgot*!' The boy sounded genuinely shocked. 'I don't believe I'm hearing this! If I said I'd ring and then forgot you'd really have a go at me. You'd go on and on and on about it.'

'I know, darling, I'm sorry, really I am.' It made her very uncomfortable, knowing her son had the moral high-ground. And he didn't even know about her spending the night with Oliver... 'Look,' she said, 'I promise I'll phone you tonight.'

Silence from Joe but the sound of Jean's radio in the

background and the rasping noise of someone scraping toast.

'Joe?'

'What?'

'I said I'll phone you tonight - promise.'

'I might be out.'

'Out where?'

'Football practice.'

'Who with?'

'The school.'

'Well,what time will you get back?'

'Dunno.'

'What d'you mean, you don't know?'

'Depends.'

'Depends on what?'

'Lots of things.'

'Oh, come on, Joe, don't give me that.' Leanne snapped, losing patience. 'You just make sure you get back when Jean says so. And I'm going to check on you later.'

'What for?'

'Have you had any breakfast?'

'Don't fuss.'

'Shouldn't you be getting off to school?'

'Back off. I'm just going.'

'All right, make sure you do,' Leanne said. 'And Joe...'

'What?'

'Don't forget. I'll ring this evening. I'll speak to you then.'

There was no reply.

'Joe?'

Leanne raised her voice. 'Joe, can you hear me?'

But the phone was dead.

While Leanne was on the phone to Joe, Aubrey Atherton had joined the others in the Lounge Bar. He was still in his night attire - a green silk, monogrammed robe over a pair of lemon pyjama trousers with a tunic style top with a rolled neck. His small feet, encased in green leather moccasins with red and gold thread-work across the toes, looked cold, lifeless, translucent, the colour and texture of alabaster. Though his face was even more pallid and embryonic than usual, he seemed in high spirits, smiling at everyone before taking his seat at the table:

'Ah, Mrs Duckett,' he called, seeing Thelma skulking in the doorway of the kitchen, partly concealed by the bead curtain. 'I won't partake of your excellent repast this morning, if you don't mind. I shall be having a little something later on, prior to my performance at eleven. Just a little of your excellent coffee will be an ample sufficiency.'

Mrs Doggett, grim-faced, served Atherton his coffee, after which he took a sip, then, turning to Oliver, he said.

'My goodness, you look deliciously debauched this morning. Did you have a bad night? By the way,' he added, looking round, 'where *is* Ms Phillips - don't tell me she's still upstairs panting for more?'

Rev Pinny looked up sharply and frowned whereas Duncan lowered his eyes and dabbed at his moustache with his napkin. Oliver simply laughed and reached for his coffee cup.

'I've always considered envy such an unattractive emotion, Atherton,' he said, looking directly at Aubrey. 'Especially in a middle-aged man. I can only conclude that your own little soiree turned out to be infinitely less memorable than mine.' He looked across at Rae and smiled.

'Oooh, you've got a *vicious* tongue, young Oliver. And so masterful with those gorgeous flashing eyes!'

A moment later his attention was drawn towards Leanne as she returned to the table.

'Ah, there you are,' he said, pushing the coffee pot in her direction. 'and looking quite radiant, I must say.'

Whilst leaning towards her, as though about to embark on an intimate conversation, he nevertheless made a point of raising, not lowering his voice.

'Tell me, Ms Philips, forgive me for prying but I've so often wondered how you single mums manage to cope with the socio-sexual side of life.'

'What d'you mean?' Leanne's voice was guarded.

'Well, put it like this,' Aubrey explained. 'Surely living in a dreary battery-coop in the sky with a gruesomely acned adolescent scowling in a corner must vastly cramp your style - in matters of the heart, I mean. Terribly inconvenient, one should have thought.' He paused, took a sip of coffee and continued. 'Do you find it deters potential suitors or am I being hopelessly naive and out of touch with the moral morass of the lower echelons of modern life?'

'What the hell are you babbling about now, Atherton?' Rae asked, frowning.

'I am talking to your friend, if you don't mind, not you,' Aubrey replied, his tone petulant. Turning back to Leanne, he went on. 'Does it mean that one has to curtail or, heaven forbid, even forgo, one's baser instincts? I must say it's most dreadfully sad if it does.' He paused. 'On the other hand, it does curb the wretched birth-rate, which, in the circumstances, is no bad thing.'

Pushing aside his coffee cup, he dabbed his lips with the edge of a napkin and rose from the table. Lifting the bronze bell from the bar he shook it vigorously several times.

'Thelma, my dear,' he called. 'Is that dear old Leonard I see lurking in the gloom of the other bar? Don't tell me the poor soul's been banished again? Oooh, you're a hard woman, Mrs Doggett, a heart of stone.. Please tell him to send my driver up to my room the moment he arrives. I shall now go back upstairs and take a leisurely bath and prepare myself for my public, some of whom, or so Fiona tells me, have travelled from as far afield as Japan. Amazing, isn't it?'

As he walked towards the stairs he turned and then, looking directly at Duncan, said, 'I do hope you have a reasonable turn-out, Duncan, dear boy.' He paused, with one foot on the bottom step.

'Oh, by the way,' he said, 'my driver's absolutely convinced he saw you on the television the other night. You know, on one of those channels that churn out hours of dreary repeats that nobody bothered top watch first time round The man's a fool - said he recognised your voice. Rubbish, I told him, what on earth would an actor of Duncan Wainwright's calibre be doing dressed up as the Yummy Breakfast Bunny? Why, the idea's preposterous, I said, quite preposterous.'

*

As Duncan cut through the alleyway by the church and hurried towards the School at twenty to two that afternoon he was relieved to see a queue of some fifty or sixty people waiting to go in. Rae, Oliver and Leanne were close behind. Although they'd all left *The Hare* together - Oliver and Leanne in the Aston Martin and the others crammed into the Volvo - they'd lost Rev Pinny in the crowds soon after reaching the town centre. Mrs Doggett had promised to make an appearance saying that if they weren't too busy she'd leave Leonard in charge and pop along for a while. She arrived soon after the others but chose to sit at the back, near the door, saying she couldn't stay long.

As she sat down she nodded to one or two local people she knew and then, seeing Duncan sitting alongside Claire Fenton and the other speakers on the platform, she gave a little wave.

The poor man. She'd felt so sorry for Duncan when that dreadful Atherton creature had mentioned the Yummy Breakfast Bunny in front of everybody. It was a horrible thing to do. Duncan had gone all red and she'd felt terrible. Let's hope he didn't think she'd said anything. She'd never do that, especially to Aubrey Atherton. Besides, she liked Duncan, even though he did go on a bit about his theatrical friends and everything.

What a shame he wasn't married - she'd said as much to Len the night before last. Perhaps it was just one of those things - too busy in the theatre and somehow missed the boat. Such a nice man and such a lovely voice. No sign of that Fiona Bridewell, she noticed, no doubt too busy fussing round Aubrey Atherton down at *The Crown.*

'Ladies and gentlemen,' Claire Fenton was saying, 'May I welcome you all on behalf of the four speakers we have lined up for you today. Our subject is, as you will, of course, know, *The Courtroom Drama*, a topic of particular interest to the experts at this table. On my far left, Chief Inspector Martin Freeman, of the Metropolitan Police; next to him an historian and writer with a special interest in post-war trials at the Old Bailey, Professor Keith Raglan; on my right, Ms Maria Gibbons, lecturer in Law at Sussex University, who has written a number of articles on this fascinating topic.'

'And finally, Mr Duncan Wainwright, writer and actor, short-listed for this year's *Birkett Bronze Award* for his book entitled, *The Theatrical Portrayal of Murder*. Good luck with that, Duncan. Right, now that we all know each other, may we begin with you, Chief Inspector Freeman?'

Well used to having to sit for hours in dreary halls listening to other members of the cast endlessly rehearsing their lines, Duncan had no difficulty whatever in allowing his mind to wander. He started by counting the number of persons in the hall. Fifty-eight. Not bad - about twenty-five empty seats, that's all - no, twenty-four, a lady in a cherry red coat has just come in and sat down next to Mrs Doggett at the back. My God, he thought, I'm only sixty-three and the old eyes are getting weaker by the day. I'll be blind as a bat by the time I'm seventy at this rate. I could see perfectly well a couple of years ago. How depressing. Teeth next, I expect. He looked again at the back of the hall. He couldn't see Thelma Doggett's face at all, just a blur. He fished out his spectacles and put them on. That only made it worse. He was confronted by a sea of out-of-focus blobs.

He was aware that Rev Pinny had just sidled in and slunk into a seat on the side. Good man - he'd promised to show up. Man of his word, was Pinny. Duncan made a note on his pad to remind himself to have his eyes re-tested.

He felt uncomfortable. The smells of the school hall made him uneasy, tapped half-hidden feelings of sadness and loss. With an escalating sense of panic he tried to turn his thoughts around, resist thinking about the past. Children's voices in the playground, under the window.

The numbing effect of pea-green paint and the evocative smell of municipal polish, the censorious school clock, always Friday afternoon slow, the hymn number 271 heralding those interminable, terminally boring assemblies and paralysingly dull prize days. He turned to look at the piano that had been pushed to one side of the platform, redundant, silenced. The top was littered with songbooks, sheet music, an indoor watering-can, brass with a green rubber nozzle and a dirty duster rolled up in a ball like an old sock. Someone arriving late - the clank and thud of the double doors, the echoing sound of high-heeled shoes on the shiny parquet floor.

He used to imagine his mother being tall and willowy and wearing high heels. He'd only seen one photograph of her which had been taken in the garden and she was wearing wellington boots. He'd wanted to ask his father what she was like but he never did. In fact, he didn't see him that much and when they did spend a hour or two together once in a while there was never time to talk. Even in the school holidays he'd been dumped with an aunt. His mother had died soon after his birth and, after being handed over to a nanny for the first five years, he was enrolled in a prep.school for a further two before being shunted off to a boarding school at the age of seven.

He had never been an academic type of boy or particularly sporty; he just sort of muddled through, living mainly in a fantasy world, always imagining exciting things that never actually happened.

Each day was pretty much the same as the one before and just as boring. He had no burning ambitions, no obsessions to keep him going and the mundane routine of his life was such that he had never savoured the joy of anticipation. He had few inner resources but he was kindly, inoffensive, easily led, liked well enough but never destined to shine. He never inspired admiration, love or hero worship. That was pretty much the story of his life, really. He was eighteen when he inherited his father's money - not a fortune but a sizeable sum.

That same year he signed on to join the Army. It was 1955 and he would have been called up for National Service, anyway, but he didn't really know what else to do. He'd rather hoped he'd be sent somewhere exciting, where he could be in the thick of things - he even volunteered to be posted to Suez but no such luck - he spent the whole of the first two years stationed in barracks on Salisbury Plain. Then, when he signed on for another five years, he ended up in a camp in Colchester and never once saw active service or had the chance to travel, not even a day trip to Calais.

But Duncan had felt at ease with the camaraderie of army life for it was rather like boarding school, all chaps together. It was in the army that he started acting, small parts mainly, and he also wrote a few plays that were well received by the lads but which were, frankly, pretty mediocre.

But that had been years ago. He'd recently had a great idea for a really brilliant, one-man, three act play. He'd already started writing it but there was still quite a way to go. He could even put it on, hire a small hall somewhere, take the part himself - if only he could win that £25,000. No chance. He'd never won anything in his life. Atherton was the sort who won things, got what he wanted out of life, sod anyone else.

When he eventually left the army he decided to try to land a job in a repertory company. He was turned down more times than he could count but a provincial company about to go on tour subsequently agreed to take him on - mainly, he realised, because he was prepared to take a small salary, didn't mind the travelling and made an excellent butler, vicar or bank manager. He was a good all-rounder, always ready to muck in and do whatever was asked of him - no massive ego, no histrionics. And he loved every minute of it. The theatre provided him with a large family of transient friends, always changing, never constant but, nevertheless, a family of sorts.

He forced his thoughts back to listen to Chief Inspector Freeman - not that he was saying anything new. Duncan had picked his brains dry when he was researching his book - nice chap, instant rapport, ex-army like himself. He turned round to look at the clock. Freeman had been talking for fifteen minutes and he'd barely heard a word. He made an effort to concentrate.

'...the ultimate result, of course,' the policeman was saying, 'was that the man we really needed to talk to, a man called Fisher...'

'Fisher, Humber, White, Portland, Plymouth, Biscay, Sole, Finestair, Lundy, Fastnet...'

Once he'd started Duncan couldn't stop his brain finishing the sequence. Strange, he thought, how everyone could recite the Fishing Forecast if they really put their minds to it. At school Duncan had spent countless hours reciting it under his breath in the most boring lessons and sometimes, if he couldn't sleep, he'd go through the whole lot from the beginning and always fell asleep before the end...

Irish Sea, Shannon, Rockall, Mallin, Hebrides, Bailey, Fairisle, Pharoahs, Helligoland, Ronald's Way, Channel Light Vessel...

What the hell did it all mean? A meaningless mantra; it was only many years later, when he was well into middle age, that he realised they were islands and areas of sea that served as markers for fleets of fishermen.

Duncan, seeing that Professor Raglan was already on his feet, felt a quick rush of adrenaline. Putting on his glasses again he rummaged through his notes, satisfied himself that he knew what he was going to say, then fell to checking the audience again. He was perplexed to note that several of the number had disappeared. He did a quick count - yes, he thought so. There were now twenty-eight empty seats.

As he was doing a recount he saw three women seated in the middle of the second row get up and crab walk their way to the end of the line; once free they made for the door. One of them poked another woman in the back as she squeezed past her and then whispered something in her ear with the result that the woman got up immediately to join her familiars and in doing so, more or less ran from the hall.

Resigned to there being only Oliver left by the time he rose to speak, he fell to thinking about the lady who lived in the mansion block opposite his flat in Prince of Wales Drive, near Battersea Park. All last summer he'd watched her leaving the building at twenty to nine each morning, driving off in her little red Renault, with a box of multi-coloured tissues on the back seat and a Springer Spaniel sticker in the window. She always returned shortly after six. Sometimes she went out again in the evening but she never came back much later than eleven - and always on her own.

Duncan knew her name - he'd sneaked up the steps to her block and read the name plates beside the bells - Mr and Mrs Brian Richards? No, he'd never seen her with a man, so he was fairly sure she wasn't married. Nigel Mortimer? Hardly. Dolly Cavendish? No, he knew it wasn't her because a card addressed to Mrs Cavendish had been delivered to him by mistake the previous Christmas and he'd taken it across the road.

Dolly Cavendish turned out to be an old lady of ninety-six who'd been a chorus girl at *The Brixton Empire*. She was really glad to have a visitor and when she found out Duncan was an actor she made a pot of tea and sat talking about the old days in the theatre for three hours or more. He helped her pull out a trunk from under her bed - she called it her *'treasure chest'*.

It was that, all right, crammed full of treasured memories - but, my God, the dust! Inside were dozens of photographs, spotted with damp and faded with age, theatre tickets and rolled posters, some dating back to the 1920's. There were several pictures of Dolly when she was no more than seventeen or eighteen and Duncan had to agree that she'd had a wonderful pair of legs. Best pair of pins in the business, she said, sadly looking down at her thin, knobbly legs encased in thick woollen stockings and two pairs of socks. Duncan coming round like that had made her Christmas, she said.

After that he went round every Sunday afternoon, took her a cake or a bit of chocolate and had a good natter. Out would come her 'treasure chest', every time, without fail, yet Duncan never tired of listening to Dolly's fascinating reminiscences as she lovingly sorted through the contents.

She was dead now. Died the following March. Duncan went to the funeral but there were only three other people there; her sister-in-law, a social worker and a woman who lived in the same block of flats. He didn't like to ask what had happened to the 'treasure chest'.

Anyway, that's why he knew the woman's name wasn't Dolly Cavendish. And it certainly wasn't Royston Fairweather. No, it could only be the name on the top bell. *Miss Jennifer Keebles*.

For months he'd watched her, so much so that he felt as if he knew her. She was small, about forty he guessed; sandy coloured hair, sort of curly. Some might think she looked a bit mousy but he'd noticed that her spectacles had fancy, blue frames and she always wore brightly-coloured lipstick. He knew she liked reading - he'd often seen her taking a pile of books back to the library.

He'd followed her to the launderette one Saturday afternoon and plucked up the courage to say, *'hello'*.

Close up, he could see that she had a nice face, quite pretty, really. When he'd spoken to her she'd looked at him in surprise and then quickly turned away, looking embarrassed.

He'd often wondered where she worked, where she went every day and then, quite by chance, when he was drawing his dole money - at a time when he was resting between parts - he saw her walk through the door of the staff entrance at the DHSS. She was walking briskly, efficiently, carrying a wodge of files under her arm. It didn't take him long to find out she worked as a co-ordinator for the Social Services and everyone called her Jenny.

Soon after this she'd acquired a little dog. It may have been a Springer Spaniel, he wasn't sure but it meant he saw a lot more of her that summer. He found that if he stood by the window of his third floor flat overlooking the park, he could watch her out walking with the little dog.

Sometimes, she'd sit on a bench and nibble from something she kept hidden in her pocket - perhaps it was a bar of chocolate, a cheese and tomato sandwich or a digestive biscuit. She'd stay out there for an hour or more if the weather was warm, and would sometimes laugh and clap her hands with delight when the dog came bounding across the grass to greet her with a ball, a stick or an old glove in his mouth. He envied that little dog. Anyone could see how much she loved it.

A loud bang broke Duncan's reverie. Looking up he saw that one member of the audience was in such a hurry to leave the hall he'd walked straight into an upturned PE bench, knocking it over and sending a cascade of tennis balls cavorting around the ankles of those that remained. It seemed as if everyone was leaving, even Mrs Doggett, like lemmings over a cliff. Only the old and infirm were left, unable to escape.

'Where are they all going, for Christ's sake?' Duncan whispered to Claire Fenton.

'To *The Crown Imperial,* of course,' Claire said out of the corner of her mouth. 'Aubrey Atherton's performance starts at three. Damn and blast - I just knew this would happen,'

Standing up abruptly as the last speaker, Ms Maria Gibbons, sat down to a short burst of applause, she said, brightly.

'And for those who have wisely chosen to stay may I introduce out last speaker, the eminent author and actor, Mr Duncan Wainwright.'

There followed an enthusiastic round of applause from Oliver and the others in the front row. Even Rev Pinny managed to look up, focus on the platform and permit his face muscles to form a reasonably acceptable expression of expectancy. As the sound of clapping died down there was a pause as Duncan adjusted his glasses, cleared his throat and looked at his notes.

From outside the open window came the sound of a sharp slap, of flesh meeting flesh, followed by a loud female voice shouting, very loudly:

'I said get in that car this minute !' the harassed mum was heard to shout, 'I said - GET IN! - you ungrateful little sod!'

Several members of the audience giggled and everyone immediately looked towards the window hoping to hear the sequel or, better still, catch sight of the irate owner of the disembodied voice.

'Ah, the joys of motherhood!' quipped Duncan, using his loud but well-modulated voice to good effect. All heads swivelled back to the front. 'May I just say, ladies and gentlemen, that I feel it is a great honour to address you all this afternoon - to be part of this, the ninth *Literary Festival* to be held here in the charming town of Chiselfordam. Before I begin to explain the tenure of my recently published book I should like to suggest that now our numbers are greatly diminished perhaps the lady at the back - yes, that's right, the lady in the red coat. Would care to move forward into the main body of the hall?'

He smiled encouragingly into the middle distance. At first he thought the lady in question hadn't heard for she remained in her seat but then she suddenly got up, walked down the aisle and sat on a seat at the end of the second row, which was now empty.

Duncan's benign smile encompassed all eleven persons in the hall. Adjusting his glasses once more he looked down and saw the woman in red coat clearly for the first time. He felt faint and held on to the edge of the table. He must be hallucinating - was this the final slip into the abyss of insanity? It couldn't be her. Jennifer Peebles. *Jenny.* Not here in Chiselfordam. *Could* it?

He looked directly at her face. It was undoubtedly her. She gave him the briefest of smiles before lowering her gaze to her lap. He was aware that Claire Fenton was looking at him irritably and Oliver was laughing with his eyebrows raised. Another member of the audience got up and left. The entrance doors clanged behind him. Down to ten. No matter.

He was looking directly into Jenny's eyes. She suddenly looked up and he saw they were a soft, greeny-grey colour behind her blue spectacle frames, and, was it his imagination or were they looking at him with a mixture of kindly interest and, to his great astonishment - *admiration?*

*

Chapter Twelve

As soon as he'd finished speaking Duncan was earmarked by an enthusiastic reader who, after buying a copy of his book, not satisfied with his signature alone, insisted on a lengthy inscription to his wife which he proceeded to dictate. Duncan was half way through this tedious process when he saw Jenny Peebles walking towards the door. Hurriedly finishing the inscription he handed back the book and dashed after her catching up with her just as she reached the school gates.

'I say - just a moment!' he called.

She turned and waited, her head tilted to one side and an expectant look on her face. Duncan felt old, out of breath and decidedly foolish in front of a queue of some thirty people waiting to get in for the Cubs' *Bring 'n Buy* sale at three.

'I'm so sorry,' he said, 'It's just that it was so nice to see a familiar face. You do live in Prince of Wales Drive, don't you? Don't tell me I'm wrong - I know my eyes aren't what they used to be but...' he gabbled.

Someone in the queue giggled. Jenny Peebles echoed it with a little laugh.

'No, you're not mistaken,' she said, kindly.

Her voice was soft and soothing as one might expect a district nurse to sound. It reminded him of Matron's at his boarding school. He had liked Matron. She was always kind to him and smelled of starched cotton. Her voice had been soft, too.

'Yes, I do, indeed, live in Prince of Wales Drive. In the block opposite you, in fact. I've seen you a number of times - in the park and in the library.'

She stopped and averted her face. She seemed to be blushing.

'And *I've* seen *you* many, many times...' cried Duncan, impulsively.

She turned to look at him again and the surprise in her voice was unmistakable.

'*Have* you? Have you really?'

'Oh, yes, many times…'

'Well, how extraordinary!' Miss Peebles exclaimed.

'You drive a red Renault, don't you?'

'Yes, yes, I do!'

'And you have a little dog...'

'Yes, I *do* indeed. A little spaniel. She's called Marcia and she's the love of my life,' she cried, clearly delighted.

'AAAHH!' said someone in the queue.

'Bless,' said the stout lady standing directly behind Jenny Peebles.

'Stop listening to other people's conversations, Madge Wigginton,' countered an elderly woman near the end of the queue with a very loud voice, her remark causing her companions to cackle in unison.

Both Duncan and Jenny laughed, too, after which there was an awkward silence. She moved as if to go. The queue shuffled forward as one body. Duncan held open the heavy, cast-iron gate.

'Thank you - and goodbye. I did enjoy our little chat,' Miss

Peebles was saying.

'May I?' Duncan ventured. 'I wonder, would you...I mean, may I ask if you'd care to have tea with me?'

'Tea? When? Today?'

'Yes, this afternoon – would you?'

'Well, how nice. Yes, I should like that very much indeed.'

*

There was a spring in his step as Duncan walked back across the school yard and into the hall. Unfortunately, the man whose book he'd signed a few minutes before was still there and he looked extremely annoyed.

'I'm afraid,' he said to Duncan as he climbed back onto the platform. 'But you'll have to do me another one. I can't read a word of this...the writing's bloomin' diabolical.'

He thrust the signed copy under Duncan's nose and stood, legs apart and arms akimbo, clearly showing he wasn't the sort to stand any nonsense. Duncan took the book, brought it close to his face and tried to decipher his writing. The man had a point. It was, quite frankly, illegible. But he shouldn't have asked him to write the stupid thing in the first place. Damn it, now he'd have to give him a replacement copy. That'd be £10.35p down the drain. Bloody cheek. As he grudgingly signed the second copy he felt a nudge in his back.

'We're off to catch the second half of Atherton's lecture,' Oliver announced. 'D'you want us to wait for you or what?'

'Ummm, no, don't wait,' Duncan thought for a moment. 'As a matter of fact I've arranged to have tea with a lady acquaintance of mine.' he said. 'I'll watch it on the box tonight. Anyway, thanks for coming, all of you. I do appreciate it. Hope you weren't too bored. See you later.'

*

'I should like you to sign my copy,' Jenny was saying an hour later as she poured tea from Mrs Doggett's best Spode pot in the Lounge Bar at *The Hare*. 'I'd bought my copy already, you see, in London, just as soon as it came out.'

'Oh, really? How nice. Just a little milk, no sugar.'

'It may surprise you to know but I'm a great fan of yours, Mr Wainwright, and have been for some time.'

'Duncan - please.'

'I've read all your books - all five of them,' Jenny went on. 'And I think the one on the Craig and Bentley case was masterly, quite masterly. It was so sad and so unfair. He should never have been hanged - but Pierrepoint said a few kind words to him, didn't he? You know, at the end. Oh, it's all so terrible...and now I've embarrassed myself by talking too much,' she finished lamely, colouring again. 'It's just that one doesn't often get a chance to meet someone one admires so much.'

'My dear,' said Duncan, gratefully, 'why on earth didn't you introduce yourself? All those times we passed each other in the park and sat on the same bench in the launderette - why?'

'Oh, I don't know,' Jenny Peebles said. 'I'm quite shy, really,' she added, splaying her left hand and looking at it intently.

Duncan noticed how pretty her hands were and that the nails, which were beautifully manicured, were painted the same shade of bright pink as her lipstick. Not in the least bit mousy, Duncan thought.

'I even spoke to you once, didn't I?' he said. 'But you just looked the other way.'

'I know. I'm sorry. It's just that I thought you must get so tired of people coming up and speaking to you all the time, invading your privacy - it's not fair.'

'Nonsense, my dear,' said Duncan, wiping his mouth with his napkin. 'Many years ago, when I was appearing in *As You Like It* at The Royal Shakespeare Theatre, I couldn't step through the stage door without someone running up to me, begging for an autograph. It's just something you get used to - you have to learn to live with it, I'm afraid. Meeting you, however, has been an unmitigated pleasure.'

Reaching over, he patted her hand and then quickly rose to his feet.

'Now,' he said, 'shall I ask Mrs Doggett to rustle up some more of her splendid toasted tea-cakes? I think we can make room for just once more, don't you?'

*

By the time Oliver, Rae and Leanne (Rev Pinny had managed to give them the slip once more) reached the Conference Room at *The Crown Imperial* the place was packed - every seat was taken and there were even people standing in the aisle and along the sides.

No fewer than three sets of TV cameras were directed on the platform and teams of reporters with flash cameras were squatting in huddled groups below the podium. The back of the stage was sumptuously swathed in red velvet drapes and on one side, near the front, was a mock-marble pedestal on which stood a flamboyant fake floral display. With so many people crammed into the room the air had become heavy and infused with a mixture of conflicting perfumes and after-lunch breath.

Aubrey Atherton, heavily made-up for the cameras, was

standing behind an ornately carved lectern in the centre of the stage, dramatically spotlighted from above. Fiona Bridewell, also done up to the nines, was wearing a smart navy suit with a delicate, floral nosegay fashioned in felt in her lapel. She sat upright on a chair near the edge of the platform, her slender legs nicely positioned and a rapt expression on her face.

Atherton was in full swing, his eyes and hands raised as he emphasised a point, his voice rising and falling in line with his text, fully aware that his audience (there must have been four hundred or more) were lapping up every word, every gesture and nuance.

It really was extraordinary that such an obnoxious man could project such a false image - that of the dedicated investigative journalist, with an impressive track record in his search for the truth and for successfully righting all the wrongs he chose to select for his incisive attention. It made Oliver mad to listen to him and see him posturing and parading before his adoring public when he, and many others, knew full well that the man had years since forgotten what it was like to interview police, witnesses or convicted criminals, leaving even the most sketchy research to a battalion of assistants.

Looking at the programme notes, Rae laughed and, nudging Leanne, pointed to the photograph on the cover.

'Jesus!' she whispered. 'He's been using that photograph for years - it must have been taken bloody years ago.'

'Probably using zinc plates...' muttered Oliver, squeezing Leanne's hand as she began to giggle.

'Shhhh!' someone hissed and several women looked round, their eyes bulging with annoyance.

Atherton was still talking twenty minutes later - the usual clap-trap, nothing new. Then, when he finally extended his arms in an encompassing, yet intimate, gesture of affection for his fans, the silence exploded into a crescendo of spontaneous clapping. Several members of the audience stood up, holding their hands aloft as they clapped, the expressions on their faces smiling and appreciative, eager for more. As he watched them Atherton's face glowed with pride and as he threw back his head he extended his arms once more, instigating another burst of renewed clapping.

When it finally died down and people resumed their seats, Atherton laughed indulgently before going to sit at the table at the back of the stage which was piled high with copies of his latest book. Still smiling, he mopped his glistening brow with a silk handkerchief and thankfully accepted the glass of water handed to him by a festival steward. Between sips he looked intently into the nearest TV camera, affecting a frank, knowing but quizzical look.

'I think I'm going to be sick,' groaned Rae, as Fiona Bridewell rose and stood by the piles of books, smiling appreciatively at Atherton, and making little clapping movements by tapping her free hand with the clip-board she was carrying.

'Aubrey Atherton, what can I say?' she breathed.

This sparked a fresh burst of applause which she quelled with a raised hand and a little shake of her head. When the room was silent once more she moved to the lectern and cleared her throat:

'And now, ladies and gentlemen, before you all rush forward to purchase your signed copies of *The Ultimate Chronicle of Crime*, and, if you're lucky, have a few words with Mr Atherton, I should like to introduce you to the three eminent personalities who have so kindly agreed to act as judges for this year's *Birkett Bronze Award*. Many of you will, of course, be familiar with the aims of this prestigious award. The bronze bust of Lord Chief Justice Birkett, plus the £25,000, will be presented to the person who, in their most recently published work, the judges feel has contributed most to further our understanding of the criminal mind in all its compelling complexity.

'Firstly, may I introduce Mr Max Wilbur, the well-known critic, whom many of you will remember from his controversial lecture at last year's Festival. Also Mr Theodore Rigby, the current President of The Crime Club Committee, an acclaimed crime writer for many years and one of the instigators of the first *Birkett Bronze Award* way back in 1987.

'Finally, will you please welcome a lady who has, at very short notice, put aside her other engagements to serve as a replacement for Beverley Holden who, as you will see from your brochures, was to have been our third and final judge. Unfortunately, and with much regret, she has had to stand down on account of an illness in the family. It is with gratitude, therefore, that we welcome that most popular and prolific of fiction writers - *Ms Rachel St Clair*.

The camera switched to the back of the stage. Through a gap in the curtain came a small, slim figure. She was an attractive woman, perhaps in her late fifties or early sixties, but her make-up was a little too thick and her hair, worn in a sleek French pleat, had been dyed a shade too dark, almost black. She was wearing a pert velvet hat with a short veil, once very chic but no longer in fashion, a fur wrap draped across the shoulders of her smart, black suit, a pencil slim skirt and very high heels. Amid loud applause she stood in the spotlight centre stage, her mouth open in a slight, diffident smile.

Then, after nodding briefly to the audience, she walked across the stage to join the other judges. As she did so the camera suddenly switched to Aubrey Atherton and in that split second caught the look of profound shock on his face. His whole demeanour had completely changed but, showman that he was, by the time the applause had died down and all three judges were seated, Aubrey had recovered his composure, though his face remained deathly pale.

'And now, ladies and gentlemen,' Fiona was saying, 'as we are running a little late and to be fair to everyone may I ask you to form an orderly queue and come up to the table two or three at a time. This will allow Mr Atherton to have a few words as you bring your copies to be signed.'

She turned and watched in surprise as Atherton, still agitated, gathered up his notebooks, grabbed his coat and scarf and, without a word, flounced through the curtains at the back of the stage.

There was an astonished *'Oooh'* from members of the audience and an immediate ripple of murmuring. Fiona caught up with him just as he was striding towards his car. Turning to her, he shook his head vigorously.

'Cancel everything!' he hissed. 'The signing, the press conference - *every*thing. I shall be returning to London tonight.'

With a final toss of his head, he climbed into the back of the Bentley and was driven away at speed.

*

Meanwhile, in the Lounge Bar of *The Hare*, Duncan and Jenny Peebles were deep in conversation. She confessed to having seen him whilst he was performing in a theatre in Manchester many years before - she'd been at the university at the time - and the more they talked the more they realised that certain aspects of their lives had strangely overlapped. It transpired that not only did Jenny know all about Duncan's visits to Dolly

Cavendish every Sunday, *she* had also been spending most Tuesday tea-times with the old lady. In fact, the old dear had established a rota of visitors; her sister-in-law, Betty, who lived not four doors away in the same street, called most Fridays on her way back from the shops with a bit of fish for her supper, Meals-on-Wheels called Monday to Friday (but they never had time for a chat) and the District Nurse popped in at least once a week.

'So you see,' Jenny said, laughing, 'she had us all worrying about her when in fact there was barely a day went by without someone calling in.'

'I didn't mind,' Duncan said. 'I really liked Dolly.'

'So did I,' agreed Jenny. 'and I was very sorry to miss the funeral. I was on a two week course in Birmingham and couldn't get away. I was going to say *'poor old soul'* but she wasn't, really, was she? She had a marvellous life by all accounts. I suppose she showed you her 'treasure chest'?'

'Oh, yes, many times! The memories those things must have brought back. I often wonder where it went. I just hope that sister-in-law of hers didn't throw it away.'

'Oh, *I've* got it!' said Jenny. 'Betty, the sister-in-law, didn't want it and after the funeral she asked me to take it. She had no interest whatsoever in the old music halls, the theatre or anything like that. It meant nothing to her and she was glad to get rid of it.' She paused, fiddling with the edge of the tablecloth. 'You know, you can always come round and look through it again, if you like.'

'I should like that, my dear,' whispered Duncan, touched by her kindness. 'Very much indeed,' He suddenly reached over and patted her hand.

'And there's something else I'm sure you don't know,' Jenny went on. 'Leanne Philips - she's short-listed as well, isn't she? Yes, well, I know her through Social Services. I deal with most of the referrals from her school - some of her kids are on my *'At Risk'* register. We see each other quite a lot really. She lives in the tower block by the park, doesn't she? I had no idea she knew you. My goodness, it's a small world.'

'It most certainly is,' agreed Duncan, happily. 'But tell me, what brought you to Chiselford? Have you relatives here?'

'Oh, no,' Jenny said, shaking her head. 'I meant to come last year but never got round to it. But then I picked up one of the Festival Brochures in the library and when I saw your photograph I decided, on impulse really, to make the effort this year. I've left my little dog with a neighbour. I just hope she's all right. I've always been a great admirer of yours, you see, and, as I told you, I never liked to speak to you when I saw you in the street - it just didn't seem right.'

Duncan noticed that Jenny had, once again, become a little flustered and to cover her confusion he folded up his napkin and rose from the table. Holding out his hand, he said.

'Why don't we go over and sit by the fire? The others will be back shortly. I think the plan is to watch the Aubrey Atherton interview on the television - the one he did just before the lecture - and perhaps go on for a couple of drinks somewhere. Why don't you stay and watch it with us? Much better, surely, than going back to a poky little *Bed and Breakfast*. Unless, of course, you have something else planned?'

'Well, no, as a...'

As she was speaking the swing doors whirled round and expelled a very angry Aubrey Atherton. Seeing them as he progressed round the curve of the bar towards the stairs he stopped abruptly.

'Well, well, Duncan, so you've found an audience at last,' he sneered. 'The poor creature! Don't believe a word he says, my dear woman. All his theatrical nonsense - all lies - it's farcical. Pure fantasy. He's never had a speaking part in anything worth mentioning and has yet to write a decent book. He's not even a '*Has-been*' - he's a '*Never-Was*'. Why don't you ask him about his latest starring role on the telly? There's a hoot if ever there was one.'

With that, Atherton hurried up the stairs and a moment later they heard the slam of his bedroom door. Almost immediately, Fiona Bridewell, accompanied by one of the judges, Theodore Rigby, barged through the swing doors and ran up the stairs. There followed more banging of doors and raised voices.

'God, what was *that* all about?' whispered Duncan, his red, flustered face betraying his anger and shame.

Jenny leaned over and touched the sleeve of his jacket.

'My goodness,' she whispered. 'I had no idea Aubrey Atherton was such an unpleasant character. He always comes over as really nice, doesn't he? You know, on the television. Fancy saying things like that! I suppose we should feel sorry for him - he's obviously a terribly unhappy man.'

'Rev Pinny would, I'm sure, agree with you but I'm afraid I'm not nearly so compassionate.'

'You should try to ignore him.' Jenny Peebles suggested. 'Don't give him the pleasure of getting to you. Has it ever occurred to you he might be jealous? Perhaps he secretly fears you might win the *Birkett Bronze*.'

'Oh, I don't expect to win, my dear. Aubrey's the sort that always wins. Just being short-listed is quite good enough for me.'

'Nonsense; I think your books are far more interesting than Mr Atherton's.'

'Really? How nice of you to say so,' Duncan exclaimed,

genuinely surprised. 'But as for Atherton being jealous of the likes of me - never. I'm sure I have nothing that he could possibly want.'

Jenny shook her head. 'But how can you say that when you don't really know him?' she observed. 'After all, everybody knows that people who sneer at others are usually feeling insecure and unhappy about themselves.'

'I'm sorry, I just can't excuse him that easily. He's so unnecessarily rude, except, of course, when he wants something. It's not just me, we all feel the same about him. He's rude to everyone, one way or the other.'

'Exactly,' said Jenny. 'Well, anyway, I think you make an excellent Breakfast Bunny.'

'Oh, no!' Duncan was mortified and looked away.

'Oh, yes, I realised it was you the second time I saw it. It was the voice, you see. You've got a very distinctive voice,' Jenny said. 'Distinctive and extremely distinguished.'

'How very sweet of you to say so, my dear,' Duncan replied, surprised and, it must be said, greatly relieved at her response.

'Have you got anything else lined up?'

'Well, as a matter of fact, I hope to have a small part in pantomime at the Margate Hippodrome this year, playing the Baron Harding in *Cinderella*...fingers crossed. I should know by the end of the month.'

'Margate!' Jenny Peebles exclaimed, clapping her hands together. 'What an extraordinary coincidence. That's where my parents live. Perhaps I'll be able to drag them along.'

'That would be wonderful - I'd be delighted to meet them,' said Duncan, feeling absurdly elated. Then, lowering his voice, he added. 'But I would appreciate it if you'd keep it under your hat while we're here. I do hope you understand. Baron Harding, indeed! Can't you just imagine Aubrey Atherton's delight if he found out? I'd never hear the end of it, and that's the truth.'

*

At six that evening Jenny and Duncan were still chatting by the fire, joined now by Oliver and the others, Rev Pinny included. Surprised at seeing Jenny Peebles in Chiselford, Leanne was reminded to phone Joe and after all the introductions had been made and a round of drinks ordered they settled down to watch the interview Atherton had given shortly before his performance. Mrs Doggett had made Len remove the old black and white television set (Aubrey had commandeered the larger, colour one on the evening of his arrival) from the Public Bar and bring it into the Lounge.

'They're more interested in their precious darts,' Thelma said, 'and probably won't even notice it's gone.'

She watched as Len positioned the TV set and plugged it in. Then, just as he was making for the stairs, she called out sharply, 'And where d'you think you're going?'

Len stopped in his tracks as though stung. 'I thought someone ought to go up and see if Mr Atherton will be eating here tonight,' he mumbled.'

'You'll do nothing of the sort,' Thelma's tone was icy. 'Anyway, Fiona Bridewell's up there. If he wants dinner he's perfectly capable of ordering it himself or getting *her* to do it, more like. You pander to him, that's your trouble.'

Len looked across at the group by the fire and gave a helpless little shrug as Thelma swished back into the kitchen, lips sealed and wattles a-quiver.

The television programme covering the Festival began at six thirty but there was still no sign of Atherton, Fiona or

Theodore Rigby.

'They're probably watching it up there,' said Rae, sitting crossed-legged in front of the set. 'Can't see him missing a chance to look at himself.'

'Shhh, everybody - it's starting,' said Oliver. 'Look - there he is, doing his lounge lizard bit.'

'God, that make-up's clever,' muttered Rae. 'He looks almost human.'

In fact, Atherton's performance was polished and impressive though he failed, of course, to mention the teams of researchers who made his books possible. Reading from his notes, the interviewer broached the subject of Atherton's immense wealth.

'It has been rumoured in literary circles.' he said, 'that you are able to command a six figure advance for one of your books, in addition, of course, to the world and film rights. Is that correct?'

'That is correct.'

'So an award of £25,000 would be a quite derisory amount for someone who is, presumably, already a multi-millionaire?'

'A drop in the ocean, as they say.'

'I can't bear to watch,' groaned Rae, her lips curled in a sneer.

'Just think - £25,000! And he won't even notice it,' cried Leanne, covering her face with her hands.

'Don't even think about it,' murmured Oliver.

After discussing Atherton's books and making lengthy reference to his films, the interviewer returned to the subject of the *Birkett Bronze Award*. Asked about the other five finalists, Atherton pretended he'd forgotten their names.

'I do apologise,' he murmured, 'I *was t*old the names at some stage but I fear they have completely slipped my memory.

I do remember that the list included works by two women and three men but as to the subject matter, I haven't a clue, I'm afraid. I suppose that's rather naughty of me,' he added, looking roguishly into the camera, 'but I've been so frightfully busy recently, working on the screenplay of my next film. There are only so many hours in a day, after all.'

He paused as the interviewer leaned over to offer him a light for his cheroot.

'Of course, if you should win again this year,' the interviewer said, 'in addition to the £25,000, you will be entitled to keep the original of the *Birkett Bronze* bust and, moreover, be entered in the record books as the first writer to win three years in a row.'

'I believe so - yes,' said Atherton, affecting a nonchalant tone.

'Do you expect to win again this year, Mr Atherton?'

Aubrey laughed dismissively. 'Who knows?' Turning to look once more into the camera he said, 'What can I say, except that may the best man win.'

'Or woman,' said the interviewer.

'Well...' Aubrey said, his smile faintly derisive, as he held up his palms and raised his eyes to the ceiling.

'Yuk! What a creep!' hissed Rae, burying her head in her knees.

'Shhh! Let's watch Atherton's lecture,' Oliver urged. 'It's quite a performance..' Turning to Duncan, he said, 'You didn't see it, did you?'

'Er, no, we - Miss Peebles and I - thought better of it,' Duncan said, apologetically. 'And came back here instead.'

'Well, watch the bit at the end when the judges are being announced. Take a close look when the camera switches to Atherton's face as the third judge, Rachel St Clair, walks in...'

*

Twenty minutes later, having watched Atherton's lecture from start to finish, accompanied by a chorus of bitter asides, everyone was staring intently at the screen, watching as Fiona Bridewell wound up the proceedings by introducing the judges for *The Birkett Bronze* award.

'Right, this is it,' Oliver announced. 'Watch carefully. It's amazing...'

'It is with gratitude, therefore,' Fiona was saying, 'that we welcome that most popular and prolific of fiction writers - Ms Rachel St Clair.'

They watched again as, for a split second, the expression on Atherton's face changed from one of triumph to one of shock, disbelief and what seemed like fear.

'Did you see that expression on his face?' cried Oliver, looking round at Duncan. 'Weird. Downright weird.'

'Yes,' agreed Duncan. 'I see what you mean. Most extraordinary.'

'Ummm, quite bizarre,' said Rae. 'I've never seen him look so - so, well, what would you say?'

'Vulnerable?' suggested Leanne.

'Yes, that's it,' said Rae. 'V*ulnerable.* Most unlike Atherton.'

'Completely out of character,' agreed Oliver. 'And I'd love to know why.'

*

Chapter Thirteen

Leanne crept back to the room she was sharing with Rae in the early hours of the following morning. After she left, Oliver lay on his back, unable to sleep. Instead, he switched on the radio by his bed and waited for the day to begin. He'd been feeling uneasy all day, in a way he found difficult to define. Was it being with Leanne? He wasn't sure. There was something about the way she laughed, that teasing laugh, that reminded him of Sarah.

Something was resurfacing, uncomfortably so. Not only that, though he was loath to admit it, he was a little nervous about his lecture the next day and this had made him tetchy and restless. Added to which, the night had been stormy, with high winds and lashing rain, and in the circumstances neither he nor Leanne could sleep. They had lain in silence for a while, listening to the rattling of the window frames, before Leanne gave him a final kiss and then crept back along the passage to her own room.

There was no sound coming from the room next door, which Duncan was sharing with Rev Pinny, but Leanne noticed that there was a thin line of light showing under the door of Aubrey Atherton's room and as she passed she was surprised to hear the low murmur of voices inside. Waiting for a lull in the wind she put her head to the door and listened. Of the three voices she could hear, Aubrey's high-pitched whine was instantly recognisable but the other two were lower in tone. She managed to recognise the voice of Len Doggett but not the other. How odd, she thought.

Going into the bathroom opposite she sat on the lavatory and looked at her watch. Two thirty-five. Back in the corridor a moment or two later she caught a glimpse of someone hurrying towards the stairs. The retreating figure was elderly, white-haired, and unmistakable - Theodore Rigby. When he had turned the corner, Leanne paused outside Atherton's room once more but could hear nothing.

Rae woke up as Leanne climbed into her bed which creaked and groaned like an old ship.

'Sorry,' whispered Leanne. 'I didn't mean to wake you.'

Rae was propped up on her elbow, peering into the dial of her alarm clock.

'Blimy,' she whispered. 'Separate beds already? Hardly a grand passion.'

'Oh, don't you worry,' said Leanne. 'There's nothing wrong in that department. It's just that he seems really nervous, tossing and turning and virtually monosyllabic. But I know how he feels. I was much the same on Sunday night and he's bound to get a much bigger audience than me. I think they're televising it as well, aren't they? That must be pretty nerve-wracking.'

'Are you sure that's what's troubling him?'

'Well, I assumed so. Why? What d'you mean?'

'Oh, nothing,' Rae said, cautiously. 'It's just that he does get a bit moody sometimes. Has he said anything about Jane yet?'

'Not really, no - except that they've decided to spend some time apart for a while. By all accounts she's out of the country more often than she's here and he's always being sent all over the place at a moment's notice chasing some news story or other. It must be pretty difficult keeping something going like that.'

'She's OK. I like Jane, but she's a rolling stone just like him. You won't want to hear this, I'm sure, but they suit each other really well and the reason he doesn't feel guilty about playing around is that he's fairly sure she's doing the same.'

'Oh, I see,' Leanne cried, feigning outrage. 'What you're saying is that I'm just another bit on the side. Don't worry, I know, that's exactly what I am. We both know it's just a bit of fun and nobody' will get hurt. But I really like him and I just hope we'll at least stay friends when we get back to London.'

'I don't see why not; he tends to hold on to his friends. Mind you, I've known him for about four years, I suppose, maybe five, but I can't say I *know* him or anything about him really. You know, where he was brought up, went to school and that. I just wondered if he'd opened up a bit with you, that's all.'

'No, not really,' admitted Leanne. 'He doesn't often talk about himself; now I come to think about it, he talks about his work most of the time. He's really ambitious, isn't he?'

'Sure is. And prolific. He's already produced six books in what - in ten years? And he's only thirty-one and works full time. Not bad going, is it? After Atherton's crown, maybe...'

'Which reminds me.' Leanne said. 'You'll never guess who Aubrey's been entertaining tonight?'

'Go on, give me a clue - man, woman or beast?'

'Len Doggett.'

'Len Doggett?' cried Rae, surprised. 'You must be joking! Did you actually see him?'

'No, but I heard him,' Leanne confirmed. 'Creepy, isn't it? Can't think what he and Atherton could possibly have in common. And.' she went on, 'the other guest was none other than - wait for it - Theodore Rigby!'

'Christ! Fraternising with one of the judges? Do I smell collusion here or a bit of gentle persuasion? I can just see it, Atherton applying the thumbscrews or resorting to a really nasty Chinese burn? Mind you, he and Theo have known each other for years - but *Len Doggett?*'

'It's a bit odd, I must say.'

'I wonder if Thelma knows?'

'We'll soon know when we get a look at the size of her mouth at breakfast tomorrow. Not a pretty sight. It was reduced to a millimetre slit last time he annoyed her, poor sod.'

'Or if we notice poor Leonard's walking around the Lounge Bar with a kitchen knife in his back.'

'God, I wish this blasted wind would die down,' Leanne whispered as she pulled the duvet up to her chin. 'What with the rattling window frames and the creaking beds, it's like something from a B-movie horror film.'

'No marks for guessing who gets to play Count Dracula,' murmured Rae, smiling to herself as she finally settled herself for sleep.

*

It was still raining the next day and *The Hare* was encased in a perceptible gloom. Added to which, the moisture in the air seemed to have unlocked the unpleasant aroma of the pugs, recently released by Thelma, an act of vengeance that marked Aubrey Atherton's ultimate fall from grace. As she served breakfast, Leanne and Rae couldn't help noticing that Thelma Doggett had managed to compress her mouth into the narrowest of slits and Len was keeping his distance, hovering in the darkened Public Bar like a chastened ghost. Everyone was relieved, however, to hear from Mrs Doggett that they would, at least, be spared the company of Aubrey Atherton, as he was having his breakfast in his room.

'Probably still sulking after his tantrum yesterday,' said Rae. 'I'd love to know what that was all about. Has he said anything to you about going back to London, Mrs Doggett?'

'Who?'

'Aubrey Atherton.'

Thelma compressed her lips even further before opening them just wide enough to give vent to her vitriolic contempt.

'Oh, don't talk to me about that man!' she snapped. 'First he's going, then he's staying - I've had that Theodore Rigby in and out, I've had that Fiona Bridewell on the phone must be a dozen times.'

She slammed down a jar of marmalade and then nodded towards the stairs. 'And now they tell me they've persuaded *that man* to stay for the presentation on Saturday. Smells like a fix to me. Strikes me they're more or less saying he's got it.'

'Well, we all know that,' moaned Duncan, spreading butter on his toast. 'No doubt Atherton does as well, that's way he's decided to stay. He couldn't possibly deny himself his moment of glory.'

'The man's a positive pest, you don't know the half of it. He's wanting room service day and night, first this and then the other. Always asking Len to bring him tea, bring him wine, bring him matches, never a moment's peace. I can't think why,' she sniffed, 'he doesn't employ a full time slave.'

'He could certainly afford it,' Rae remarked. 'Mind you, I wouldn't wish that job on anyone. A fate worse than death.'

'Well, I'll tell you something for nothing,' Thelma confided, 'There's no way I'd have that man here again next year. No way. *Never.*'

And the fractious rasp of Mrs Doggett's nylons as she marched back to the kitchen, a pampered pug under each arm, left them in no doubt that she meant it.

Before Duncan had said goodnight to Jenny Peebles the previous night she'd promised to call for him at nine thirty the next morning to take him to Oliver's lecture in the Marquee. They'd had such a pleasant evening. After watching Atherton's television performance, they'd left the others in the bar, preferring to go for a walk by the river, followed by a night cap in *The Dog and Whistle*.

They got on so well; Duncan found her remarkably easy to talk to and she made him feel good about himself, not such a dead loss. So much so, in fact, that he didn't feel the need to exaggerate half as much when he was with her and, with a conscious effort on his part, he even managed to curtail his customary name dropping.

Though normally fairly solitary in their habits, they nevertheless found they were enjoying each other's company so much they hadn't wanted the evening to end. When he finally gave her a tentative kiss on the cheek and then watched her drive away, he couldn't resist giving a little skip as he hurried back into the hotel.

Not wishing to break the spell of his new-found happiness, Duncan went straight to bed without a word to Pinny, but once he'd snuggled beneath the blankets, he succumbed to one or two romantic thoughts of Jenny Peebles which carried him through until he fell asleep and experienced such a pleasant dream that he called out her name.

Rev Pinny looked across at the sleeping Duncan, puzzled to see a rapturous smile on his face. He closed his copy of

Meditations On Faith and removed his spectacles. Laying them both on the bedside table he closed his eyes and said a final prayer before switching off the side-light. He lay on his back, his hands by his sides and his eyes closed, like a body lying in state.

For a moment Joan crossed his mind and he wondered if she'd done as he'd asked and contacted someone to sort out all the hymn books that needed replacing. Effortlessly drifting into a deep, dreamless sleep, he remained still throughout the night, untroubled, never turning, either to the left or to the right. immobile

*

Promptly at half past nine, as arranged, Penny Peebles's little red Renault pulled up in the driveway of *The Hare*. Duncan immediately jumped up from the breakfast table and fairly ran to the front door to meet her. They greeted each other warmly, then Jenny reached up and, removing the napkin which was still tucked into Duncan's collar, used the end of it to wipe some toast crumbs from the side of his moustache. He was blushing like a schoolgirl as he brought her through to the Lounge Bar, guided her to the table and poured her some coffee.

By the time everyone left for the journey into town, shortly before ten, Aubrey had still not appeared.

Leanne went with Oliver in the Aston Martin. He was still tense and pre-occupied and she expressed her sympathy by giving him a little squeeze on the thigh as the car drew to a halt at some traffic lights. Then she leaned over and lightly kissed his ear but he continued to tap out a rhythm on the steering wheel with his right hand and his only response was a barely discernible smile.

Rae was travelling close behind in the Volvo with Rev Pinny sitting bold upright in the passenger's seat looking like an undertaker. Jenny and Duncan arrived soon after, she in a lilac linen suit and he sporting a bright pink shirt and floral bow-tie. In complete contrast to their light-hearted mood the weather was truly abysmal. The torrential rain during the night had reduced the grassed area around the Marquee into a quagmire and although council workmen had been out early scattering loose straw around the entrance and along the pathways, it had proved useless. It was already flattened and saturated by the crowds converging on the Marquee.

Everyone was carefully picking their way towards the entrance, their ruined shoes squelching horribly in the mud and with so many people walking with their heads down there were several incidents where umbrellas became interlocked like warring antlers. These awkward clashes, which occasioned a number of apologetic shouts, curses and exasperated laughter, were accompanied by further shrieks each time a fresh gust of wind whipped across the green, relentlessly exposing the bald patches of the men and lashing the women's strands of hair across their reddened cheeks and stinging their eyes.

Leaving the others to sort themselves out in the front row, Oliver took his place on the platform and listened while Fiona Bridewell, in a fetching cerise suit and green beads, ran through the proposed order of speaking.

Looking down he saw Rae and Leanne giggling and, glancing at one of the other speakers on the platform, the pathologist, Professor Alistair Whittal, he saw why. The professor had left his hotel that morning with his sparse strands of hair combed carefully across his bald pate, but a particularly vicious gust of wind had whisked it out of place and it was now sticking up on one side of his head like the Bakerlite indicator on a vintage Morris Minor. Aware that he was the object of some amusement, he soon realised what had happened and tried to flatten the offending hair and tease it back across the top of his head, at the same time affecting to give his undivided attention to what Fiona was saying and nod in agreement.

Oliver also inclined his head towards her and assumed an intelligent expression, at the same time scanning the faces in the audience. The Marquee, the seats were arranged in semi-circular terraces, was packed and still more people were filing through the main entrance.

The reason for such a large attendance had more to do with the presence of the TV cameras than the assembled speakers though many were perhaps intrigued to see what Kevin Doubleday, reformed armed robber turned novelist, had to say for himself. He was already seated on the platform, staring ahead, stony-faced. He had a prominent tattoo of an eagle on his fore-arm and another, in the shape of spider, on his neck.

Having interviewed him on a number of occasions, Oliver knew him to be a man of few words and wondered how he intended to entertain his audience for the required minimum of fifteen minutes. Aware that Oliver was looking at him he turned and caught his eye. He nodded briefly before staring once more into the well of the Marquee.

Harassed stewards were shepherding latecomers along the sides and trying to squash them into the spaces on the end of each row of seats.

Several women with small children were asked to have their offspring on their laps to make room for those without seats. He spotted Max Wilbur sitting at the back, deep in conversation with Rachel St Clair. He also noticed Theodore Rigby, reading from his programme, sitting on his own in the fourth row.

As Fiona was coming to the end of her introductory speech, the double flaps at the entrance were once more drawn aside and Aubrey Atherton strode in wearing a long black PVC Macintosh, galoshes, very dark glasses and a green velour trilby. Of course, every eye and camera lens was immediately turned in his direction as he made his way to the front row, stopped, looked up at Fiona and made an exaggerated gesture of disbelief.

'Fiona Bridewell, don't tell me you forgot to reserve my seat. Really, it's more than I can bear.'

At a signal from Fiona, a steward appeared and, after a few whispered words to some insignificant soul sitting next to Duncan, the seat was quickly vacated and Atherton, with a little wave to the audience, sat down and gave Oliver a triumphant smile.

No sooner had the first speaker, Professor Whittal, risen to begin his address when several members of the audience broke into suppressed giggles; still more sniggered as the flaps on the part of the Marquee that formed the back of the stage began to bulge. There was a frenzied yanking, like the frantic antics of an escapologist in a sack, followed by a loud 'Oh, *blast!*' and then the figure of Rev Pinny, with his hair plastered down by the rain and his glasses opaque and misted, stepping through the gap onto the stage.

There was a spontaneous round of derisive applause as poor Pinny, blinking in the spotlight, realised where he was and stood as though paralysed, like a rabbit looking down the barrel of a gun. Then he suddenly turned and was just about to scramble back the way he had come when Fiona's sharp, authoritative command stopped him in his tracks.

'Rev Pinny, *please*! Would you kindly stand somewhere along the side? I'm afraid we're rather full. Do hurry,' she said, irritably, as Rev Pinny sloped across the stage and half-fell, half-slithered down the steps at the side, red in the face and almost bent double with embarrassment.

Oliver looked down at Leanne and Rae and winked. Next to them Duncan and Jenny had their heads together, giggling but Atherton sat with his arms folded, immobile, expressionless and still wearing his trilby and dark glasses.

By the time Professor Whittal resumed his address the weather had worsened and a gale force wind had risen. He had to raise his voice to be heard above the flapping, wind-lashed canvas of the Marquee. The ropes were stretched taut to accommodate the tremendous force of each gust of wind.

The subterranean atmosphere inside the Marquee made Oliver feel uncomfortable, yet strangely excited. The smell of wet earth and saturated, cold-stiffened canvas reminded him of school camps - frozen hands, icy water, tin kettles, dollops of barely edible food, gritty and tasting of soil and smoke, heaped onto chipped enamel plates. It brought back the excitement of first sleeping away from home, where familiar faces looked strange so late at night and seemed somehow alien, other-worldly and threatening, the stuff of children's nightmares.

And later, when he was eighteen, a quite different camping holiday with a pretty fellow student called Maggie - the warm, claustrophobic womb-like tent, barely room for one - the sound of the rain, new and exciting sensations, the first time he'd had a girl's warm body at his disposal, the heady prospect of uninterrupted sex, clinging together in a single sleeping bag, the fug of the pre- and post-coital cigarette, shared cans of lager and a steamy repeat to come. Just thinking about it made him feel randy.

He was aware that Atherton's awful eyes were focused on his face yet obscured by the black orbs of his glasses. Jesus, the smell of the canvas, the sound of the rain, damp straw, warm wet wool, soft body. And Maggie was hot for it.

The air in the Marquee was stifling and he felt uncomfortably warm. He must think of something else. His eyes focused on the living equivalent of the cold shower - the hunched figure of Rev Pinny, inelegantly perched on the edge of the second row, black and dripping like someone's bent, discarded brolly.

Oliver was aware that Leanne was looking at him, smiling in a sexy sort of way. It was as if she knew what he'd been thinking. She couldn't, of course, she knew nothing of his life - nothing at all. She, on the other hand, was very open and he'd learned quite a bit about her. She'd told him all about the vicious tart Kelly and life on the estate. She wasn't exaggerating, either. He'd covered enough depressingly sordid stories during his time on *The South London Gazette* to know what she was talking about. But she could still laugh about it - just. He liked her resilience, her pluck. Pretty, too.

He thought of his own comfortable background - the only son of very liberal parents, a solicitor and a schoolteacher, a near idyllic childhood in a large Victorian house in Barnes. Private schooling, a fairly innocuous sister who, being several years older, took up music and generally kept out of his way; plenty of friends, no trouble passing examinations. He experienced a fairly easy adolescence, suffered with spots and the usual crushes and bouts of unrequited lust, but nothing particularly devastating.

There followed an equally smooth and untroubled time at University. He'd developed into an intelligent, articulate and attractive young man and by the third year he'd become President of the Debating Society, Editor of the University Magazine and played the clarinet in a jazz band. He was reasonably good at sports and quite enthusiastic about rowing, though never quite powerful enough to be picked for the team. And there were, of course, always plenty of girls - having served his apprenticeship on Maggie there was no stopping him.

This pleasant flow of reminiscence faltered and became blurred. That same unease - something surfacing, something sad, the sound of that bloody wind outside, the wet flapping canvas tugging at the ropes. Like being on a boat. He felt a moment of faintness, loss of control, alienation. It was stuffy in there, too many people, he couldn't breathe. He held his head in his hands and felt the dampness of his temples.

'....and now, will you welcome one of our brightest investigative journalists, author of no fewer than six true-crime books and now one of those short-listed for this year's *Birkett Bronze Award* - Mr Oliver Johnson.' Fiona was still standing, her head was inclined towards him and she was clapping in such a restrained manner her hands barely touched.

Oliver rose to tremendous applause, the volume of which was especially vigorous from the large number of women in the audience, a bunch of whom had clustered near one of the exit flaps; they broke into cheering, their faces pink and eager. He noticed that whereas Leanne and the others were clapping enthusiastically, Atherton merely tapped his knee with his rolled up programme and his lips were curiously puckered as though he were silently whistling.

*

Oliver's talk went very well, if, that is, the applause at the end was anything to go by. As he sat down again Fiona rose to assure the people with their hands raised to ask questions that they would be given the opportunity after the final speaker. He couldn't really remember what he'd said. He knew his subject inside out and had, in fact, already given a similar talk the week before at a writers' workshop. He was, however, greatly relieved that it was all over and settled back to listen to the final speaker, an ex-screw, who was already pointing his baton at a large poster depicting the Krays in their smart, double-breasted suits. He turned away - there'd be a picture of *The Blind Beggar* pub next - he knew it all by heart. It was all too familiar.

Yet he tried hard to concentrate, still aware of the unease inside him, the direction his thoughts were taking him, the sound of the blasted wind and the flapping of the canvas...and Sarah. He didn't want to think about her but he couldn't help it. He could see her so clearly, *feel* her almost. She'd joined his year at University several months later than everyone else. She was incredible - extremely attractive, fair-haired, warm and refreshingly open with an intelligence - she was reading Classics and Medieval English - that was at first almost intimidating. But she was also disarmingly witty and she and Oliver hit it off immediately, loving every minute of being together.

After university - they both got good degrees - they moved to London and lived in a converted torpedo boat moored under Richmond Bridge. It didn't take them long to find out why the rent was so cheap. The noise of the trains was not only deafening but frequent and the plumbing primitive. Having pumped out the effluent it floated offensively on the surface of the water, bobbing about outside the galley window for all to see, sometimes for days.

But they'd been so happy - everything was fun, nothing depressed them or got them down, not even the plumbing. Oliver was working on *The South London Press* while Sarah was teaching English part-time to foreign students in a crammer in South Kensington and spending the other three days each week working on her PhD.

And then Oliver was offered a job on a national newspaper and was so overjoyed at the thought of no more write-ups on missing dogs, planning protests and council cut-backs, they celebrated by getting married by special licence.

Ten months later, their daughter, Annie, was born and they were ecstatic. But it seemed that such joy couldn’t last, happiness such as theirs demanded some perverse retribution, some vengeful levelling, some heart-breaking equilibrium. When Annie was barely two, a friend lent Oliver a boat and they all went on a sailing weekend in the Solent. Sarah wasn't too keen but Oliver, who'd often been sailing with his father, promised her it was far from dull. Game to try anything once, she agreed and they took all the right precautions; all three were fitted out with the regulation life-jackets, even the baby.

The first day and night were magical - glorious weather, just right for lying around but not enough wind to really get going. But it was fun and he took dozens of photographs of Sarah and the baby - the two most important people in his life.

On the second day the weather had changed. It had become squally. Like it had been earlier that morning. They hadn't ventured far, quite happy to circumvent the Fort, and once Annie was strapped in her special seat below deck. Oliver showed Sarah how to hoist the sails, regulate the boom and use the edge of the wind so that it lifted the nose right out of the water as it skimmed the surface sending glistening sprays like wings on either side.

And then - he couldn't stop himself remembering - even now - five years later - how quickly it happened and the terrible, devastating, finality of it. It was just after seven on the second evening and Sarah had taken Annie down to the cabin below.

She said she'd had a long day and needed to sleep. Oliver was struggling a bit with the ropes and the sea had begun to swell and shift with tremendous force. The wind had become angry, relentless. He called out to Sarah. He needed a hand with the ropes. Could she come up on deck for a minute?

They'd been so careful up till then. And it all happened in a split second - no chance to think again, no chance to undo it, no chance to take back that fatal request.

She came up smiling, still carrying the toddler in her arms and there was a sudden, vicious surge of water beneath the boat and it suddenly lurched to one side sending the boom crashing into her back and tossing her, like a rag doll, into the sea, with the baby still clutching her round the neck, smiling but silent, trusting, not making a sound. No time to cry out, no time to be frightened. They both went under, the sea literally swallowed them, gulped them down and they just disappeared.

*

Chapter Fourteen

The moment the ex-screw had finished speaking Oliver, muttering an apology to Fiona Bridewell, hurried out of the Marquee, white-faced and shaken.

He drove straight back to the hotel, went up to his room, locked the door and then lay on the bed, the shock and sadness of it all still with him. Even though he thought of Sarah and the accident most days, no matter how briefly, the memory could still catch him off guard and shock him to the core.

He felt numbed by the sheer senselessness of her death. The random chance cruelty of it. It could so easily *not* have happened. If the wave had been a second or two later, if the boom had not struck with such a force, if she'd left Annie strapped in her special chair down below - if he, Oliver, hadn't called her. If they hadn't been on the bloody boat in the first place. Poor Sarah - she hadn't even wanted to go. She only went to please him. He felt as though it had been *his* whim, not that of the sea, that had killed them, and the terrible image of their faces was indelibly branded on his brain with the agonising permanence of guilt.

Tears had dried on his face, making the skin taut and he felt cold, defeated. After smoking a joint he dozed for a while but was vaguely aware of the sound of Rae's car as she and Leanne returned soon after one to change out of their damp clothes and freshen up before meeting Fiona at three. It had been arranged for all six finalists to meet her in the foyer of *The Crown Imperial* to discuss their combined book signing session the next morning - an event Aubrey Atherton had naturally threatened to veto.

Leanne looked around for Oliver.

'He's in his room,' confided Thelma Doggett. 'He didn't say a word when he came in. White as a sheet, he was.'

She clamped her hand over her mouth and widened her eyes. 'He hasn't had an accident in that car of his, has he?' she asked.

'No, he'll be all right, Mrs Doggett. He's just a bit upset about something, that's all.' said Rae.

'Upset? Has someone upset him?''

'No, don't worry – he'll be fine.'

'Don't tell me that Aubrey Atherton's been at it again,' Thelma said, indignantly. 'He's got a vicious tongue, that man.'

'No, honestly, don't worry, it's nothing to do with Atherton,' replied Rae. 'Now, would it be possible, d'you think, for us to have a pot of tea? Just for Leanne and myself - I think Rev Pinny's gone off to a prayer meeting somewhere or other and Duncan and Jenny Peebles are at a seminar given by the Romantics. Let's hope it's sufficiently sentimental, but I doubt it somehow.'

'Oh, it's *ever* so nice, isn't it?' Thelma Doggett cooed, putting on a soppy voice. 'You know, seeing him with a lady friend and they seem to get on so well.'

Still smiling, she scuttled over to the fireplace and tried to resuscitate the embers with a poker. 'Now come along, you two, come and sit down by the fire,' she ordered. 'Leonard's fetching some more logs and I'll bring the tea over as soon as it's ready.'

Once they were seated and out of ear-shot, Leanne turned to Rae.

'What's wrong with Oliver?' she asked.

'How d'you mean?'

'Why did he rush off like that?'

'How should I know?' Rae protested.

'Oh, come on, Rae, you *do* know.'

'Well, I do know but it's not up to me to say anything, is it?'

'Why not? If something's bothering him I might be able to help.'

'Why don't you ask him when he comes down?'

'But why can't *you* tell me?' Leanne demanded. 'You *do* know, don't you?'

'I've got a pretty good idea,' Rae admitted. 'I told you he was inclined to be moody.'

'Oh, come on, Rae! We all get moods, for Christ's sake,' Leanne persisted.

'Well, he had a bad – and I mean a *really* bad - experience some time ago,' Rae went on, keeping her voice low. 'And it catches up with him every so often, you know how it is, something reminds him of it, that's all. He'll be fine again by this afternoon, you'll see.'

'But how can I ask him about something that obviously upsets him so much?' Leanne went on. 'Just tell me what it's all about and I promise I won't say anything.'

'Well, he'll probably tell you about it anyway if you go on seeing each other when you get back.'

She looked up as Thelma approached. 'Oh, thanks, Mrs D,' she said, reaching to take the tray, at the same time blocking the attendant pug's progress with her leg. Thwarted, it plonked itself down a short distance away and began to drool, its supplicating eyes fixed on the tray.

Just then Len Doggett came up from the cellar preceded by the other pug who, thinking that its rival was being fed with biscuits from the tray, tossed itself (the effort involved occasioned some unpleasant grunting noises) into the air and landed on the other, forcing it onto its back and sending the tea things flying - tea pot, water jug, milk, sugar - the lot.

The up-ended pug, recovering from the shock, retaliated by grasping one of the other's fleshy lips in its teeth and, digging its trotters into Mrs Doggett's thick pile carpet for extra leverage, pulled with all its considerable might.

'Now look what you've done!' Thelma screamed at Len. 'You can just go and get the Hoover and a cloth and clear up this mess. Trust *you!*'

With that, she reached up and deftly clipped him round the ear. 'Why didn't you stop them, you silly bugger? You're useless - good for nothing. Your head's always full of stupid nonsense, that's your trouble.'

As she berated her husband she fell to her knees and, pinning one of the dogs between her thighs, she prised its jaws apart with both hands. Releasing the other dog's lip left her, of course, free to bite back. The two dogs immediately threw themselves at each other with tremendous ferocity, becoming one writhing, growling heap.

Everyone stood back while Thelma, screaming and shouting, tried to spank their plump bottoms with a rolled-up magazine; but this merely fuelled their rage. Leonard's solution to the crisis was inspired. He simply went to the bar and ripped open a packet of *Cheese 'n Onion* crisps. The two pugilists immediately desisted, the battle forgotten as they sat at his feet, slavering shamelessly while their eyes bulged from an excess of activity and their blatant, all-consuming greed.

*

By the time everyone met in the Lounge Bar that evening all was quiet once more. The dogs were nowhere to be seen and Len Doggett, it seemed, had been banished, yet again, to the kitchen. Oliver, having spent the afternoon in the town seemed fine, almost cheerful again. Aubrey Atherton was standing alone at the bar nursing a gin and tonic. He seemed preoccupied.

As Rae ordered a round of drinks, she was aware that Atherton's cold eyes were swivelled in her direction and that his gaze had rested on the stud in her nose before proceeding to encompass her lean, athletic body and sleek blond head. This silent, steely surveillance irritated her, as he knew it would. She turned and looked him in the eye.

'Something troubling you, Atherton?' she demanded.

'I'm so sorry – did you speak?' Atherton said, affecting surprise.

'If you've got something to say, just say it. Not that

anyone's the least bit interested in your opinion.'

'Oh, now, that's not nice. There's no need to be so snappy. I was just thinking about that frightful *Birkett Bronze* bust. To be quite frank with you I was only too glad to hand it over to Ms Bridewell this morning. It's a ghastly thing, isn't it? Quite gruesome. In fact, I rather hope I *don't* win the damned thing again this year.'

If Atherton was hoping for a reaction from Rae he was disappointed for she merely stared at him with undisguised loathing.

'Of course, if I do win I'll be obliged to *keep* it, perish the thought.'

He paused and looked at her once more.

'You never know, my dear, you might just be lucky enough to win it this year, though I rather doubt it, somehow. Such a shame. Think what a difference it could make to your life. Who knows? With £25,000 under you belt you might even present quite an attractive proposition for someone or other. A minority appeal, of course.'

'Piss off.'

'Now, now, vulgarity is *so* unattractive in a female.'

'So what was *your* little tantrum all about yesterday?' Oliver asked, who had just come over to help Rae with the drinks. 'I meant to ask you yesterday but I didn't get a chance. You shot out of the hall like a rocket. I had no idea you could move so fast.'

'Tantrum?' Atherton said, feigning surprise. 'The boy's rambling. I'll have you know I had a rather unpleasant attack of asthma and had left my ventilator in my room. That was all.'

Turning to the others he announced, 'Take my advice; always cultivate some ghastly affliction - asthma or migraine - it's invaluable for getting one out of sticky corners, if you know what I mean.'

'But you weren't in a sticky corner, Atherton - *were* you?' said Rae.

Atherton drained his glass and looked at her disparagingly.

'My dear, there is no situation on this earth that I cannot handle with ease and, I might add - a certain panache.'

He paused as he adjusted his silk scarf. *'Panache.* It means style, flair.' Having pulled on his gloves, he smoothed his chestnut hair and then rose to leave. 'Now I must go,' he said. 'I am meeting a charming lady for cocktails and have no wish to keep her waiting. Good evening.'

'Pompous sod,' said Rae as they watched Atherton summon his driver from the Public Bar and leave the hotel.

Once Atherton had gone the others fell to talking about the award and the probability that he would win yet again. The judges were due to meet to decide the winner the following morning at nine-thirty.

It was Duncan's suggestion that Oliver should ask one of them, Rachel St Clair, to lunch afterwards and try to find out in advance who had won. Leanne went on to suggest that if Atherton *was* chosen again they should all go back to London on Friday afternoon as a form of protest. By not waiting for the official announcement on Saturday morning they would be demonstrating their feelings about Atherton and the press might even allow them to air their grievances in print. Rev Pinny, who had earlier rejoined the group in the Lounge Bar, wasn't keen on what he considered to be such 'radical and underhand tactics' but Oliver, Rae and Duncan were all for it.

Oliver didn't take much urging therefore to go and phone Rachel right away. The telephone rang about seven times and he was just about to put the receiver down when a weary voice answered:

'Yes?'

'Rachel? It's Oliver,' he said.

'Oliver? Oliver who?'

'Oliver Johnson - Brighton Festival last year.'

'Brighton Festival?'

'Last year – we shared a table at the hotel.'

'Who is that speaking?'

'Oliver. Oliver Johnson. I spoke to you this afternoon - in the foyer with Fiona.'

'Oh, yes. Oliver. I think I remember now.'

'Did I wake you?'

'Pardon?'

'I said, did I wake you?'

'Oh, no, not to worry. I was just lying on the bed for a little rest.'

'Well, I won't keep you for more than a moment.'

'How nice of you to call.'

'I was wondering if you'd care to have lunch with me?'

'Lunch?'

'Yes, if you're free and feel like some company.'

'When?'

'Tomorrow?'

She gave a short laugh. 'Ah, you mean, *after* we've made our decision.'

'How d'you mean?'

'You know perfectly well what I mean!'

She made a tutting noise and then said: 'You know, you're a very naughty boy....'

Her voice trailed off. 'Hang on a minute - there's someone at the door....don't go away.'

Oliver could hear voices as Rachel opened the door of her hotel room. When she picked up the receiver again she sounded quite different, clearly upset.

'Oliver? Sorry about that,' She lowered her voice to a whisper. 'It's Aubrey Atherton - I must go.'

'What about lunch tomorrow?'

She seemed distracted, wishing to end the conversation.

'Yes, all right, if you like. Where?'

'Giovanni's at one?'

'Right. I'll see you there.'

*

Chapter Fifteen

Shortly before nine the next morning the finalists arrived at *The Crown Imperial* for the book signing session. Fiona Bridewell was already there and in between whispered consultations with the hotel manager, Mr Popperwell, she used her clipboard to indicate where she wanted everyone to sit. Six tables had been set at intervals around the foyer.

Rev Pinny was disconcerted to see that he had been allocated a small collapsible card table just inside the door. The position was such that once the door was opened, he would be virtually obliterated from view.

Naturally, Aubrey had been allocated a highly polished refectory table at the base of the grand staircase, directly in line with the entrance. Having warned everyone that he had no intention of attending - he objected, he said, to having to 'hawk his wares in the market place shackled alongside writers of little worth' - they were surprised to see that Aubrey was already installed at his table, his glossy toupee looking even more luxuriant after recent washing and his face had relaxed into the semblance of a smile as he chatted amicably with Popperwell.

He was wearing a pale mauve shirt under an oatmeal linen suit and his dark glasses were folded into his top pocket alongside the mauve and lemon spotted handkerchief. His complexion was less pale than usual and his eyes more defined. On closer inspection Leanne noticed a tell-tale smear of stage make-up just below his jaw-line and the faintest hint of Kohl about his eyes.

Taking up their inferior positions the others did their utmost to look lively and interested. The muscles of his face peevishly tensed, Rev Pinny settled himself behind the door with as much grace as he could muster. After laying his eight copies before him, he cupped his head in his hands and stared gloomily at the dreary, shop-soiled publicity board mounted at one end of the table. The blurred black and white snap of him leaning on a rake in the Rectory garden, circa 1959, didn't help by emphasising his beaky nose and disappearing eyes and the overall inelegance of his bent and bony frame.

Further along, Rae had spread her dozen copies as enticingly as possible and tried to avoid looking at the equally unflattering photograph of herself, taken several years before, when her hair was much longer and her ears and nose un-pierced. She was dismayed to see that it made her look, not only oddly feminine, but also embarrassingly conventional.

She looked further down the foyer towards Leanne's table and, catching her eye, pointed to the offending portrait and made a face. Leanne countered this by pointing to her own and, putting her fingers in her mouth, made a gagging motion. Rightly so. The photograph of her had been taken after the publication of her first book and showed her with a nest of permed, black hair, and, despite the heavy eye make-up and reddened lips, the overall impression was one of doleful innocence.

Oliver had laughed out loud when he saw it, pleased that his own publicity shot, which had been taken quite recently, had, he told everyone, captured the essence of his particular charm and revealed his natural warmth, intelligence and sophistication. Both Rae and Leanne had inspected it at close range, hoping to find some blemish or other, a spot, wrinkle or blackhead with which to deflate his ego, but found none.

Duncan's photograph was quite bizarre. His publisher's publicity department had used an old theatrical shot, tinted in the manner of an early *Picture Post* magazine, in which he looked like a 1940's bomber pilot, smiling jauntily beneath his manly moustache, on the verge of delivering a rakish wink. He was a little embarrassed by it until, that is, Jenny Peebles saw it and was captivated - so much so that she had extracted a promise from Fiona Bridewell that she could have it to take home for the wall of her flat in Prince of Wales Drive. Duncan, of course, was both thrilled and gratified.

Whereas everyone else had only a few copies of their books on display, Aubrey's table was piled high with copies of his *The Ultimate Chronicle of Crime* and there were no fewer than three large, free standing publicity boards already in position, complete with close-up colour shots of Atherton in dark-glasses and a striped double-breasted suit, in which, thanks to the liberal use of the air brush and other camouflaging techniques, he looked quite presentable. When Rae protested about the unequal state of affairs, referring to the size of the photos and the position of the tables, Fiona Bridewell gave her short shrift.

'We must be practical, Rae,' she snapped. 'Let's face it,

you'll be lucky to shift a dozen copies between you. People just can't afford to buy several hardbacks at a time, even at festivals - and if it comes to a choice I think you'll find most people will go for Atherton's. The films were really popular and people think they know him because he's constantly in the press. Bad news for you, I'm afraid, but, needless to say, simply great for his publisher.'

'But he's got *three* publicity posters with blow-ups - in *colour* - and we've only got *one* board with pictures the size of bloody postage stamps!' protested Oliver. 'I wouldn't mind so much if he weren't so fucking ugly!'

'Oh, come on,' Fiona protested, 'you must admit, the studio's done a brilliant job. I think he looks very distinguished. You're only jealous.' As she spoke, she laughingly reached up as though to ruffle Oliver's artfully dishevelled hair but he ducked away and looked sulky.

'But it's just not fair!' he persisted, aware of the demeaning petulance in his voice.

'I know, I know,' Fiona said, adopting the soothing tone one might employ when placating a recalcitrant child. Raising her finely arched eyebrows, she looked up at him apologetically. 'But, Oliver, sweetheart,' she went on. 'Life *isn't* fair, is it? Surely you don't need me to tell you that?'

*

By nine-thirty quite a crowd had gathered on the steps of *The Crown Imperial* and there was a certain amount of good-natured pushing and shoving when the doorman eventually beckoned everyone in. Predictably, the first batch made a beeline for Aubrey Atherton's table where, flanked by Fiona Bridewell, Mr Popperwell and Claire Fenton, he sat imperiously with a benign smile on his face and an expensive tortoise shell Waterman pen poised in his right hand. The others watched glumly as ladies, flushed at finding themselves talking to a celebrity, clucked and chatted, fumbling in their handbags for their chequebooks and purses. And while Claire collected the money, Fiona smiled encouragingly along the line and, passing each copy to Aubrey, stood back and surveyed the scene with obvious satisfaction.

After a while a small queue of some seven or eight ladies had formed by Duncan's table, headed by Jenny Peebles, clutching her copy of his book. Duncan was looking especially spruce and roguish, and, having been encouraged by Jenny's liking for his publicity photo, had decided to affect a more debonair look. Spurred on by Jenny's admiring looks, he applied his signature with a theatrical flourish and, to each recipient's delight, he made some little quip or personal comment. The ladies clutching their books loved it, surprised that even a relatively unknown author would treat them so cordially. They cheekily responded with equal familiarity and before long their spontaneous chuckles echoed through the foyer, eliciting a fiercely disapproving glare from Fiona Bridewell.

'*Whooops*!' whispered Duncan, winking at the ladies. 'We mustn't upset teacher, must we?' and they all cackled some more, slapping their hands to their mouths and rolling their eyes at Fiona like naughty school-girls.

Tucked away behind the door, Rev Pinny was feeling depressed although, remarkably, he had managed to sell three copies of his book. But his mind was back at the Rectory and he was wondering how Joan was getting on at the prayer meeting, which they held in his study every Friday morning. They enjoyed this chance to get together with some of the more spiritual members of the congregation and Joan always provided refreshments - tea and home-made scones. With his being away he'd suggested they cancel the meeting but she'd insisted she could cope. She was a tower of strength, was Joan. He smiled as he thought of her. Sometimes he felt he'd just crawl away like a hermit crab if it weren't for her.

'Poor old Pinny looks quite deranged,' said Leanne, coming over to Rae's table which was as empty as her own. 'How many have you sold?'

'Three. Five left. I reckon that bloody Atherton's sold at least sixty already - just look at him! Talk about gloating. Makes you sick, doesn't it?'

'Duncan's doing quite well,' said Leanne, looking across at his table. 'And Oliver's sold about fifteen, I think. One woman asked him to write his phone number as well. Bloody cheek. I bet he did, too.'

'Did you see the judges go through to the conference hall?'

'Ummm,' said Leanne, looking at her watch.

'I wonder how long they'll be?' Rae said. 'What time's Oliver meeting Rachel St Clair?'

'One, I think,' Leanne replied. 'D'you reckon she'll tell him the winner?'

'Of course she will!' cried Rae. 'They've met several times before and you must have heard about her liking for presentable young men, especially writers. You never know she might take him on as one of her '*walkers*'. Whenever she ventures out for a function - you know, dinner, the theatre or some private view or publication party, she's always clutching onto the arm of some good looking 'walker' or other. Mind you, these days it's never her own publication party. She's nowhere near as popular as she was. In fact, I don't think she's had a book out for several years.'

'It's a bit sad, really, isn't it?' said Leanne.

'Not really,' said Rae. '*We* should be so lucky! After all, she had it all once. She was beautiful, feted and successful, which is a damned sight more than most people can say. Like Atherton, she's made a lot of money out of her books in the last twenty years or so, which is more than we ever will. She's been luckier than most - after all, life's pretty grim for most people. No money, no job and ugly as sin - either that or it's just plain boring.'

*

As soon as Oliver entered Giovanni's shortly after one he saw Rachel St Clair sitting at a table for two in an alcove. She was dressed in a well-cut midnight blue suit on the lapel of which was a large, brightly enamelled brooch in the shape of a bee. Her expensive fur wrap was thrown carelessly over the back of her chair, exposing the frayed lining and she seemed unaware that the end of it was caught under the leg of her chair. She was furtively touching up her make-up using a small powder compact on the front of which was a striking Art Nouveau design of nasturtium leaves. Although she looked up as he approached she did not recognise him until he was standing directly in front of her.

'Rachel,' Oliver said, softly. 'I'm so sorry I'm a little late. I'd love to be able to say that I was delayed by hordes of fans lining up to buy my book but alas - that would be a miserable lie. Besides, you've been to enough book signings to recognise it as such. No, the truth is that I felt obliged to stay and help remove the tables and carry the remainders to Fiona's car. Rev Pinny has extraordinarily weak arms and Duncan, having become besotted fairly late in life, is incapable, not only of rational thought, but of performing the most mundane task. Needless to say, Atherton refused to lift a finger and was whisked away in his car the moment he'd signed his last copy.'

'Oh, please don't apologise, darling,' Rachel said, snapping shut her compact and reaching for the still smouldering cigarette in the ashtray. 'At my age one is perfectly content merely to *anticipate* the arrival of a gorgeous young man - besides, the surroundings here are really quite pleasant and I have been amply supplied with some very good wine.'

'What on earth do you mean *'at your age'*?' teased Oliver, bending to retrieve a silk scarf that had slithered from her shoulders onto the floor. 'You're looking delightful - absolutely delightful.'

'Come now, Oliver. It's very sweet of you but I *am* sixty-two, you know,' Rachel said, challenging him to express surprise. He looked into her once-enticing eyes, now already glazed by alcohol, and at her expertly camouflaged, time-ravaged face yet, party to the predictable politeness of the game, he protested as convincingly as he could.

'Oh, come on!' he cried, shaking his head as though in disbelief. 'Rachel, you're having me on.'

'No, really - sixty-two.'

'Well, I find that hard to believe but anyway, whatever your age, you look fantastic. Now, down to business - shall we order? And what would you like to drink while we wait?'

Rachel briefly lifted the menu to her face, then replaced it on the table without interest.

'Order for me, darling,' she said. 'I can't be bothered to read that now. Such tiny, spidery writing - too tiresome.'

'What would you like - a meat dish, fish, pasta?'

'Oh, anything, except red meat - or dead flesh as I call it. It makes me throw up. Just order me something nice. I leave it to you,' she said, impatiently, as she reached for her glass and drained it. 'And another bottle of Muscadet, if I may?'

Her eyesight may have weakened, thought Oliver, but

there was certainly nothing wrong with her constitution. He noticed that she'd already drunk two thirds of a bottle of wine already. Nor was her hearing in any way diminished. The couple at the next table had, apparently, recognised her and, in the course of their conversation, she managed to pick up the whisper of her name. When the pair next looked her way she gave them the briefest of smiles, more like a quick, perfunctory grimace. After which, she took another cigarette from the packet and lit it with an exquisite silver filigree lighter.

'I see you haven't been de-programmed to abhor the evil weed, Rachel,' said Oliver, taking his own packet from the inside pocket of his leather jerkin. 'May I?' he asked, reaching for the lighter.

Rachel shrugged. 'Oh, I know one shouldn't,' she groaned. 'Everyone gets so ridiculously hot under the collar about it these days, don't they? In some ways, I suppose, they're right, but for heaven's sake, why can't we choose our own death? After all, we don't get any damned say in our birth, do we?'

She drew heavily on her cigarette, pursed her lips and blew the smoke above her head. 'Anyway,' she went on, 'I *can't* stop. It's as simple as that.'

She paused to drink from her wine glass. 'Besides,' she went on, 'it's one of the few pleasures left in life. Everything's such a misery - all these wretched aches and pains, eyes going, teeth falling out, wrinkles galore - oh, what the hell? And, for heaven's sake, at my age, how else can I live dangerously? I don't drive fast cars or jump off poles with a piece of rope round my ankle. A few cigarettes and a drink now and then, that's all. My God, if I can't do that what is there? I might as well be dead.'

'I'm sure you're right, Rachel.' Once he had lit his cigarette he fingered the lighter appreciatively.

'Wonderful, isn't it?' said Rachel. 'A present from an ancient lover.' She giggled girlishly. 'I mean, from a lover many years ago. He was far from ancient, as it happens, just splendidly rich and - ' she opened her expressive eyes even wider. '...madly in love with me.'

'I can well imagine,' offered Oliver, sipping his wine.

Rachel looked at him intently, unsure of his sincerity.

'That may be difficult for you to believe,' she said, 'but I assure you it's true. And he wasn't the only one. Oh, Oliver, it was such *fun* being young and beautiful. Such incredible fun.'

She paused while the waiter replenished their wine and seemed lost in her thoughts. Then she looked up and smiled: 'But I must admit, I *was* a bit wild, darling.'

'I bet you were!' Oliver exclaimed, stubbing out his cigarette. 'And why not? You're a long time dead, as they say!'

They paused in their conversation as the waiter arrived with their lunch and Rachel looked wistfully at Oliver. How extraordinarily sad, she thought, lunching with such a charming young man, one equipped with those gorgeous melting brown eyes, and not feeling the need to flirt outrageously in anticipation of some sexy denouement. In some ways being old was nothing but a bore - yet, she had to admit, it made things so much easier, far less complicated. One's options were curtailed, the possibilities few. No risk of getting hurt, immune to emotional pain. Lost dreams traded in for rheumatism, chilblains and hip replacement.

'Were you ever married, Rachel?' Oliver asked, breaking his bread roll and then retrieving Rachel's wrap which had finally slid to the floor. She laid down her knife and fork and laughed.

'Oh, yes, I was married all right,' she replied. 'Twice, as a matter of fact. Both charmers, impossible to live with, of course. And we writers aren't the easiest of bedfellows, are we? And masses of lovers - well, one could in those days - gorgeous, all of them. How I ever found time to write my books I shall never know.'

'Any children?'

At first, it seemed that Rachel hadn't heard Oliver's question, for there was a prolonged silence during which she kept her eyes downcast as she pushed her food around the plate with her knife. Finally, she looked up and her eyes, no longer bright with laughter, were now sad and dull.

'A daughter, Melanie.'

'And what does Melanie do?' asked Oliver, taking a sip of wine.

'Do?' Rachel stared at him for a moment. 'Do? She made a terribly unsuitable alliance,' she said, her voice coarse with distress. 'And paid for it with her life.'

Oliver was shocked to see that she was crying. Tears were seeping into the thickly-caked layer of powder on her cheeks and a small rivulet of diluted mascara had appeared under her left eye. Before he could reach for the napkin, she had dabbed at her face with a piece of green tissue and in doing so exposed a patch of raw flesh. Devoid, now, of make-up, he saw that the skin was finely meshed with tiny thread veins. Realising what she had done, she uttered a sort of strangled whimper, pushed back her chair and rose unsteadily to her feet.

Muttering something about powdering her nose, she tottered off towards an exit door in search of the lavatory, only to find herself in the street. As Oliver was half way across the floor of the restaurant to help her, she reappeared, looking wild-eyed and confused.

'It's over there,' Oliver said, quietly, drawing alongside her. Taking her elbow he gave her a gentle push in the right direction before returning to his seat. But she was unable to recognise the LADIES sign and, after flitting from one door to the other, she was eventually guided through the right one by a sympathetic waiter who realised her predicament.

She was in the lavatory for ages but when she did appear she made a supreme effort to overcome her intoxication and remember where she had been sitting. She managed to negotiate the tables remarkably well and, Oliver noticed, she had done a remarkable repair to her damaged make-up and seemed more than game for round two.

'You look a million dollars!' said Oliver. 'Here - have another glass of wine.'

'That's what I like about you, Oliver - devil may care - to hell with it.'

She was slurring her words. She laughed and, reaching over, covered his hand with her own. Then, looking down, she saw that her hands, though still shapely and well-manicured, with several layers of puce varnish on the nails, were disfigured by a profusion of age spots and knotted blue veins. Mortified, she withdrew them immediately and then, restlessly reaching for her napkin ring, she started to twist it around in her fingers until, having loosened her grip, it shot over the edge of the table and clattered to the floor.

'But tell me,' she said, as Oliver bent to retrieve it for her. 'all about your life and how you came to write about your Fifties' movie gangsters. I did enjoy it by the way. And no,' she added, playfully tapping his hand with the end of her napkin. 'I shan't tell you who's won until you've told me all I want to know - about you, the other finalists and all the latest intrigues in Fleet Street. I'm quite out of touch these days. You are at my mercy until you do.'

'But first you must tell me about your latest offering,'

Oliver demanded, knowing full well she hadn't published a book in years. 'When can we expect the latest *Rachel St Clair* to appear or is it a well-guarded secret?'

'Oh, there's no secret,' Rachel declared. 'I haven't written a word for three years and I doubt very much I'll ever produce another novel now.'

'Oh, don't say that,' Oliver protested, refilling her glass.

'Come on, Oliver,' Rachel chided, trying to look stern. 'I know perfectly well you never read romantic fiction - you told me so when we had our little chat at Brighton. No, I must admit it's not from choice - I just don't get the ideas anymore but I do miss it. I've published so many books over the years that the routine of writing had become so much part of my life, my '*reason d'être'*, if you like.'

She took a small mouthful of food which she delicately chewed, clearly finding no pleasure in the taste. As she did so, she seemed lost in thought.

'I suppose it's a way of hiding from some of life's disappointments,' she said. 'Especially in fiction, being in control, making people do what you want them to, making things end as you wish them to end. Not like real life where we have no control,' She paused to look intently into Oliver's face before finishing her sentence. 'And endings can be so cruel. Don't you agree?'

Oliver nodded and refilled their glasses. 'Indeed, they can,' he said.

'But one's imagination, like everything else, dries up eventually. We fight it, disguise it, but we can't deny it. But you, dear Oliver, how I envy you, for you're still young, and, hopefully, have many more books to write.'

Seeing that Rachel seemed close to tears again, Oliver launched into a round of Fleet Street gossip that soon had her smiling once more. They chatted amiably throughout the meal and were just finishing their coffee when Oliver encouraged her to talk about literary life in London during the late Sixties. Her face came alive again as she recounted early affairs with warmth and gaiety but she soon sank into a mood of mawkish nostalgia which, in turn, gradually developed into despair.

'Oliver, you may think it was all fun and parties but it was not. There were heartaches and bitter disappointments. Not all my lovers were gentlemen - not by a long straw.'

'That's the whole point of nostalgia, isn't it? You forget the boring times, the painful times, the times you'd never wish to live through again.'

She made a small, gasping noise deep in her throat and Oliver noticed that her lower lip was quivering as it latched on to the rim of her cup. He wondered if this was a good time to bring her back to the present and ask her who had won the *Birkett Bronze*. He knew she'd tell him. But he could see she was still somewhere back in the past and her face had become contorted with anger.

'One of them deceived me very badly,' she said. 'I was utterly, *utterly* betrayed in the most hurtful way - in a way that only another woman would truly understand.' She looked beyond his face, fighting back a fresh flow of tears. 'More than twenty years have passed but it still saddens me and the memory of the pain he caused still makes me tremble.'

'Do you want to tell me about it?' Oliver asked, secretly dreading she would further unburden herself. The restaurant had emptied now except for the couple at the next table who were deliberately, or so it seemed, dawdling over their coffee, determined to hear as much of Rachel's conversation as they could before leaving. It was therefore some relief to Oliver when she stopped talking, held his gaze for a moment, then shrugged. Lighting another cigarette from the smouldering stub between her fingers, she shook her head.

'No,' she said, quietly. 'No. It's over. Past. Dead. Be an angel, Oliver, and pour me the last of that wine. And then I shall tell you the name of the winner. After all, that's the reason you brought me here, isn't it?"

Oliver smiled triumphantly as he emptied the last half inch of wine into Rachel's glass and called for the bill.

'I'm sure this will be no surprise to you,' Rachel said, emptying her glass. 'The voting was two to one. Needless to say I was the one who voted against him. I'm sorry, but Aubrey Atherton has won for the third time.' *Aubrey Atherton*. She repeated his name, very quietly. Then her voice faltered and, for a split second, the expression on her face was one of restrained agony - or was it utter revulsion?

The next moment she was laughing again, remembering some little morsel of gossip fed to her by Oliver. But by the time he had walked her back to *The Crown Imperial* and handed her over to the care of the capable Mr Popperwell, who showed no surprise whatsoever at seeing her legless, she was in tears again, weeping silently into the folds of her wrap as he coaxed her gently up the sweeping staircase to her room.

*

Chapter Sixteen

Early that evening Rae and Leanne were sitting in the Lounge Bar of *The Hare,* waiting for Oliver to come back. He'd promised to meet up with them after his lunch with Rachel St Clair but they'd somehow missed each other. At one point during the afternoon, however, Leanne had caught sight of his back as he joined a queue that was filing into the Schoolroom for a lecture on *Poetry in the Vernacular*. As this held no appeal for either of them, she and Rae decided to join the audience at a discussion on *The Contemporary Novel* instead.

By ten past seven Oliver still hadn't returned, despite arranging earlier that morning to meet them at seven to go out for a meal at a small restaurant called, for some unfathomable reason, *The Nutcracker Grill.* Duncan and Jenny Peebles had decided to go on ahead and secure a table and Rev Pinny, who was not entirely sure that he was included in the evening's arrangements, was in the passage talking to his wife on the telephone. Leanne was waiting to ring Joe, having forgotten again that morning.

As she and Rae waited, their conversation naturally turned to Oliver and, having listened to Leanne relating one of her erotic fantasies, Rae admitted to cultivating one of her own since her arrival in arrival in Chiselford. It concerned, she confided, the killing of Aubrey Atherton, and she outlined the theme with evident enthusiasm.

'I'd do it partly for pleasure and partly to ensure I got the maximum publicity at my trial. You know, all the tabloids and the mass media out in force. Doubtless I'd be found guilty but no matter,' she went on, between sips of beer. 'Just imagine, the absolute luxury of free board and lodging, locked in a cell at *Her Majesty's Pleasure* for twenty-three hours a day, with my nifty little Desk-Top computer provided by the Social Services and the time in the world to write my best-seller entitled, *Why I Killed Aubrey Atherton*.'

Rae paused, her eyes shut, imagining it all. 'I can see it now - the great publishing conglomerates making wildly extravagant bids for the copyright, then the TV series, the film rights - the book goes straight to the top of the Best-sellers List, a run of tens of thousands and translated into thirty languages.'

She opened her eyes. 'And naturally, once the powers that be realised what an absolute shit Atherton had been when he was alive, they'd release me immediately, with a free pardon and probably give me a public service medal for good measure.'

Leanne laughed. 'I don't suppose you're the first person to nurse a similar fantasy. In fact, I'm surprised somebody hasn't bumped him off before now. He does seem to go out of his way to be as obnoxious as possible. I suppose it's a form of attention seeking. As for me, I think if I were to contemplate murdering someone I'd automatically turn to poison.'

'Oh, no,' Rae said vehemently, 'I think if my temper were really up - you know, really *spitting* mad, I could quite easily throttle someone with my bare hands.'

As she was speaking, Oliver came through the bar, gave everyone a cheery wave and called, 'be down in a minute' before bounding up the stairs two at a time.

'Well, at least he hasn't *forgotten* he's meant to be meeting us,' said Leanne, feeling her face flush.

'I just hope he doesn't keep us waiting for hours while he tarts himself up...' Rae stopped when she saw Leanne's face. '*Leanne Philips*!' she cried. 'You're blushing!'

But before she could tease her friend further she was interrupted by the sound of raised voices from the kitchen. One of the regulars in the other bar looked across at Rae, jerked his head towards the bead curtain, raised his eyebrows and laughed. Someone said, 'They're starting early tonight' and Rev Pinny came back into the Lounge saying he'd heard some 'quite dreadful language' coming from the kitchen.

Leanne went off to phone Joe and found herself apologising once again for neglecting to ring earlier.

'Doesn't matter,' Joe said.

'Is everything all right?'

'Yes, fine.'

'Don't you even want to know when I'm coming home?' Leanne asked, trying to keep her voice light.

'Well, when?' came the reply.

'Tomorrow,.'

'Okay.'

'Probably won't be until late afternoon, depending on what time we can get away.'

'Okay.'

'I can't wait to see you, Joe.'

'Okay.'

'Are you sure everything's all right?'

'Course it is.'

'Miss me?'

'What?'

'I said - have you missed me?'

''Suppose so.'

‘Well, that’s something, I suppose.’

‘What?’

‘Doesn’t matter.’

‘Can I go now?'

'What's the hurry?'

'Football.'

'With the school?'

'Yes.'

'Is Jean looking after you all right?'

'Yes.'

'Everything OK, then?'

'Yes. I told you.'

'I'll see you tomorrow then.'

'OK.'

‘You won’t forget, will you?’

‘Forget what?’

‘I’m coming home!’

‘Course not. Don’t fuss,’ Joe said.

‘Make sure you're in, won't you? And tell Jean to expect me. Tell her I'll ring as I'm leaving.'

‘OK.'

'Bye, then, Joe, see you tomorrow.'

'Bye, Mum, see you tomorrow.'

‘Bye, Joe. See you tomorrow.’

Replacing the receiver, Leanne realised that the tempo of the row between the Doggetts had increased while she’d been on the phone to Joe and some sort of confrontation was taking place. Walking along the passage she could hear Thelma’s harsh voice issuing a command to her husband.

'Give me that tray,’ she was saying. ‘I said, *give me that try!*

By the time Leanne had joined Rae and Rev Pinny in the bar Thelma was in full voice and Len Doggett was backing through the beaded curtain gripping a tray on which he had laid a copy of the local newspaper, a green apple and a bottle of sparkling wine. His wife had her finger hooked into one of the button-holes on his old fawn cardigan and was pulling so hard that one side had fallen away from his shoulder and the much-darned and misshapen sleeve hung down like a withered wing. Len, it seemed, was taking a stand at last. He refused to relinquish the tray, backed through the gap in the bar, turned and, surprisingly quickly, made for the stairs.

Whilst Thelma's face had gone white, her neck had broken out in fierce pink blotches. She stood on the other side of the bar and, seemingly oblivious to the rapt attention of her customers, yelled.

'Come back this minute. I've told you, Leonard Doggett, and I mean it. I said, *give me that tray.'*

Despite the dangerous rise in the tone of Thelma's voice, Len ignored her and began to mount the stairs. All five customers in the Public Bar were leaning over the counter to watch and someone sniggered as Thelma shouted.

'If you so much as step foot in that man's room I'm finished with you. Don't say I haven't warned you. Finished. This time you can bloody well move on your own - I'm staying. This time *you* go. Out. Once and for all. OUT!'

'God, what's that all about?' whispered Leanne, looking across at one of the regulars. But he merely grinned, shrugged and shook his head. Thelma, meanwhile, had made a dash for the stairs with the two pugs at her heels. Catching up with her husband already half way to the landing, she stood full square in front of him and tried to wrench the tray from his hands. He managed to steady the bottle of wine but the apple shot off and rolled down the stairs, the pugs in furious pursuit, snarling and snapping at each other like fractious children after a tossed sweet. Grabbing the newspaper, Thelma ran back to the bottom of the stairs and bent down to whack the dogs.

This momentary distraction gave Len his chance to escape. Without looking back, he skipped up the remaining stairs and turned the corner towards Atherton's room.

It was here that he ran into Oliver as he was coming out of the bathroom. Len passed without a word, reached Atherton's door and knocked several times in quick succession. As the door opened and Doggett went in, Oliver heard the sound of the key turning in the lock.

As he reached the landing, Thelma came barging round the corner, her mouth set and her thighs rasping dangerously.

'Blimy, I don't fancy his chances when she gets hold of him,' Oliver said, as he joined the others at the bar. 'Talk about guns a-blazing - poor man.'

'Ah, but you don't know what he's done to upset her, do you?' cautioned Rae. 'Who knows what he's been up to?'

'Len Doggett?' cried Oliver, derisively. 'What d'you reckon? She caught him with a pile of porno mags or what? The mind boggles. I mean, be honest, the options for sin must be pretty thin for someone like Doggett.'

'Ah, but surely that depends on one's interpretation of sin?' said Rev Pinny, his voice rising thinly from the depths of the wing-backed chair by the fire.

'God, I didn't know the praying mantis was in here,' whispered Oliver. 'I was going to say 'wanking in front of the telly' - just as well I stuck to the porno mags.'

Just then Thelma Doggett came back downstairs, carrying a pug under each arm. As she passed the people in the bar, their sorrowful eyes swivelled from one face to the other, seeking approval. Mrs Doggett, however, looked at no one, but it was clear that she was simply seething with frustration. Once behind the bar, she released the dogs and, her brow furrowed, she began to attack the surfaces with a dish-cloth but every time she looked towards the stairs, her eyes narrowed and she muttered something unintelligible under her breath.

*

A little later, just as they were about to pile into the taxi Rae had ordered, they were surprised to see Theodore Rigby turn his car into the driveway and park near the front entrance of the hotel. Looking back, Oliver watched him as he hurried through the swing doors of the hotel, carrying a small suitcase. Fraternising with Atherton again, he thought, before joining the others, nudging Rae out of the way so he could sit next to Leanne.

The Nutcracker Grill was pleasant enough but everyone felt flat and dispirited. As soon as they had joined Duncan and Jenny Peebles and ordered their meal, attention centred on Oliver. He had been maddeningly reticent about his lunch with Rachel St Clair. To maintain the suspense still further he began by describing her appearance and demeanour but was soon halted by Rae.

'Cut all that crap,' she snapped. 'Did she tell you who's won?

'Yes, she did tell me, as a matter of fact...' he said, slowly sipping his wine.

'Well?' demanded Leanne.

They all stared at him - even Rev Pinny seemed to understand the magnitude of the moment.

'I'm not sure that I'm at liberty to say.' Oliver teased. 'She did tell me in the strictest confidence.'

'Oh, come on, stop pissing about!' Rae shouted. 'Who is it, for God's sake?'

'Guess.'

'Atherton,' they all said in unison.

"Fraid so.'

'Surprise, surprise,' groaned Duncan, shaking his head like an old donkey. Jenny Peebles gave his arm a sympathetic squeeze.

'Shit,' said Rae, lighting a cigarette and throwing the packet onto the table.

'It was two to one, apparently. Rachel voted against him.'

'Well, we knew it, didn't we?' Rae said. 'He was bound to get Machete Max and Theo's vote. Talk about arse-licking! You can stuff the effing bronze but God, what I couldn't do with that money.'

'Me, too,' said Duncan, ruefully. Turning to Jenny he added, 'Well, there goes my play; I'll never get another chance to put it on.' Jenny leaned over to whisper something in his ear. He looked pleased and started fingering his moustache.

Noticing that she hadn't said anything, Jenny asked Leanne what she would have done with the money.

'Oh, I can hardly bear to think about it,' she said. 'What would I do? I know exactly what I'd do. I'd use it as a deposit on a ground floor flat, any condition so long as it had a garden and a shed. Jesus, bang goes my last chance to get out of that bloody awful estate. How else could I raise the money? And what makes me so mad is that Atherton doesn't need it. He's loaded, more money than he knows what to do with. It seems so unfair...'

At this point, however, Leanne stopped, hating to hear the whinging tone of her voice.

'What would you have done with the money, Pinny?' Oliver asked. Joseph Pinny was dabbing at a trickle of grapefruit juice on his chin. He didn't answer directly but thought for a moment.

'Oh, that's easy,' he said. 'I'd have used it for the Lord's work, of course, what else? I have all my basic needs.' He looked directly at Leanne: 'I have a roof over my head and sufficient to eat. My wife and I would have used the money on people who have nothing - nothing at all.'

'Don't you ever get really mad?' Rae enquired, genuinely perplexed by Pinny's complacency.

'I agree that it hardly seems fair that someone as wealthy as Atherton should acquire yet more money - but then, who are we to judge?'

'Oh, for God's sake!' snapped Rae, losing her patience with Pinny. 'There's no justice! How can you be so sanguine?'

'Ours is not to reason why...'

'Rubbish!'

'Well, anyway, we expected it, didn't we?' said Oliver, draining his glass. 'What shall we do? Shall we boycott the presentation or would that be seen as sour grapes?'

'Which it is, in a way, I suppose,' said Leanne. 'I reckon we should go. It'd be pretty petty-minded not to. I mean, we don't have to go over the top with enthusiasm when they make the announcement.

'No, but we'd have to watch his silly face smirking in triumph as he pockets the cheque,' Rae moaned, bitterly. 'No kidding, I don't think I could bear it.'

They sat in silence, feeling envious and resentful.

'Never mind,' said Duncan, cheerfully. 'Look at it this way, at least we'll get paid for coming here, it made a nice little break and ...' He opened his arms to encompass Jenny Peebles and winked at Oliver. '...there *have* been one or two compensations.'

'I haven't noticed any,' grumbled Rae. Then, turning on Rev Pinny, she added, 'And don't you dare say there's always next year because you know damned well it'll be at least another two years or more before we get anything else published.'

'She's right, of course, but hell - what can we do?' said Oliver, with a shrug. 'Nothing. I'll order some more wine. Come on, drink up. Don't let Atherton spoil our last evening as well.'

But despite everyone's efforts to dismiss the thought of Atherton's undeserved success, their resentment remained and they left the restaurant early. Pinny insisted on walking back at eight-thirty saying he'd promised to ring Joan at nine. Duncan and Jenny Peebles left soon after and when the others reached *The Hare* shortly after ten they found them already ensconced, deep in conversation, in the Lounge Bar.

Leaving them to it, Oliver and Leanne went straight up to bed and Rae did likewise - but in her case to read. The affirmation of Atherton's success somehow sapped any enthusiasm, even for illicit sex, and after an unsatisfactory coupling, Oliver and Leanne lay together without speaking, each lost in their own private regrets. They were also trying to contemplate the return to London, the resumption of their separate lives.

Neither said anything. Oliver was loath to make promises that might be soon be forgotten once he picked up the threads of his life with Jane. Leanne, though obviously looking forward to seeing Joe again, was somehow dreading the return to her usual feeling of isolation. She knew that, not only would she miss Oliver, her life would seem even more dreary than it had before she'd met him - the dismal estate, the perennial problems of the classroom, the strain of being the mother of a teenage boy. She wanted to ask him if they'd see each other occasionally but, fearing a negative reply, she said nothing.

They lay listening to the sounds of the bar downstairs. It was evident that Thelma Doggett was in no mood for chat for she'd cleared the premises and bolted the doors less than five minutes after calling last orders - and no sooner had the last drinkers turned into the road than she was upstairs knocking on Atherton's door. Quietly at first, but receiving no answer, she started to hammer at it with her fists.

'Len!' she was saying, her voice distorted as though she had her mouth close to the door panel.

Receiving no response, she banged on the door again. 'You'd better bloody well come out,' she called. 'Len, can you hear me? I'm warning you.'

She waited, her ear to the door. After a short while she started again. '*Len*! ' she called again, even more loudly.

Still no answer from within but, then, the hint of a stifled giggle. Thelma was furious.

'Don't pretend you can't hear me,' she bellowed. 'I know you're in there. You'd better speak up now, this minute, before I get really mad.'

Suddenly, from behind the door came Atherton's shrill voice.

'Oh, go away, you stupid woman, and stop being such a silly, old spoil sport. Go on, push off!'

'How *dare* you!' screamed Thelma. She put her ear close to the door once more.

'Is that Theodore Rigby still there?' she shouted. 'The old pervert. That's it, I've had enough. Can you hear me? Enough.'

With that, she started to bang on the door again, loud enough for the whole street to hear.

Sitting up in bed like eavesdropping children, Oliver and

Leanne heard the door to Atherton's room suddenly open. This was followed by a tirade of abuse from Thelma as she ordered her errant husband upstairs to their bedroom on the second floor.

'Just look at you,' she shouted. 'You're pathetic, that's what you are. You look downright ridiculous. How *dare* you touch my things. Get up those stairs this minute - go on - I said *get up those stairs!'*

This was followed by the sound of shuffling feet and the slam of a door, after which everything was quiet.

Oliver and Leanne lay in the dark, still listening, sure that all the other guests were doing exactly the same.

'But what's the betting old Pinny's sleeping through it all?' Oliver whispered.

'Probably is,' said Leanne. 'But I bet Rae's having a good laugh - can't you just see her face?'

Hearing Atherton's door opening once more, Oliver shot out of bed and quickly ran across the landing to the bathroom. He'd timed it well for as he did so he nearly collided with Theodore Rigby as he headed for the stairs.

The old man looked agitated on seeing Oliver and hurried by without speaking. He was still carrying his suitcase but Oliver could see quite clearly that, under his overcoat, Rigby was wearing a duck-egg blue, candy-striped blouse with a Peter Pan collar and pearl buttons.

A few moments later, just as Oliver was settling back into bed with Leanne and telling her about Rigby's unusual get-up, a woman came up the stairs and walked quietly but firmly along the passage towards Atherton's door. Without knocking she turned the handle and went in, closing the door quietly behind her.

Chapter Seventeen

Thelma Doggett found Aubrey Atherton's body the next morning at seven thirty when she went up to his room with a pot of tea. The other guests were just about to sit down to breakfast when they saw her run down the stairs, call Leonard from the other bar, grab hold of his arm and whisper something in his ear. His face was ashen as he followed Thelma into the kitchen.

'What's that all about?' asked Leanne. 'Did you catch what she said?'

'No,' said Rae, who was sitting nearest to the bar. 'Shush, a minute, if you're quiet we might be able to hear something.'

'Just don't say anything,' Thelma was saying. '*Anything* at all. D'you hear? I'll phone the doctor. Now get out there and finish the breakfasts. And remember, keep your mouth shut.'

When Len came back through the bead curtains his face was taut, like a mask and as he gathered up the empty fruit dishes they rattled under his shaking hand.

'What's happened?' asked Oliver, reaching for the butter.

'It's Mr Atherton,' he said, his voice little more than a whisper. 'My wife says she can't wake him. She thinks he might be dead...'

Everyone stared at him, disbelieving.

'You must be joking!' cried Oliver, putting down his knife.

'Damn! Someone got there first,' muttered Rae.

'What?' quipped Duncan. 'Don't tell me someone's given him what for at last!'

Rev Pinny shook his head, sorrowfully: 'Perhaps there *is* some justice in the world, after all?' he muttered.

But the look on Len Doggett's face told them that this wasn't a macabre joke.

'Len!' came Thelma's voice. She came through the bar carrying a pot of hot water. Her face was flushed and she was blinking rapidly.

'Mrs Doggett,' cried Duncan. 'Tell us the truth - Atherton isn't *really* dead, is he? Or is it some sort of joke?'

'He's dead, all right,' came the terse reply. 'I saw him with my own eyes. Dead as a blinkin' dodo.'

'I don't believe it!' Oliver said, getting up to walk around, his hands jammed into his trouser pockets.

'You must be mistaken,' said Leanne, incredulously. 'Are you sure he's not just sleeping heavily?'

'Everybody knows he's a pill-popper,' Oliver announced, 'always dosing himself with uppers, downers and as a chronic insomniac he must have tried every brand of barbiturate on the market.'

Thelma Doggett shook her head. 'I told you,' she said, grimly. 'He's dead.'

'Mrs Doggett, this has been a terrible shock,' said Rev Pinny, getting up and knocking his side plate to the floor. 'Would you like me to pop up and take a look at him?'

'No, I've sent for the doctor. She'll be here in a minute.'

'But how can he be dead?' Duncan said, clearly distressed. 'I just can't believe it. Poor old bugger.'

'Much as I loathed the man,' Rae said, drawing heavily on

her cigarette, ‘it’s still a bit of a shock.’

‘Perhaps he’d been ill,’ suggested Leanne. ‘Does anyone know?’

‘He seemed perfectly all right yesterday,’ Oliver asked, looking round at the others. ‘Well, didn’t he? I don’t know.’

‘No more pasty than usual, I suppose,' said Rae. 'What happened, d'you think? Was it an overdose? A stroke?'

'Heart, I should think,' said Thelma. She made her way around the table filling the coffee cups. Her hand was remarkably steady. 'After all,’ she said, ‘he was carrying a fair bit of weight. Drank like a fish. Smoked like a chimney. Poured pills down his throat, by all accounts, like there was no tomorrow. What d'you expect?'

Leonard stood transfixed, white-faced, as though incapable of moving until the sound of a car drawing up outside broke his trance, making him jump.

'That'll be the doctor. Len, you stay here and see to the guests. Make sure the dogs stay in the kitchen. I'll take her upstairs.’ She looked at him coldly. ‘And just remember what I said.'

Dr Margaret Evans hurried upstairs behind Mrs Doggett but came down again a few minutes later to use the telephone. When she returned to the Lounge she took Len Doggett to one side.

'The Police are on their way,’ she said. ‘I'll ring the Coroner from the surgery. He'll probably want a post-mortem - you know, suspicious death. An ambulance will come for the body in due course when forensics have finished.’

She rested her bottom on a bar stool and looked around. ‘I'll just hang on here till the police arrive - shouldn't be more than a minute or two.’

She looked more closely at the landlord’s face. ‘If I were

you,' she suggested, 'I'd have a nip of brandy to calm you down. Things like this are a terrible shock, aren't they?'

Len Doggett poured himself a double whisky and downed it in one go. He reached to pour another but Thelma shot him a venomous look, pushed him through to the kitchen and followed him in. Then she quickly closed the door, thereby preventing everyone in the lounge bar from hearing the gist of the heated exchange that followed.

*

Inspector Bill Crocker arrived within minutes, accompanied by PC Ian Richards. As they passed through the lounge he summoned the Doggetts and told them to ask all the hotel guests to remain on the premises until the preliminary examinations were complete. Len was further instructed to send the police photographer upstairs as soon as he arrived.

'Perhaps, Mrs Doggett,' Crocker suggested, 'you would lead us to Mr Atherton's room?'

Walking ahead of them up the stairs and along the passage Thelma opened the door to Atherton's room and stood aside for the police to enter. Following them in, she pulled back the curtains and tutted as she saw that the place was a mess. There were clothes strewn everywhere. Women's clothes, mainly.

Then, with the morning light now flooding through the window onto the bed, she had a clear view of Aubrey Atherton's body; the top half was hanging over the edge of the mattress with one arm extended, the clenched fist almost touching the floor. The bed covers had been pulled back to his waist. He was wearing oyster grey silk pyjamas, the top having a rolled neck. His green silk dressing gown was lying across the foot of the bed.

Crocker bent over the body and inspected the face.

The pale, lifeless eyes were bulging, the whites showing a network of tiny haemorrhages. The lips and ears were tinged with blue and there was a small bubble of bloodied froth oozing from his left nostril and another from the corner of his open mouth. The tongue that protruded through the discoloured lips was swollen and livid. His chestnut toupee had become dislodged and was lying upside down on the pillow, leaving his bald head exposed, the numerous tiny haemorrhages showing clearly on the unnatural whiteness of the skull.

Carefully lifting the extended arm, Crocker felt the resistance of the rigor mortis which had already stiffened the body. He looked closely at the clenched fist on the fingers of which were two heavy gold rings and noticed that the nails had turned blue. An ornate gold chain lay on his hairless chest.

On the bedside table there was a Rolex watch, an empty wineglass, a bottle of barbiturates, three quarters full and an envelope. Though much of the postmark was indistinct, the date was just decipherable and showed that the letter had been posted some years before. There was nothing inside the envelope, only a name and address on the front, which Crocker copied into his notebook before replacing it on the table.

Turning again to the body on the bed, Crocker hooked his little finger over the neckline of Atherton's pyjama top and eased it down to reveal a black nylon suspender belt pulled tightly around the throat.

PC Richards, looking over his shoulder, made a slight hissing noise between his teeth but Crocker remained silent. Bruising had already begun to appear on either side of the ligature and there were several small scratches under the chin. Before releasing his finger, Crocker peered more closely at Atherton's throat and then beckoned Richards to do likewise.

Then, leaving the body he started to work his way around the room, picking up various items of clothing, some of which were draped over the chair beside the bed whilst other garments were strewn along the ottoman at the foot of the bed. He turned to Mrs Doggett who was standing by the door, her podgy feet neatly together, her eyes wide and her ring-encrusted hands clamped over the lower part of her face.

'Married gentleman, was he?' Crocker asked, holding up a pair of tights on the end of his biro.

'Not so far as I know, sir,' said Mrs Doggett, tight-lipped.. 'Leastways, he came on his own.' To this, she added, primly, 'I don't allow any female visitors - or gentleman callers for that matter - in my rooms after ten o'clock. Those are my rules.'

'When did you last see Mr Atherton alive, Mrs Doggett?'

'When he came in about seven last night. I didn't see him after that. He didn't order dinner. As far as I know he stayed in his room.'

'Did he usually stay in his room?'

'No, he usually went out,' Thelma replied, sniffily. 'He only ate here once as far as I can remember. He wasn't my only guest, don't forget. I've got five others to worry about and the pub to run. It's not easy, you know.'

Inspector Crocker was looking in the wardrobe, fingering Atherton's expensive suits.

'Umm. Very nice. Quality stuff.'

Then, going across to the ottoman at the foot of the bed he caught up a limp fawn cardigan between his thumb and forefinger. Lifting it level with his face, he looked quizzically at the landlady.

'Hardly in keeping with the rest of his gear, would you say?'

Recognising Len's old cardi, Thelma closed her eyes and

appeared to sway.

'Richards - a chair for Mrs Doggett,' said Crocker. 'No, not *that* one!' he snapped, as PC Richards went to remove the clothes from the bedside chair. 'There's one on the landing, I believe. I remember seeing it as we came up.'

Once Thelma Doggett was seated, he said, 'There now - bit of a shock, isn't it, finding a dead body in one of your rooms?'

He paused while the landlady took a deep breath and tried to regain her self-control. 'I'm sorry I have to ask you to stay, I know it's not pleasant, but you're the only person who can tell me if anything's missing, or been disturbed in any way, or - how shall I put it - whether there's anything here that shouldn't be, if you catch my drift.'

Thelma nodded and made a point of looking round the room.

'Have you any idea, for instance,' he said, 'who this fawn cardigan might belong to?'

The landlady regarded the object with some distaste. 'No,' she said, firmly, 'none whatsoever.'

'One of your other guests, perhaps?'

Thelma looked directly at the inspector and shook her head. Crocker looked at her intently. 'It's just that a garment such as this doesn't seem to fit, somehow, with the other items of clothing. D'you know what I mean?'

'It is a bit odd, I must say,' agreed Mrs Doggett, folding her arms.'

Then I take it you've never seen it before?' he said, holding the drab garment at arm's length.

'Not that I remember. No.'

Handing the old cardigan to PC Richards, Crocker started calling out a list of the items of men's clothing in the wardrobe.

'One charcoal grey, feint stripe Worsted double-breasted

suit. One pale beige, heavy linen single breasted jacket. One camel hair - the real McCoy, by the way - overcoat. Two pairs of trousers - one, pale grey, the other mauve.'

Moving over to the chest of drawers, which was close to the window, he continued, 'Three polo-necked cashmere - lucky chap - sweaters - one pale lemon, one pale grey, one white. Vests, two - silk. One cream silk shirt - one white cotton, one mauve. Spare pair of pyjamas - lemon yellow satin.' Looking at the back of the door, he added, 'And one PVC Macintosh, black. Green velour trilby.'

Crocker's attention returned to the bedside table,

'One watch - Rolex,' he said. 'Three rings - gold - still on body. Likewise, a heavy gold chain.'

Walking round to a chair on the far side of the bed, he said, 'Now the female attire. I hope you're getting all this down, Richards. Two long sleeved blouses - what would you say these were made of Mrs Doggett? Cotton?'

Thelma Doggett felt the sleeve of one of the blouses,

'Well, this one's definitely Seersucker,' she said, 'and the other looks like polyester to me - synthetic, anyway.'

'Did you get that, Richards?' Crocker asked, as he went back to the wardrobe. 'One navy, lady's costume - wool, I should imagine. Very nice.'

He bent down and picked up a pair of sling-back sandals and held them up with the straps hooked over his little finger. 'One a pair of ladies' shoes - dark pink, wouldn't you say?'

'Raspberry,' said Mrs Doggett.

Crocker was bending down once more,

'And another pair - ladies' again, different style, black patent leather - I know that because my wife's got a pair very similar.'

He looked at the rest of the garments laid across the seat

of the chair. 'Female undergarments, Richards - bras, pantie girdles, petticoats, the lot - two sets by the look of things...'

'And there's a whole load of make-up and costume jewellery in the drawer, sir,' said PC Richards. 'And these...'

He held up two wigs - one was made of curly brown hair, medium length and the other was straight and ash-blond in colour.

'Well,' said Crocker, looking across at Mrs Doggett. 'Either he had a lady visitor or he was planning on going to a fancy dress party. What do you think? Did he ever invite friends to his room?'

'Fiona used to go up to see him.'

'Fiona?'

'Fiona Bridewell,' said Mrs Doggett. 'She's a PR working for the publisher - Mr Atherton's publisher - she's in charge of him over the Festival. Shouldn't someone tell her what's happened?'

'And where might we find her, this Fiona Bridewell?' asked Inspector Crocker.

'She's staying at *The Crown Imperial,*' said Thelma Doggett, helpfully. 'And Claire Fenton - that's her assistant - she used to come up to see him sometimes but she had more to do with the other finalists.'

'Other finalists? How d'you mean?'

'For the *Birkett Bronze Award* - they're all crime writers. They're going to announce the winner today - one o'clock at *The Crown.*'

'Where might I find these other finalists, Mrs Doggett?'

'Downstairs,' the landlady replied. 'They're all staying here. They're down there having their breakfast. Surely you must have seen them as you came through the bar?'

'Ah, yes,' Crocker said, nodding. 'I should like a word

with them before I leave. Now, Mrs Doggett, I must ask you again. Are you sure Mr Atherton's spent last evening alone in this room?'

'As far as I know.'

'Could he, d'you suppose,' Crocker went on, 'have slipped out without your seeing him and returned, say, with an acquaintance? A lady - or even two?"

'I don't see how,' Thelma said. 'He'd have to come through the bar and either me or Len - that's my husband - would have seen him. It's always busy on a Friday night,' she explained, 'and we're both behind the bar from six till closing time.'

'So you would have seen anyone going upstairs?'

'Bound to.'

'Through the bar's the only way up?'

'Yes.'

'I see,' said Crocker. 'Perhaps I could have a word with your husband just in case he remembers seeing anyone? Richards, go and fetch Mr Doggett, will you? And while you're downstairs, get on the blower and get forensics over here and tell them to hurry.'

Turning to the landlady, he said,

'I wonder if you would let us use the room next door, Mrs Doggett? Somewhere a little bit more private so I can have a word with the other guests. I'll start, if I may, with your husband. Thank you.'

Inspector Crocker opened the door for the landlady and gave a little bow.

'That will be all for now,' he said. 'You've been more than helpful and I'll talk to you again a little later on, if I may? In the meantime, please try to keep to your usual routine as though we weren't here. As you say, running a pub's no doddle. I should know, I was brought up in one.'

Chapter Eighteen

As Len Doggett followed PC Richards along the passage he faltered when he saw Inspector Crocker waiting for him outside the open door of Atherton's room.

'Come along, we'll go in here,' Crocker said, indicating the next room. 'Once forensics have finished in there we can shift the body and get back to normal. Awful business, isn't it?'

'Yes,' said Len, taking the seat by Oliver's bed. He looked around the room, reluctant to make any eye contact with Crocker.

'Don't look so uncomfortable,' Crocker said, lightly, offering him a cigarette.

Len shook his head and folded his arms. Still avoiding his eye, he cleared his throat before asking,

'What was it? Drugs? Heart attack?'

'I'm afraid that will be for the Coroner to decide,' said Crocker. 'Now, I should like to ask you one or two questions about last night. Your wife tells me that you were both in the bar all evening. Is that correct?'

'Yes.'

'It's fairly busy on a Friday night?'

'Usually. Unless there's an away match. Darts.'

'So you were both working in the bar between, say, five-thirty and eleven-thirty.'

'More like eleven-fifteen. Depends how quickly we can get them all out. We generally get up early in the morning to finish clearing up - too tired last thing.'

'So you both went to bed about eleven-fifteen?'

'Something like that.'

'Tell me, Mr Doggett, did you see anyone going up to Mr Atherton's room last night?'

'No.'

'No one at all?'

'No.'

'Are you quite sure?'

'Quite sure.'

'Is there any other way up to the rooms on the first floor except through the bar?'

'No.'

'What about the other guests - all finalists for some award or other, I hear.'

'Crime-writers. They're all staying here. Mr Atherton was one of them.'

'Were they all in the hotel last night?'

'As far as I know,' Doggett said. 'Sometimes they drink in the bar, sometimes they go out.'

'What about last night?' asked Crocker. 'Which did they do? Go out or stay in?'

'Not sure. The wife'll know. To be honest, I don't take much notice. The vicar was in, I know that, 'cos I took him up a glass of warm milk.'

'What time was that?'

'About nine... nine-thirty, something like that.'

'What's his name, this vicar?'

'Pinny. Rev Pinny. Don't remember his first name.'

'And which room does he occupy?'

'The one on the end, next to the bathroom.'

'So you must have walked past Mr Atherton's room when you took the milk to Rev Pinny at nine-thirty last night?'

'Yes.'

'Did you see anyone either going in or coming out of Mr Atherton's room?'

'No.'

'Did you hear voices from inside the room? Anything to indicate that Mr Atherton was in, alone or in company?'

'No.'

'Nothing at all?'

'No.'

'And had you, at any time during Mr Atherton's stay,' Crocker continued, 'heard any argument between him and anyone else? You know, raised voices, an altercation of any kind?'

'No.'

'When was Mr Atherton due to check out?'

'Today. After the announcement. He was going back to London straight after. That's what he said, anyway.'

'How would you describe Mr Atherton?'

'How d'you mean?'

'What sort of person was he?'

Len thought for a moment, then said, 'He was all right.'

'All right?'

'Well, you know.'

Crocker waited for Doggett to elaborate but he simply pulled at the frayed cuff of his jumper and stared at the floor.

'One last thing,' said Crocker, 'and then I'll let you go about your business. I can see you're still in a state of shock. When you had taken the glass of milk to Rev Pinny's room did you return immediately to the bar?'

'How d'you mean?'

'Did you go back downstairs straight away,' explained Crocker, patiently, 'or did you go anywhere else?'

'Like where?'

'Well, I don't know,' Crocker's voice rose slightly. 'To anyone else's room - to check on towels, take the orders for breakfast, that sort of thing.'

'No. The wife does all that. It's not up to me.'

'So you went straight from Rev Pinny's room to the bar and stayed there the rest of the evening until closing time?'

'Yes.'

'Thank you, Mr Doggett, the Inspector said. 'I shan't need to ask you anything else for the moment. Perhaps you would ask your wife to come up as there are a few things I'd like to check with her before I go any further.'

*

As Mrs Doggett came into Oliver's room she was trying to unfasten the tie on her apron. Inspector Crocker was standing by the window staring at the cars parked in the drive. He turned as Thelma came in,

'There's no need to take your apron off, Mrs Doggett,' he said, 'I won't keep you more than a moment. I know how busy you are. I was just looking at that little Aston Martin out there. Very nice.'

'That's Oliver's. He's staying here - this is his room, as a matter of fact. He's one of the finalists. Nice boy but a bit of a fidget.'

'You strike me as the sort of person to be a pretty good judge of character, Mrs Doggett...'

'You see all sorts from behind a bar,' she said, blinking

rapidly.

'Indeed,' agreed Crocker. 'And what about Mr Atherton? What sort of person was he, would you say?'

'Not my cup of tea, to be honest. A trifle big-headed, if you know what I mean.'

'Was he ever involved in any argument? Unusually heated discussions - rows?'

'Well, I didn't hear any, but he had what you might call a sharp tongue. He was always saying spiteful things and annoying everybody. Never stopped. It was just the way he was. Bumptious.'

'So, in your opinion, he was the type of man who might well have a number of enemies?'

'I'd say so - yes,' she agreed, firmly. 'Quite possibly.'

'There's just one other thing I'd like to ask you, Mrs Doggett. Did your husband leave the bar at any time last evening? You know, pop out for a few minutes?'

'No. We were both in the bar all night. I told you - Friday's always busy.'

'Could he have popped upstairs to check towels, take orders, that sort of thing?'

'No, I do all that.'

'You always attend to room service?'

'Yes. It's more of a woman's job, if you know what I mean.' She paused. 'You know,' she went on, 'going into the guests' bedrooms and that.'

'Then why did your husband respond to Rev Pinny's request for a glass of warm milk?'

'How d'you mean?'

'At approximately nine-thirty, Rev Pinny rang through for a glass of warm milk and your husband, apparently, was the one who took it to him. Why was that?'

Thelma nodded. 'Oh, yes,' she said, 'you're right. He did go up about that time. I remember now.'

Inspector Crocker looked at her intently, waiting for the answer to his question.

'Well?' he said.

'Well what?' asked Thelma Doggett.

'Why did he go instead of you?'

'I told him I'd do it but he insisted on taking it himself.'

'Why was that?' asked Crocker, evenly.

'How should I know?' Thelma's tone was sharp. 'You'll have to ask him yourself. That's if you can get a straight answer. He can be quite stubborn when he wants to be.'

'Is that so? Tell me, now that you have had time to reflect, are you quite sure you didn't see anyone go up to Mr Atherton's room last night?'

'Positive.'

'And did your husband come back to the bar immediately after he'd delivered the glass of milk to Rev Pinny's room at nine-thirty?'

'Of course he did!' Thelma Doggett retorted, 'where else would he go?'

'Oh, I don't know. Would he have popped in to see Mr Atherton or one of the other guests?'

'There was only Rev Pinny up there and I don't think he'd have much to say to him!'

'I wonder, Mrs Doggett, if you can recall where the other guests were? I know it's difficult, but please try.'

'Yes, I can. I know exactly where they were. Duncan - he's an actor, you know, and *ever* so nice; he was in the bar with his new lady friend from Battersea just before closing time and as far as I know the others went to bed as soon as they got in.'

'What time was that?'

'Not long after ten.'

'And you're sure your husband returned to the bar at nine-thirty?'

Thelma was adamant. 'Quite sure,' she said. 'I told you - where else would he go?'

'Might he have gone to Mr Atherton's room?' Crocker suggested.

'What for?'

'You tell me, Mrs Doggett, your guess is as good as mine.'

'I told you. He came straight back down to the bar. And stayed there all evening.'

*

Inspector Crocker asked to see Oliver next and waited for him in the passage. After shaking hands and introducing himself he had a few words with the forensic team who had just arrived to begin their work in Atherton's room. Crocker led the way, apologising to Oliver for commandeering his room.

'I need to have a word with you all and I don't want to disrupt things even more by talking to people downstairs,' he said. 'Not good for business. Please sit down - cigarette?'

'I'll keep to mine, if you don't mind,' Oliver said, lighting up.

'Nice little car. The Aston Martin. Yours, I'm told. Very nice. I also hear that you are one of the finalists for some award or other.'

'Yes, the *Birkett Bronze Award* - the winner gets £25,000.'

'Not bad, not bad.'

'Atherton won it - *would* have won it, I should say.'

Inspector Crocker seemed surprised.

'But I was told the winner was going to be announced at

one o'clock today,' he said.

'It is,' Oliver replied. 'Rachel St Clair told me yesterday that Atherton had won.'

'And who is Rachel St Clair?'

'She's one of the judges,' Oliver said, lighting a cigarette. 'I took her to lunch yesterday.'

'And she's staying at *The Crown Imperial*?'

'That's right.'

Inspector Crocker drew a piece of paper from his top pocket and looked at it. 'Rachel St Clair,' he said. 'Does she live at 27, Melrose Avenue in Maida Vale?'

'I know she lives in Maida Vale but I don't know the address.'

'Tell me if you can - did you see anyone going into Mr Atherton's room last evening?'

'Yes, I did,' Oliver said. 'I was coming out of my room to join the others?'

'What time was that, would you say?'

'Oh, about twenty-past seven, something like that. I saw Len Doggett carrying a tray into Atherton's room.'

Crocker glanced across at PC Richards who was making notes.

'And a few minutes later,' Oliver continued, 'as we were leaving, we saw Theodore Rigby arriving. He's one of the other judges.'

'Was he visiting Mr Atherton, do you think?'

'I should think so. I can't think of any other reason why he'd come here. In fact, I know he was visiting Atherton...'

'Oh? Why?'

'Because I saw him leaving his room later that night, about eleven-thirty or there abouts. I remember it distinctly because he was wearing a woman's blouse underneath his overcoat. And very nice it looked, too. It really suited him - you know, it went very well with the white hair and florid complexion.'

He looked at Crocker and, smiling, said, 'Whatever turns you on, Inspector.'

Hearing PC Richards clear his throat, Crocker looked up sharply.

Then, turning to Oliver again, he asked, 'Was there any sign of Mr Atherton?'

'What? When I saw Theo?'

'Yes.'

'No. No sign at all.'

'So you didn't see him at all that evening?'

'No, but I *heard* him - at closing time. Mrs Doggett was hammering on his door and he was telling her to stop, telling her to bugger off, basically.'

'Why would Mrs Doggett be hammering on his door at that time of night?'

'Trying to get Len out, I suppose,.' Oliver said, laughing. 'Poor sod - she'd warned him earlier on not to go there. Surprised he had the nerve to disobey. She was giving him hell, apparently, threatening to chuck him out - the lot.'

'When was this?'

'About seven. I didn't actually hear the row. I was upstairs getting changed but the whole pub heard it. Leanne told me she was really tearing him off a strip.'

'Leanne?'

'Leanne Philips,' Oliver said. 'She's one of the other finalists. We were in bed last night - in here - when, immediately after closing time, Mrs Doggett started banging on Atherton's door.'

'And did Mrs Doggett succeed in getting her husband to come out of Mr Atherton's room?'

'Eventually, yes. They went upstairs, still rowing. I saw Theo leaving a few minutes later as I was going to the bathroom.'

'Did you see or hear anyone else coming or going that night?'

'No. Not a sound.'

'Tell me,' Crocker went on, 'what sort of person was Mr Atherton? I should like to get a picture of him, character-wise, that is. How did he strike you?'

'Frankly, he was a bastard.'

'How so?'

'Ruthless, shallow, vain, vindictive, completely obnoxious....is that enough?'

'Was that just your opinion or would you say he was generally disliked?'

'In a word, yes,' Oliver said, bluntly. 'Only some people pretended to like him because they were afraid of him.'

Crocker seemed surprised.

'Afraid of him?' he repeated. 'Why?'

'Because he was dangerous,' Oliver explained. 'Not only was he totally amoral, a notorious gossip with a vicious tongue, but he also mixed with people in powerful positions and every sort of celebrity. They lived in dread, of course, that he'd blow the whistle on them. Unfortunately, a lot of what he said was not only offensive but also true.'

'I see,' Inspector Crocker said, moving towards the door. 'Well, thank you for being so frank. Perhaps you'd ask Ms Philips - Leanne - to come up for a few moments. I should like to hear what she has to say.'

*

Leanne was able to confirm that she and a number of other persons in the bar had heard the Doggetts having a flaming row shortly after seven the night before. It was, she said, about Len taking the tray up to Aubrey Atherton's room.

'Why should Mrs Doggett object to her husband taking the tray, do you think?' asked Inspector Crocker.

'No idea.'

'Was there, perhaps, some ill-feeling between her and Mr Atherton?'

'She liked him at first,' Leanne said. 'She was all over him, you know, really fawning over him. But then, after a couple of days her attitude changed completely. She had no time for him after that.'

'Do you know why?'

'Haven't a clue. Sorry.'

'And did you also see Mr Theodore Rigby arriving soon after that?' Crocker enquired.

'I saw him as we were leaving - we were going out for a meal - all of us, you know, all the finalists.'

'And you saw him leave later that evening?'

Leanne shook her head. 'No. I didn't,' she said. 'Oliver did, though, when he was on the way to the bathroom. We were both here, in his room.'

'All night?'

'All night.'

'Did you, by any chance, see Mr Atherton later that evening - or even hear his voice?'

'You mean when Mrs Doggett was banging on the door after closing time?' asked Leanne.

'That's right,' said Crocker. 'Tell me about that.'

'Well, I didn't see him but I heard him. He's got such a peculiar, high-pitched voice I could hear him above all the noise. He was telling Mrs Doggett to go to bed and not to be such a silly old spoil sport.'

'Is that what he actually said?'

'Yes - he said, "*Oh, go to bed you stupid woman and stop being such a silly old spoil sport.*" He was laughing as well,' Leanne added, 'and sounded pretty well-oiled, to me.'

'Why would he say that, d'you think?'

Leanne shrugged. 'Oh, I don't know,' she said, with a smile. 'Perhaps they were playing strip poker or watching blue movies? Whatever they were doing Mrs Doggett was absolutely furious - really *spitting* mad.'

'Did you like Mr Atherton?'

'No, to be honest,' admitted Leanne. 'I don't think anybody did. Mind you, I only met him for the first time last Sunday so I can't honestly say I knew him. But Oliver and the others have told me a bit about him and from what they say he could be pretty unpleasant. Mind you, from what I saw of him he could be superficially amusing, I suppose, but he was always cruel - you know, he'd pick on a person's weakness and exploit it for a quick laugh. Not very nice, is it?'

*

As Rae reached the landing she had to step to one side as the body of Aubrey Atherton was carried downstairs on a stretcher to the waiting ambulance.

Looking down, she caught sight of Len slinking into the gloom of the other bar whilst Thelma, seeing the paramedics negotiating the main staircase, turned her back and began to count the glasses on the shelf above the bar.

Leanne had re-joined Duncan and Oliver at the breakfast

table; still shocked by what had happened they sat toying with the remains of the bread rolls, drinking coffee and talking about the tragedy.

Duncan, who'd needed a couple of whiskeys to steady his nerves, was fretting as he'd promised to meet Jenny for coffee before the presentation. He'd rung the Bed & Breakfast place but she'd already left to go shopping. Fretful at this unforeseen hitch, he transferred to one of the easy chairs by the empty fireplace, sighed and closed his eyes.

Rev Pinny, having already rung Joan to tell her of Atherton's death - they'd said a prayer together over the phone - was sunk into the armchair, reading the latest newsletter from a new Catholic mission in Mozambique. At one stage he closed his eyes and muttered something before bringing the paper close to his eyes, scrutinising a photograph.

Unable to sit still for long, Oliver took to pacing the area around the table, anxious for the interviews to be over so he could get back to London. Leanne, having decided not to ring Joe with the news, went back upstairs to pack her things. Oliver had offered her a lift and he wanted to be off by mid-day.

*

Inspector Crocker was waiting for Rae inside Oliver's room. He rose from the chair and introduced himself. She sat on the edge of the bed and accepted the cigarette he offered her.

'Rae?' he said, 'Rae Roberts?'

'Yes.'

'Thank you for coming. I need to ask you a few questions about last night. I take it you heard the quarrel between Mr and Mrs Doggett?'

'You bet!' cried Rae. 'It was a real hum-dinger.'

'What time was that?'

'Well, which one?' Rae asked. 'They had two that I heard.'

'Let's hear about the earlier one first.'

'Thelma was screaming at Len about the tray for Atherton's room. Screeching like a Banshee, she was. The whole pub could hear her. That was about seven - seven-fifteen, something like that.'

To this she added, dryly. 'She's got a real mouth on her once she starts.'

'Who won?' Crocker asked, smiling.

'Len, for once in his life, I should think. He just went on walking, up the stairs and into Atherton's room.'

Rae stopped to draw on her cigarette. 'It was real 'High Noon' stuff,' she went on. 'She followed him up and tried to get the tray off him but he still carried on. I felt a bit sorry for her, really. She was in a terrible state.'

'And the second row?'

'I didn't see it - only heard it. I was in bed, reading with the radio on.'

'Which is your room?'

'Next one up. I heard her banging on Atherton's door for ages; she was shouting and telling Len to come out. Quite honestly, I didn't even know he was in there. I knew Theo was, because we saw him arrive.'

'What time was that?'

'About half-seven, I suppose.'

'Did you see him leave?'

'No,' Rae said, shaking her head. 'I went to bed soon after ten - as soon as we got in, in fact. We'd been to the *Nutcracker Grill* for a meal. We all went to bed, except Duncan - he stayed downstairs clutching paws with his new lady love, unable, apparently, to tear himself away.'

She gave a little shiver. 'It's quite sickening, really. Pinny came back early and went straight to bed, as far as I know. Probably had a copy of The National Geographic under the pillow,' she said, flashing a big smile at PC Richards.

'I have yet to interview Rev Pinny,' said Crocker, 'No doubt he will do his best to enlighten me.' He paused. 'Did you like Mr Atherton, Ms Roberts?'

'No, I loathed him,' said Rae, stubbing out her cigarette.

She stood up and combed the tufts of her blond hair with her fingers.

'He was the pits,' she said. 'A vile human being and to tell you the truth, I'm surprised no one's snuffed him out before.'

'That bad, eh?'

Rae nodded, emphatically.

'That bad,' she said. 'He was dishonest, calculating, cruel, pompous, cunning, manipulative, a dreadful snob - d'you need any more? Now, do me a favour, will you? Find out that it was a woman who killed the bastard...'

'Why?'

'So I can write about it, of course,' Rae exclaimed. 'I only write about women who kill men and it'd be a great case to work on. I'd make a fortune. Promise me this,' she added, pretending to beg, 'if you find out it's a woman let me be the first to know - my pen, as they say, is metaphorically poised ready to go!'

'I will indeed, Ms Roberts. And good luck.'

He went to the door and opened it. Shaking hands, he said,

'Thank you - you've been most helpful. Perhaps you would ask Mr Duncan Wainwright to come up? After that I should like to see Rev Pinny.'

*

Duncan had little to add but answered Inspector Crocker's questions as fully as he could.

When asked about the row between the Doggetts he said,

'No, I'm afraid I missed that one. My lady-friend and I had gone on ahead to bag a table at the *Nutcracker Grill*. It's a restaurant just off the main square - very good. I expect you know it. We - that is to say, the finalists - well, not Atherton, of course, were going for a meal together to celebrate the end of the Festival. We'd planned to go back to London after lunch today - you know, after the presentation, but I don't know what'll happen now. Does Fiona know? We haven't seen her.'

He sighed and looked at his watch.

'Ms Bridewell has been informed,' Crocker confirmed. 'Have you an appointment?'

'Well, yes, I had arranged to meet Jenny at eleven,' Duncan said. 'But I dare say if I don't turn up she'll come looking for me.'

'Jenny?'

'Yes, Jenny Peebles. I only met her a few days ago but I feel I've known her for ages. You see, she lives in the mansion block opposite my flat in Prince of Wales Drive - that's near Battersea Park.'

'So you and Miss Peebles left the hotel before Mr and Mrs Doggett had their little squabble?'

'That's right,' said Duncan. 'But I've heard all about it as you can imagine.'

'Now what about later on that evening?'

'How d'you mean?'

Duncan asked, looking again at his watch. Nine forty-five. He adjusted his bow-tie.

'Apparently Mr and Mrs Doggett had another argument

later on,' Crocker said. 'Shortly after closing time. Did you hear any of that?'

'Yes, I most certainly did, Inspector.'

'And what did you hear?'

'Well, Jenny and I had left the others at the restaurant and come back here for a little night-cap on our own. It was more cosy, if you know what I mean.'

'What time was that? When you got back?'

'Oh, quite early,' Duncan said. 'Just before half-nine. We were all feeling pretty tired and a bit dejected.'

'Were you alone in the Lounge Bar?'

'Well, yes. The others came back about ten. Oliver and Leanne, *err umm*, went straight up to bed.' He tapped the side of his nose and grinned. 'Got a thing going, I think.'

'And Ms Roberts? Where was she?'

'She went up at the same time. Said she was going up to her room to read and listen to *Book At Bedtime.*'

'And Rev Pinny?'

'Oh, he'd left the restaurant early,' replied Duncan, fingering the strap on his watch, 'even before us. He probably walked back. He said he wanted to phone his wife or something. He must have gone to bed - leastways, I didn't see him.'

'How long, would you say,' Crocker asked, 'were you and your lady friend in the bar?'

'Till just before closing time.'

'Tell me, were both Mr and Mrs Doggett behind the bar when you got back?'

'Yes.'

'Did you, by any chance, see Mr Doggett leave the bar for any reason?'

'Just after we got back he went upstairs with a glass of

milk. I heard him tell his wife it was for Rev Pinny.'

'What was Mrs Doggett doing?'

Duncan looked perplexed.

'How d'you mean?' he asked.

'When her husband went upstairs with the milk?'

'She was standing behind the bar, glaring at him.'

'How long was Len Doggett upstairs, would you say?'

'He didn't come down again. Thelma - Mrs Doggett - was on her own till closing time. As soon as she called last orders I took Jenny to her car and said goodnight. Then I came in and went straight up to bed.'

'Where was Mrs Doggett?'

'Collecting glasses and rinsing them out. I called out 'goodnight' to her but I don't think she heard.'

'And did you see any more of Len Doggett that night?'

Duncan shook his head.

'No,' he said. 'I didn't see anyone when I went upstairs. I could hear Rae's radio coming from her room. I couldn't hear anything coming from Oliver's and when I got to my own room, Pinny was reading; either that or sleeping sitting up. It's difficult to tell with him. He's got these really deep-set eyes and he always closes them while he's having a think. But when I passed Atherton's room I could hear voices inside.'

'Did you recognise any of these voices?'

'No. I just walked by on my way to my room, that's all. Then a few minutes later, when I was already in bed, I heard a hell of a racket going on outside. Thelma thumping the door and Atherton was shrieking at her to go away.'

'You didn't get out of bed?'

'*What*? With Thelma on the warpath!' exclaimed Duncan. 'You must be joking! No, thanks. I just pulled the blankets over my head and kept well out of it.'

'Then what happened?'

'It went quiet. I heard Atherton's door open and close and then I could hear the Doggetts moving about upstairs.'

He nodded towards the ceiling. 'Their room's directly above this one, apparently. After that, I went to sleep.'

'One more question,' said Crocker. 'Tell me, Mr Wainwright, did you like Mr Atherton?'

'No, not really,' Duncan admitted. 'He could be terribly cruel, you know. Unnecessarily so, in my view. No compassion. No kindness. Very few will mourn his passing, I'm afraid.'

'You could be right,' said Crocker. 'Now, just one more thing before you go. May I ask you for Miss Peebles's address at the Bed and Breakfast?'

'I can certainly give it to you, Inspector, but why?'

'Well, she was here in the bar, according to you, until closing time last night. I should like to have a word with her later.'

As Inspector Crocker showed him the door Duncan grasped his hand and shook it heartily.

'I'll tell Pinny to come up, shall I?'

*

Inspector Crocker got very little out of Rev Pinny for it was soon apparent that his mind was on other things. He did see, he said, the early evening altercation between the Doggetts on the stairs but had paid little attention. He could not recall seeing Theodore Rigby in the driveway. His sense of time was weak; he wasn't sure when he got back from *The Nutcracker Grill* or what time he went upstairs to bed. He did, however, remember phoning his wife because she told him they'd made £217.83p. on the Christian Fellowship *Bring and Buy* Sale.

'What time do you think it was when you asked for the glass of milk?' Crocker asked, with commendable patience.

'Oh, I don't know,' Pinny replied. 'As soon as I got to my room, I suppose, because I remember thinking how thoughtless I was not to ask for it before I came upstairs. I could have saved him the trouble - you know, coming all the way upstairs when I could have asked before and carried it up myself.'

'Who brought you the milk, Rev Pinny?'

'Oh, it was Mr Doggett and he didn't mind a bit. Made a joke of it, in fact. Glad to get away for a few moments, he said. Stuck in the bar all night.'

'Did you hear Mr Doggett go back downstairs?'

'Oh, he didn't go back. He went into Mr Atherton's room.'

'How do you know?'

'I went out to thank him again and saw him going in.'

'Did you see anyone else?'

'Anyone else?'

'Well, did you see Mr Atherton? Or Mr Rigby?'

'No, no one else,' said Pinny. 'He closed the door behind him.'

'And did you hear anything else that night?'

'No. No, I didn't. Apparently, Mrs Doggett had a bit of an argument with Mr Doggett at closing time but I must have been asleep by then. I'd had a glass of white wine in the restaurant, you see, and then the warm milk on top of that. I'd been reading my Bible and must have dropped of. I didn't even hear Duncan come in.'

Rev Pinny looked at the floor and seemed lost in thought.

'How would you describe Mr Atherton?' asked Crocker.

'Oh, he was a large man - tall, mid-fifties...'

'As a person, Rev Pinny – what was he like as a person. The character of the man.'

Rev Pinny thought for a moment and then shook his head.

'I'd rather not speak ill of the dead, Inspector, if you don't mind. It was my view that he was a deeply unhappy man. *Deeply* unhappy. Well, he must have been to behave the way he did.'

'Not a very pleasant character, would you say?'

'I should say he was a man who was ill at ease with himself, Inspector. Very sad. Tragic, really.'

'I gather you knew, as did the other finalists, that Mr Atherton had been selected as the winner of *The Birkett Bronze Award*.'

'Yes, indeed. Might that have something to do with the fact that the poor man's been murdered?' asked Rev Pinny, earnestly.

'I really don't know,' said Crocker, evenly. 'We shall have to see. Thank you for your time.'

He drew from his pocket the envelope he'd found on Atherton's bedside table.

'Now, a visit to *The Crown Imperial* and a little chat with a lady called Ms Rachel St Clair.'

'Oh, she's one of the judges. Now *she'll* be able to tell you all about Aubrey Atherton,' said Pinny.

'They knew each other?' asked Crocker.

'Oh, yes, and in a Biblical sense, too,' replied Pinny. 'They had an affair many years ago.'

'Is that so?' Crocker said.

'Yes, indeed. In fact, it was while they were living together that he wrote his first book. And it was she who paid for the publication, or so I've heard. It's strange how things work out, isn't it, Inspector?'

*

Chapter Nineteen

By the time Inspector Crocker reached *The Crown Imperial* Rachel St Clair had gone. The manager, Mr Popperwell, confirmed that she had checked out shortly after one o'clock the night before. He said that he'd tried to dissuade her from driving all the way back to London at that time of night, especially, he added, drawing his face closer to Crocker's ear, as she had clearly been drinking.

'She was in a right state,' he confided, 'and not for the first time. Mind you, she could knock it back - you know what I mean, sir.'

He paused to watch one of his staff dealing with a guest at reception.

'Don't get me wrong, she's a nice woman,' he went on, 'but too demanding, a bit out of control.'

'Out of control?' asked Crocker. 'How d'you mean?'

'Well, she only arrived on Wednesday and on two occasions I had to get her up to her room so she wouldn't make an exhibition of herself in the foyer.'

He moved closer to Inspector Crocker. 'That sort of thing's bad for the hotel. To be honest, I'm quite relieved that she's gone.'

This said, he bent over one of the coffee tables, making

little tutting noises as he straightened a pile of magazines.

'And now this!' he exclaimed. 'Mr Atherton dead - oh, dear, what a *tragedy*, what a thing to happen here in Chiselford,' he cried, pressing his palms together to express his concern. 'He was due to stay here, you know, but there was a mix-up and Fiona Bridewell booked him somewhere else instead. Now this. She's terribly upset. Devastated. Well, one can imagine.'

'Where is she now?'

'In her room - gone to pieces, poor thing,' clucked Popperwell. 'Claire's with her. The phone's been ringing non-stop. All the nationals. The television companies. The CCC...'

'The CCC ?'

'That's the *Crime Club Committee,'* explained Popperwell. 'They're the ones who organise the *Birkett Bronze Award* every year. Mr Atherton had won, apparently. The presentation's been cancelled, of course. Goodness knows what they'll do with the money now. Oh, dear, what a mess. What a thing to happen.'

'Are Max Wilbur and Theodore Rigby staying here as well?'

'Oh, yes. Very nice gentlemen,' declared Popperwell. 'I haven't seen Mr Rigby this morning but Mr Wilbur's been an absolute godsend, dealing with the press and the CCC, that sort of thing. It's been a terrible shock to them both, of course.'

'I should like to see Ms St Clair's room, if I may?' said Inspector Crocker, whereupon Mr Popperwell raised his hand to summon a chambermaid who was just about to climb the stairs, her arms laden with freshly laundered sheets.

'Meanwhile,' went on Crocker, 'would you kindly ring through to Ms Bridewell's room and tell her I'll be along to speak to her in approximately fifteen minutes. Also, would you tell Mr Wilbur and Mr Rigby that I am here and will get along to see them shortly? Thank you so much.'

The chambermaid led the way up to Rachel St Clair's room and, at Inspector Crocker's request, opened the door with her master key. Flashing a pert smile at PC Richards, she closed the door behind them before ascending the next flight of stairs, her chin resting on the pile of bedding.

The curtains in Rachel's room were still drawn, the lights still burning and the bed made. The wardrobe was empty save for a cheap, plastic belt hanging over the rail.

On the window sill in the *en suite* bathroom Crocker found a Vodka bottle, half full, and there was an upturned glass in the sink. The cold water tap was still running. Two aquamarine bath-towels were folded neatly on the heated rail but a damp hand towel was lying on the floor near the door.

The air was still quite heavily-scented. On the cistern was a piece of green tissue and a small wodge of cotton wool, both stained with nail varnish.

Going back into the bedroom, Crocker opened the drawer of the bedside table. It was empty save for a piece of white paper, folded in two. Opening it, he saw that it was a note, written in blue biro, signed by Rachel St Clair. It read:

> *I have gone back to London. You will find me at 27 Melrose Avenue, Maida Vale. The landlady lives on the ground floor. She has a key.*

That was all. Inspector Crocker sat on the end of the bed and rang through to the local police station. Briefly explaining the situation to his Superintendent, he said he would be interviewing Fiona Bridewell, Claire Fenton, Max Wilbur and Theodore Rigby before returning to the station. He also asked for the Metropolitan Police to be contacted to send someone along to Rachel St Clair's flat, in Maida Vale. After he'd given the address he also asked for someone to be sent to *The Hare Hotel* to take Leonard Doggett in for further questioning.

*

Very little was gleaned from Crocker's interview with Fiona Bridewell and Claire Fenton. Neither of the women had seen Aubrey Atherton after he left the book signing in the foyer that morning, and as everything had already been arranged for the presentation of the award, neither of them had any reason to contact him.

No doubt mindful of their position as PR's for Atherton's publisher they were loath to openly vilify Atherton but it was clear that they had not liked him.

After taking Inspector Crocker along to Max Wilbur's room and finding it empty, Claire suggested he try the manager's office. She was going there herself, she said, to help out with the press calls, and would tell him that Inspector Crocker wished to have a word.

Leaving him at Theodore Rigby's door, she went downstairs. Just as Crocker was about to knock, he was joined by PC Richards who told him that they'd got Len Doggett down at the station and not to bother knocking at Rigby's door. He wasn't there, he said. He'd just walked into the station saying he wished to make a statement.

'Like what?' asked Crocker, giving his nose a good blow.

'Something about giving Atherton sleeping tablets,' said Richards. 'Oh, yes, and the Met are sending someone over to Rachel St Clair's right away. We should hear something soon. Odd sort of case, isn't it, sir?'

'You can say that again, Richards.'

*

When the Metropolitan police opened the door of Rachel St Clair's London flat they found her lying face down on top of the bed.

She was still wearing the dark blue suit she'd worn at Giovanni's the day before and her face was heavily made-up. The blusher on her cheeks showed up as livid streaks against the deathly pallor of her skin.

Her eyes were closed, the eyelids covered with deep mauve, frosted shadow. Her hair was only slightly dishevelled, a few strands having broken free of the pleat at the back, but at close range the grey roots were clearly visible.

One earring had come off and lay on the pillow close to her cheek and one of her high-heeled shoes was lying on its side on the floor at the end of the bed.

In the crook of her left arm was a child's toy, a lamb, the tail missing, the fleece matted and yellowed with age. Her hand covered a sheet of paper. The nails were manicured, the puce varnish expertly applied - but two were broken, the ends jagged and split.

Some seven or eight dolls of varying size, prettily dressed in gingham frocks, mop-caps and lace-edged petticoats, had been arranged around her head, propped in a line along the top of the pillow.

Photographs were scattered all over the bed, some under Rachel's head and some resting on the dolls' laps; others had slipped, topsy-turvy, to the floor.

One of the officers crouched down and picked one up. Then another. A few more. He spread them in his hand like a fan but as the heavy curtains were drawn and the only light came from a small bedside lamp, he took them across to the window.

Drawing back the curtain, he saw that they all featured the same young girl. A pretty little thing. Playing in a garden in one. Cuddling a kitten in another. And in every picture, she was with what must have been her mother, they looked so alike. The girl was laughing, her head thrown back and her arms clinging around Rachel's neck.

He gathered a few more and laid them carefully on the bedside table next to a glass tumbler and a small radio. In the drawer of the table there was a collection of pill bottles, most of them empty.

Standing up again the officer carefully slipped his hand under that of the dead woman and pulled out the piece of paper. There was writing on both sides. After a brief look, he put it into a polythene bag and handed it to his colleague.

'Suicide, sir?'

He nodded. "Fraid so. It's a sad business, suicide. Very sad.'

*

Soon after their return to London, the five remaining finalists were notified that the *Crime Club Committee* had convened an emergency meeting and decided that as Aubrey Atherton had not been in possession of the prize money at the time of his death, it did constitute part of his estate. In the circumstances it had been decided to distribute the prize money equally amongst the remaining finalists. They would receive £5000 each but *The Birkett Bronze* bust would remain under lock and key until the following year.

On May 8, the following obituary, written by Max Wilbur, had appeared in *The Independent:*

AUBREY ATHERTON

The sudden death of Mr Aubrey Atherton has shocked the literary world. His tragic and untimely departure has left an irreplaceable gap in the world of crime writing. Mr Atherton enjoyed enormous popularity and was the acknowledged leader in his chosen field, having won the Birkett Bronze Award for the previous two years. His first book, The Loner - Study of a Serial Killer, published in 1963, was an instant success; fourteen books followed, equally successful, nine of which were subsequently made into films, proving a tremendous draw at the box office.

Atherton was a prodigious writer and though meticulous in his research he had the ability, so rare among investigative journalists, to write a cracking good story. This must explain his enduring popularity with the reading public and why his greatest fans waited impatiently for each new publication. He will be sadly missed, not only by the doyens of the literary world, but by his grateful readers, millions of them all over the world, who will mourn this sad loss.

Born in Walthamstow, in 1938, he came from humble beginnings. At the age of three he was taken into care when his mother, who had several other children, had found it impossible to cope while her husband was away fighting for his country. From that time there was little contact between young Aubrey and the rest of his family. After his father's death at the front in North Africa his mother remarried and made a new life for herself - a life that did not, it seemed, include young Aubrey.

Years of institutional life were followed by one or two unhappy attempts at fostering and Aubrey grew to feel abandoned and betrayed. He regularly played truant and often ran away from the various homes in which he was placed. Bereft of the love of a proper family he withdrew into his own fantasy world. Indeed, his first crime book was about a misfit, like himself, an alienated character who became a serial killer.

At the time the book was published Aubrey Atherton was living with the well-known writer of romantic fiction, Rachel St Clair, and her daughter, Melanie. The book was an instant success and Aubrey Atherton was, at last, able to face the world on equal terms. At the time of his death Aubrey Atherton was at the peak of his career, and yet, some might say, for all his wealth and influence, he was misunderstood and much-maligned, not by his faithful readers, but by his fellow writers.

His latest book, The Ultimate Chronicle of Crime, had, in fact, been selected as this year's winner of The Birkett Bronze Award. Had he lived to receive this prestigious prize he would have been rightly acclaimed as the undisputed leader in his field, having won the award for three years running.

Sadly, this was not to be. He died last Friday, the day before the award was to be announced. Estranged from his family, Aubrey Atherton will, nevertheless, be sadly missed by his countless fans and the world of crime writing will be the poorer by his unfortunate and untimely death.

At the bottom of the same page there was a small paragraph announcing the death of Rachel St Clair. No details were given. Both ex-husbands were dead, it stated, and her only daughter, Melanie, had died in 1967, aged eighteen.

Every newspaper in the country had a field day over Aubrey Atherton's death. News that he had been murdered fuelled a deluge of speculation as to the killer but, inexplicably, a few days later, the police announced that the case was closed. They were not, they said, looking for anyone in connection with the death.

*

A couple of weeks later Oliver and the remaining finalists met for a drink in a wine bar in Battersea to celebrate receiving their cheques for £5,000 each.

Oliver and Leanne arrived late; they looked relaxed and happy, having just returned from a trip on the Norfolk Broads with Joe. Rev Pinny was also late, looking pale and withdrawn, having endured a weekend retreat in Aberystwyth with Joan.

When they were finally assembled Oliver drew from his pocket several sheets of paper covered with erratic scrawl. Through his journalistic contacts he'd managed to get hold of a copy of Rachel St Clair's suicide note which had been given as evidence at the inquest into Atherton's death. It had been written with a blue biro on several sheets of ivory notepaper. He read it out loud:

He was nothing when he met me. He was working in a Local Government office. He was younger than me and had no money but there was something about him. Tall, red-gold hair, detached. And amusing. He could be quite charming when he wanted to be. When I heard about his background I felt sorry for him. He came to live with me. My daughter, Melanie, was fifteen. She was beautiful, so bright, so happy, doing well at school. She was going to be a dancer. She'd been studying since she was four. He was good with her. Took her places at weekends. Ice-skating, the cinema and sometimes we'd all go to the ballet - she loved that.

The rest of the week he'd be writing the book - his first. He'd given up his job. I didn't mind footing the bills. I knew he'd be a good writer given the chance. But one publisher after another turned it down. He got so depressed I paid to get it published. I didn't mind - I was earning good money then and was writing one a year. I didn't realise what was happening. I can hardly bring myself to write it. But I must - to explain why I killed him. I had to. I've hated him for nearly thirty years. Hated him so much. He didn't deserve to live.

I accepted the role of judge more out of curiosity than anything else. I hadn't spoken to him for years. If ever we met socially he always made a point of avoiding me - sometimes leaving the room altogether. I asked him to come to my room. He only came to get my vote for the damned prize. Seeing him again brought back all the pain.

And the anger, the incredible anger. All the rage was still there

After two minutes in his company I realised I still hated him. And when he refused to even discuss Melanie's death I knew I wanted to kill him. Just hating him wasn't enough.

Why d'you have to drag up the past, he said. It suddenly seemed the perfect solution - he wasn't fit to live and I no longer wanted to. He is despicable - the lowest form of life. A vile creature who inveigled his way into her life and destroyed her. He deprived me of my daughter - all I had. I hated him. My life is empty. Finished. Pointless without her. My only consolation is that now he's gone too and it was I who rid the world of him.

PS. Don't blame Theo. He's a good sort. I begged him to give him the tablets just to knock him out and I'd do the rest. That bastard was threatening to expose him. He wasn't doing any harm. It was only a bit of fun. That shit Atherton would love to ruin him too. Bastard.'

*

There was a long silence after Oliver had finished reading. He folded the pages and put them back in his pocket.

Rev Pinny was shaking his head sorrowfully, deeply moved.

'God, what a mess,' said Rae, after a while. 'What happened to Melanie - did you find out?'

Oliver nodded. 'Of course, as soon as Atherton's book came out,' he explained, 'he buggered off, didn't he? Left Rachel like a shot - taking young Melanie with him. He soon introduced her to the drug scene, you know the sort of thing. Less than a year later, he dumped her and she went to pieces. Apparently, she O-deed about six months after he left. Someone found her crashed out in a derelict basement off the Fulham Road. They reckon she'd been dead three weeks. Terrible, isn't it?'

'No wonder Rachel hated him so much,' Leanne said, almost in tears. 'I'd feel the same if something like that happened to Joe. God, what a *bastard*.'

'And don't forget, she was all washed up as a writer,' said Oliver. 'And she knew she'd never do another book. She was also feeling her age and drinking herself silly. Atherton had destroyed the only family she had. It all came to a head - the balance of her mind, etc.'

'Great story!' Rae exclaimed, without thinking.

Then, seeing the shock on everyone's faces, she apologised. 'Sorry, folks, but you what I'm like - I've just *got* to write this one.'

'So what was old Theo up to, then?' asked Duncan, draining his glass. 'Why would Atherton be able to expose him? Did you manage to find out, Oliver?'

'Come on' Rae urged, 'spill the beans."

'Oh, he was harmless enough, poor old sod,' Oliver said, laughing. 'He liked a bit of cross-dressing, that's all. Never did anyone any harm.'

'Ahhh, it's rather sweet,' Rae cried. 'But no big deal, in this day and age, surely?'

'Well, to someone of Theo's generation it was clearly something he preferred to keep hidden. Atherton encouraged it, of course, and, knowing his little secret, made damn sure he'd get Theo's vote for *The Birkett Bronze.* The old boy must have been shitting bricks in case the *Crime Club Committee* found out and crossed him off the list for a knighthood.'

Rev Pinny raised his eyebrows and frowned in Oliver's direction but declined to comment.

'And poor old Len Doggett was the same way inclined,' Oliver went on. 'Atherton, of course, soon sniffed him out and got him to join the party that night. They were all a bit pie-eyed by the time Thelma started hammering on the door at closing time.'

'D'you reckon she knew what was going on?' Rae asked.

'You bet,' Oliver replied. 'Of course she did. She knew what Leonard was all about. Some women accept it, of course, even encourage it, but she obviously couldn't. Don't you remember she hinted it was all Len's fault they'd had to leave their pub in the Cotswolds? He probably got caught in Tesco's in drag or something, poor bugger. She knew Atherton was encouraging him and hated him for it.'

'So what did Theo *do* exactly?' Jenny Peebles wanted to know.

'From what I could gather,' Oliver said, 'the plan was that he'd keep Atherton's glass topped up during the evening, making sure he was pretty far gone. And he knew Atherton always took three or four sleeping tablets last thing at night. Always, without fail. So Rachel St Clair persuaded him to make sure Atherton took the maximum dose so that the combination of the pills and the booze would really knock him out.'

'Then what happened?' Rae asked, taking notes.

'Rachel left her room at *The Crown Imperial* and arrived at *The Hare* over just before twelve. Theo had left the door open on his way out. She went in, found Atherton legless as planned, already unconscious, in fact - and strangled him.'

'What?' Rae cried, almost in admiration. 'With her bare hands?'

'Not quite,' said Oliver. 'The coroner's report stated that he was strangled with a black nylon suspender belt! Quite apt, really, I suppose.'

'What a business, what a to-do,' Pinny lamented, covering his brow with his hand as though to shield himself from the wickedness in the world.

'It *is* a bit sad, isn't? The whole thing,' Leanne said, reaching for Oliver's hand under the table.

'I suppose it is - in that everybody's a victim, in a way,' agreed Jenny, linking her arm through Duncan's.

'Except us,' said Oliver. 'You could say we came out the winners in the end. The whole £25,000 would have been bloody fantastic but £5,000 isn't bad - better than a kick up the arse any day - what d'you reckon, Pinny?'

*

Two months later a small announcement appeared in *The Times:*

According to the will of the late Mr Aubrey Atherton, his estate estimated in excess of at £5.8 million, will be used to establish a Drugs Rehabilitation Centre in London's Dockland. At Mr Atherton's request, on completion, there will be no opening ceremony or any plaque commemorating his part in the financing of the Centre. All royalties from his books will be split between the funding of research projects into Drug Addiction and the day-to-day running costs of the centre.

A suitable site has been acquired and work has already begun. Completion is expected by the middle of next year.

*